The Shore and the Wave

UNESCO ASIAN FICTION SERIES

The Shore and the Wave

BY AZIZ AHMAD

TRANSLATED FROM THE URDU BY
RALPH RUSSELL

London

GEORGE ALLEN & UNWIN LTD

RUSKIN HOUSE   MUSEUM STREET

First published in 1971

This translation © UNESCO 1971

ISBN 0 04 891042 2

Originally published in Urdu under the title
Aisi Bulandi, Aisi Pasti (literally: 'So high, so low')
© Aziz Ahmad

UNESCO COLLECTION OF
CONTEMPORARY WORKS

This volume has been accepted in the Translations Series of Contemporary Works jointly sponsored by the International PEN Club and the United Nations Educational, Scientific and Cultural Organization (UNESCO)

Printed in Great Britain
in 11 pt Plantin
by Billing & Sons Limited
Guildford and London

The novel in Urdu, as in all the modern languages of the South Asian sub-continent, is of very recent growth. It stems on the one hand from the orally transmitted romances of mediaeval Islamic chivalry (reduced to writing for the first time as late as the second half of the nineteenth century) and on the other from the more realistic, but avowedly didactic, moral tale. Not until the last year of the century did a work appear which can without serious reservation really be called a novel in the modern sense of the term. This was Rusva's *Umrao Jan Ada*, first published in 1899, and as secure in its reputation today as ever it was. The major Urdu novelist of the present century is Prem Chand (d. 1936) whose stature is as great in Urdu literature as it is in Hindi; but his novels are remarkable above all for the new range of their themes, and more especially for their vivid, moving portrayal of Indian peasant life. As works of art they are uneven, and the author's moral zeal sometimes clashes with, and prevails over, his sense of realism.

In this setting the novels of Aziz Ahmad represent something of a new departure. He is a novelist whose craftsmanship is equal to the demands of his chosen literary form, and from those in the Urdu-speaking community who were alive to the importance of these things he rapidly won well-deserved praise. Upon others he made a less favourable impact, for he wrote with a straightforwardness about aspects of personal relationships which, in a society still largely primly Victorian in its moral attitudes, some found offensive. Nirad C. Chaudhuri, in his *Autobiography of an Unknown Indian*, tells us how in his youth a fellow-student of his had criticized a novel of the august nineteenth-century novelist Bankim Chandra Chatterji for being 'flooded with eroticism', and comments, 'The flood was one solitary scene of kissing within wedlock'. Times have changed since then, but old traditions die hard (kissing is still taboo on the Indian screen). So Aziz Ahmad's frankness, though quite unremarkable by Western standards, aroused a good deal of shocked disapproval in his own country.

However, his novels have more to recommend them than their very competent craftsmanship and their frank portrayal of things which the more conservative of his readers felt should have

7

remained decently veiled. *The Shore and the Wave* in particular presents a picture of an important but too little known section of Indian social history. His fictional 'Farkhundanagar', the city in which most of the scenes are set, is in fact Hyderabad, capital of the large princely state (as large in area as Italy) in central India, which survived under the aegis of the paramount British power until 1947 and disappeared as a separate entity several years later, when the redrawing of the boundaries of the Indian states on linguistic lines took different parts of it into different political units.

The politic fictional disguise was never any disguise at all to anyone who knew Hyderabad, and need no longer be maintained. Aziz Ahmad grew up in Hyderabad, and indeed, at the time when the novel was written, had spent most of his life there. He gives in his second chapter a perceptive overall account of the 'three tides of westernization' which had swept over the state, and his novel describes in the period up to the eve of independence (the book was first published in 1948) the impact upon the educated, well-to-do sections of Hyderabad society, of the 'third tide'. The title is taken from the verse in Chapter 8.

In making this translation I was fortunate in having the close co-operation of the author, when he was my colleague at the School of Oriental and African Studies in the University of London, and my sincere thanks are due to him. He took the opportunity to make revisions, some of them fairly considerable, in the original text, and these were incorporated in the translation. For the most part, these revisions consist of omissions and abridgements of certain passages, but numerous other minor changes have also been made. Most of these were made at the author's own wish, and none of them without his consent. In detail, therefore, the translation often diverges considerably from the published Urdu text.

Those who are not accustomed to Muslim names and titles find them difficult to remember, and I have therefore appended to the novel a brief account of its setting and of the main characters. I have also added a few footnotes to the text where these seemed absolutely necessary.

RALPH RUSSELL

I

Love cannot develop to the full without separation, they say, and no landscape is perfect without heights and depths. That is why there is a hill near every big city, and if God has endowed the citizens with good taste, they build their houses on the hill as well as in the plain. If He has not, they build a temple or two on the hill or discover somebody's shrine there, and go and visit it from time to time. From the top of the hill, they gaze down for a while at the city below, admire the scene, and then return to their narrow streets.

Near Farkhundanagar, capital of the princely state of that name in central India, lies the hill which now bears the name of Kishanpalli, but which in former days was called Gipsies' Hill. From the air it looks like a great spider, a spider with three symmetrical, linked bodies, and numberless legs reaching out in all directions. All around is flat country, stretching away until in the distance it once more meets the hills, and dotted about the plains are muddy bluish pools which from the air look like big pieces of blue glass set in the fields of green waving paddy. In former days there were only tracks on Gipsies' Hill, winding their way through the trees of thorny babool and bitter-leaved neem among rocks of every shape and size. There is a legend that when the Creator had fashioned the world, He flicked His fingers to free them of the clay still clinging to them. The lumps of clay fell on the Deccan plateau and formed the rocks which litter it today. Most of these rocks are black, like the Deccan's Dravidian inhabitants, or like the stone-hewers whose vigorous young women Josh Malihabadi immortalized in his verse. These rocks occur in the most curious shapes. One stands upon another, almost as though it were suspended above it. The lower rock is often small, while the upper one is very large and barely in contact with the lower. You would think that the slightest shock would bring these great rocks crashing down; but far from it; even earthquakes have failed to move them, and these jugglers of the world of stone stand fast still poising their weight as before.

These days there are houses among the rocks. Look for instance

9

at the house of Wali Chalak Jang, a small five-roomed building of so-called 'German' design. Wali Chalak Jang was no slave to tradition, and he made changes when he moved in. He had the name of the house, which had been engraved on the gate like the inscription on a tombstone, written in Kufic script on an old-fashioned Chinese lantern suspended like a street-light on the front veranda near the bougainvilia creeper. He changed the name, too. The house had been called 'Gulkada' – the 'Flower House' – perhaps from the deep pink flowers of the bougainvilia, but the 'Flower House' reminded him of the Id greeting cards fashionable in Farkhundanagar twenty-five years earlier. His family had played a great part in changing this old-fashioned style with its profusion of flowers and leaves, and introducing a simpler taste; so he dropped the old Urdu name, and on the Chinese lantern was now engraved in a sort of English Kufic script: 'The Rock'. Not that this referred to the house itself, which looked more like one of those modern Urdu poems in free verse, descending in stages from front to rear until it came to a stop at the edge of a pool. No, what gave the house its name was a huge rock some fifty feet high, which stood confronting it like a virile young aborigine. By some geological freak the breast of this gigantic rock had been cleft open; across the cleft lay a slab, ten feet long and seven feet high, and on the top of that yet another much smaller one.

Today there are houses on the hill. But two hundred and fifty years ago, when the armies of the Mughal Emperor Aurangzeb marched over Gipsies' Hill it must have been green and unin-habited. In the rear of his armies came the *banjaras* – the merchant-gipsies who supplied them, and who were to give the hill its name. They were still there when the Mughal Empire fell and the Marathas overspread the land, levying tribute wherever they went; and when the Afghans invaded and far to the north defeated the Marathas at Panipat and cut off their commander's head; and when the Sikhs rose to power in the Panjab; and when the Dogras conquered Ladakh; and they were still there when the soldiers' tread was heard no more on Gipsies' Hill, roaming as before and trading where they could. There, where the smoke rose from their huts near the sheer rock, three hundred feet high, that curves towards the valley like the thigh of a giant negress, the poet Nazir warned them of their approaching doom:

Give up your greed of worldly gain, your ever-restless wandering.

'Oh, shut up!' said the banjaras, and went on with their trading. Nazir tried again, at the place where you suddenly find yourself looking down over the plain below, where the great rocks come to an end, and give way to hundreds of thousands of useless little stones, littering the slopes like little tombstones. He tried to frighten them:

Your wealth will lie abandoned there when Death the Trader
    goes his way.

'Oh, go away,' said the banjaras; and they went on their accustomed way, roaming from town to town and from village to village. They came down from the heights of Gipsies' Hill towards the valley; they knocked at the door of Amir Karim Khan, and spread out the wares they had brought from Delhi:

The screens and curtains, carpets, rugs, the carved and painted
    beds of state.

They bowed low before the gatekeeper of the Rajah of Rajahs Himmat Shamsher Singh Bahadur, were granted audience, and paraded before him:

Fine horses, saddles chased with gold, and elephants with trappings
    red.

Nazir again tried to frighten them:

Your sons and grandsons – yes, your wives, will shun your corpse
    when you lie dead.

And in fact not all of them waited so long – these banjaras' wives, decked in the jewellery they had brought with them from Tibet and Central Asia, wearing in their ears, on their arms, on their ankles, in their noses, on their foreheads, ornaments of brass which jingled as they walked. It was a banjara's wife who deserted her husband to enter the harem of the Rajah of Rajahs and to become the grandmother of the present Rajah. But the banjaras went on trading, selling their wares, their women, themselves, until the day when the Honourable Englishman entered the market and prospered to such an extent that Nazir's prophecy came true, and not only Nazir's banjaras, but all the banjaras were wiped from the slate of history. The footpaths of Gipsies' Hill fell silent. Their women entered the harems of rajahs and nawabs and their children ceased to be their own. Even the Khan Hazrat, the ruling prince of Farkhundanagar, stopped buying their vessels of gold and silver and went over instead to the glass-ware displayed in the English-style shop windows.

> Your wealth will lie abandoned there when Death the Trader
> goes his way.

Then came the aborigines from the nearby plains; stone-hewers, bird-catchers, and eaters of carrion flesh. It was they who robbed the hill of its trees, so that today there are no trees on Kishanpalli except those which the new residents have planted in their gardens or those in the avenues laid out by Dr Qurban Husain. The aborigine women lopped and felled the trees and uprooted the thorn bushes for fuel. That is why in the summer months Kishanpalli is burning hot, and the earth on the hillsides seems to turn a deeper black, and the ringed snakes come out from under the scorching black rocks, those rocks which, in Josh's poem, suckled the young Dravidian women of the Deccan plateau. Here and there you can see a pair of mongooses courting, or you may hear the cry of the hares, with their deep blue eyes, as they run past the bird-catchers' huts. . . .

It would be about a hundred years after the last banjaras departed from Gipsies' Hill that one afternoon early in the rainy season Ahdi Husnkar Jang happened by the merest chance to go walking there. The Deccan rains, the Malwa nights, evenings in Oudh and mornings in Banaras are all proverbial, but the first two were made by God, and the other two by man. It was July, the month when in northern India it seems to be raining fire, but when in the country around Farkhundanagar the earth becomes a paradise. The grass was lank and green, the air cool and fragrant; and the Rajah of Rajahs Shujaat Shamsher Singh Bahadur, Prime Minister of Farkhundanagar State, decided to postpone the business of government until the next morning and to spend this beautiful afternoon in the gardens of the Royal Tombs picnicking with his Rajput consort and one of his Muslim wives and three of his concubines. His Secretary-in-Waiting, Ahdi Husnkar Jang, bowed low and asked leave of absence for the afternoon.

Ahdi Husnkar Jang drove out of the city to the foot of Gipsies' Hill and went for a long walk. He climbed to the top, and splashing through pools of mud, passing from track to track, and from hanging rock to hanging rock, made his way past the bird-catchers' mud-and-straw huts, to the spot where the solitary house of

Dr Qurban Husain – the first to be built on Gipsies' Hill – was already standing.

It so happened that at this moment the sky took a fancy to see what was going on in the city. It tore a gap in the clouds and looked down with its deep blue eyes. The Rajah of Rajahs' Hindu cook was soaking gram cakes in yoghourt. His Muslim cook was grilling shish-kababs on the spit. His youngest wife was thinking of the handsome young Arab who had eyed her appreciatively from the corner of the road. The British Resident was confiding to the Finance Minister his distrust of the Prime Minister. The ruling prince, the Khan Hazrat, had just taken another tablet of opium, and was picking his nose and trying to make up his mind whether to sign the papers sent by the Resident or to write an elegy on the Grandson of the Prophet, martyred thirteen hundred years ago. Near the Four Turrets the horse-carriage drivers were making fun of a group of eunuchs dressed as women. A labourer was carrying on his back a fifty-four pound sack of cement. A man was putting up a poster advertising a Charlie Chaplin film. In short, all was right with the world. Ahdi Husnkar Jang looked up at the sky and smiled in gratitude. The sky laughed back graciously and the clouds spat out the mild sun.

The view over the city was beautiful – the minarets of the mosques, the spires of the temples, the thousands of dwellings sprawled out beneath his gaze, and the great lake of Shahid Sagar, brimful of monsoon rain. At his feet lay a little pool, and on the slopes below it rolling fields of paddy with not a square inch of barren land to be seen. Grass was growing round every stone and rock, grass and creeping vines, studded with bright yellow flowers and swarming with hundreds of thousands of insects whose mingled chorus could be heard clearly in the still air.

Ahdi Husnkar Jang closed his eyes and opened them again. He had conjured up a picture of the hanging gardens of Malabar Hill in Bombay, overlooking the sea. He looked again at Shahid Sagar with its muddy blue water, and in his mind's eye he saw hundreds of houses being built among these hanging rocks on the top of Gipsies' Hill, and on its slopes and in its hollows. He saw the tracks being widened, roads being built, descending to the valleys and climbing up to the heights, hanging like lace on the skirts of the hill. The most picturesque rocks could, he thought, be left as they were or surrounded with gardens; and the rest could be broken up for building stone. He saw thousands of aborigine stone-hewers driving their wooden-wheeled buffalo carts loaded with heavy stone, their women bare from the waist up and with breasts as firm as the rocks around them, carrying baskets of stone on their heads and passing them to the masons. He saw hundreds of houses going up, modern and bizarre and exotic, combining 'German' abstract designs with arabesques and marble trellises, enclosed by hedged gardens; here and there would be a house resembling a pagoda or even one reminiscent of far-off South America. There would be orange gardens, and tree-lined avenues. . . .

The following day Ahdi Husnkar Jang was again on duty, laying various papers before the Rajah of Rajahs for his decision. The Rajah of Rajahs was very, very old. His false teeth were old, the eyes that peered out of his dyed eyelashes were old; his arthritic backbone was old, and held artificially straight by a surgical belt. When he had signed all the papers which had been laid before him, routine orders, orders for promotion, demotion and transfer, schemes motivated by patriotic fervour – or by nepotism – he put down the fountain-pen which the British Resident had presented to him, tilted back his head and closed his eyes. God knows what lay behind those eyelids, in the recesses and vacant spaces of that brain: boundless love and loyalty to the Khan Hazrat; boundless love and loyalty to the British Crown; philanthropic concern for the poor; consideration for the rich; condescension towards his courtiers; and love for every woman in the world – love for the slanting eyes of his young Rajput Rani, love for the big moist eyes of his Muslim Begum, love for European women, love for low-caste aborigine women, love for other men's daughters and daughters-in-law, love for the dark-skinned maidservants in their grubby sarees. . . . The air was full of the fragrance of the hookah. The Rajah opened his eyes and said with dignity, 'Long may the Khan Hazrat live! Long may his Kingdom endure!'

He took another pull at the hookah and blew out the smoke, wafting the aroma across the Persian carpets. Ahdi Husnkar Jang, who had been waiting to catch his eye, bowed low, by which he meant, 'Your servant awaits your command,' . . . that is, wants to go. The Rajah motioned to him with the mouthpiece of the hookah to stay, and with a gesture towards a nearby chair indicated that he should sit down. The Secretary-in-Waiting again bowed respectfully and took his seat. The attendants saw at once that the Rajah of Rajahs was in a gracious mood.

With his eyes half-closed, the old man said, 'Call them in.'

14

This was the signal for audience. Courtiers and petitioners who had been waiting outside for an hour or more in the cool, spacious veranda patiently gazing at the Kashmir carvings on the wooden columns, were now brought in. Each of them bowed deeply and salaamed as he entered. The Rajah acknowledged each salutation with a nod; for the senior officers such as Zijah Jang, the Home Secretary, Araish Jang, the Chief Engineer and Khaqan Jang, the Royal Physician, there was a gracious smile as well.

One of the petitioners – a somewhat untidily dressed young man who looked as though he drank heavily – was presented to him: 'This gentleman has brought a letter from Iqbal. He is himself a very promising poet.'

'God be praised! God be praised!' The hookah gurgled and the aroma again filled the room. 'So you have a letter from my friend Iqbal. He knows me for a mystic like himself, whose soul is not with the things of this world.'

'Your Lordship is indeed a mystic,' said the Royal Physician, bowing deeply. 'A most just, as most true observation.'

The Rajah smiled contentedly. The petitioner was about to hand over Iqbal's letter to the Rajah of Rajahs, but the great mystic was now in a mood of abstraction, pulling at his hookah and reflecting on the vanity of vanities. With an understanding smile Ahdi Husnkar Jang took the letter from the petitioner's hand.

The hookah again gurgled. Zijah Jang and Khaqan Jang were whispering together, and the Rajah of Rajahs returned from the ecstasy of Life Divine to the banalities of this world. He laid the mouthpiece of the hookah on a silver dish and asked kindly, 'What is it, Nawab?'

'Your lordship, Zijah Jang was telling me about his case.'

'What case, Zijah? Let us hear it.'

Zijah Jang was an impressive figure. Six feet tall, fair-complexioned, haughty, and an aristocrat by birth, he never adopted a humble tone with anyone except the Rajah of Rajahs, and, of course, with the Khan Hazrat.

'May your lordship live for ever! The Finance Minister, who as your lordship knows does not like me because of my devotion to your lordship, has made two complaints against me: First, that by my order the two parts of the Secretariat have been connected by a bridge between their upper storeys; and second, that there is an inscription on the bridge saying that this was done by my order.'

'Excellent! A bridge with an inscription. A most fitting plan. I must be sure to come and see it one day. Eh, Ahdi?'

The Rajah of Rajahs had already seen it half a dozen times at least; in fact it was he who had laid the foundation stone.

'Indeed,' said Ahdi Husnkar Jang, 'your lordship should most certainly see it.'

Zijah Jang continued. 'The Finance Minister has refused to sanction the expenditure.'

'Set your mind at rest. I shall speak to him about it.'

'God grant your lordship long life.'

'Well, Ahdi, what has Iqbal written to me, his unworthy mystic friend?'

Ahdi Husnkar Jang began to read out the letter. As he listened, the Rajah of Rajahs began to doze, and before the letter was finished he had fallen fast asleep in his chair. The petitioners tiptoed out. Ahdi Husnkar Jang whispered to the bohemian poet who had brought Iqbal's letter of recommendation: 'That is all that was needed. I shall write to the Education Department to find you a post as lecturer.'

A little later the Rajah of Rajahs awoke. 'Yes, Zijah,' he said, 'you were saying about Averroes that there was no greater scholar in Sicily. . . . What, Ahdi? Have they all gone?'

'Yes, your lordship. It was time for your lordship's luncheon.'

'Very well. Have you anything else to tell me?'

'Nothing of importance, your lordship. But yesterday when I was out walking I saw a wonderful sight. I went to Gipsies' Hill. The summit commands a beautiful view over the city, and it occurred to me that if your lordship felt interested a fine suburb could be planned there for the nobility and the higher government officers. Have I your lordship's permission to submit a scheme?'

'Do so by all means. I shall take it personally to the Khan Hazrat, may he live for ever, and obtain his approval. Tell me something of the scene on Gipsies' Hill. You know that romance I am writing these days?'

'*The Magical Tale of the Magnet and the Straw*? Yes, your lordship.'

'You know Munshi Gyan Chand? He told me that Sri Krishna had appeared to him in a dream and handed him some parts of this romance saying to him "Give these to Rajah Shamsher Singh; they are his work written in a former birth." '

'Just so, your lordship.'

'Well, describe the scene on Gipsies' Hill to Munshi Gyan Chand. I may have described it somewhere, I don't remember. Munshi Gyan Chand will receive his instructions from Sri Krishna. . . .'

In *The Magical Tale of the Magnet and the Straw*, reckoned among the masterpieces of the Rajah of Rajahs, Maharaja Sir Shujaat Shamsher Singh Ji Bahadur, Munshi Gyan Chand, in accordance with the instructions received in his dream from the blue-bodied god Lord Krishna, describes Gipsies' Hill in these words:

'The story-tellers of olden time and the chroniclers of the traditions of ages long past tell that on Gipsies' Hill in former days there stood a great city, the twin in splendour and in population of its neighbour Farkhundanagar. Such was the charm of its dwellings and its gardens that those were gleaming white as the faces of the houris of paradise, while in these the dense shade of the trees was as black as their long tresses, the envy of the long black night of separation. Only the great and the noble dwelt in the city. Commoners could not enter, and no barking of dogs grated upon the ear. There was no market-place, no commerce. It seemed an enchanted city where none laboured, yet all were blessed with wealth and high estate. If there were any who worked, they worked in Farkhundanagar, and the sweet-tongued chroniclers relate that they, too, dozed in their offices. In this earthly paradise the women would sit adorning their beauty at eventide, and the younger among them would sigh for the love of some swain. The peri Gulandam would sit writing love-letters or reading lovers' tales in the old romances, and would keep secret tryst with her demon-lover, Khanna Dev, behind the black rocks. But the fairest among these peris was the enchantress Nur Jahan. Her skin was like ivory, her cheeks bloomed like the rose, her delicate body was slender as the cypress, and her fragrance was the fragrance of musk; and the sweet-tongued chroniclers tell her story in this wise. . . .'

2

The real Nur Jahan's skin was not at all 'like ivory'. 'Delicate'? Yes, if you like, but only because every six months when the doctor examined her, he diagnosed anaemia. (Once or twice he had suspected T.B., but when her chest was x-rayed her lungs were found to be quite clear.) All her life she had had to take vitamin B. 'A face like a peri'? I cannot say. I could only give an opinion if I had ever seen a peri. Still, she was not bad-looking; rather a long face, with rather large front teeth; but not so large that you could see them peeping out even when her mouth was shut. 'Fragrant with the fragrance of musk'? That was something of an exaggeration; but it is true she did use perfume. But then the real Nur Jahan, when you come to think of it, could not have been the model for the enchantress Nur Jahan of *The Magical Tale of the Magnet and the Straw,* sublime creation of the Rajah of Rajahs, Maharajah Sir Shujaat Shamsher Singh Bahadur; because at the time when Ahdi Husnkar Jang laid his scheme for the development of Gipsies' Hill – henceforth to be called Kishanpalli – before the Rajah of Rajahs, Nur Jahan was still only a little girl, and in fact it was on that same day that her grandfather Qabil Jang died. The Rajah of Rajahs had attended his funeral the same evening and the Khan Hazrat himself had been graciously present for a few minutes.

There are very few people who still remember Qabil Jang. He belonged to the age when Sir Sayyid Ahmad Khan used to wear his medals and stars on his breast, when Hali in his Urdu prose used English words quite freely, and when Nazir Ahmad's Ibn ul Waqt still used to dine upon ox-tongue and had not yet repented of his English ways.[1]

---

[1] Sir Sayyid Ahmad Khan (1817–98) was the leader of the first Indian Muslim movement which sought to come to terms with the modern West. Hali (1837–1914) poet, critic and biographer, and Nazir Ahmad (1836–1912), who helped to lay the foundations of the Urdu novel, were two of the best-known writers who supported Sir Sayyid's general aims. Ibn ul Waqt ('Son of the Age') is the main character in Nazir Ahmad's novel of that name. In it he ridiculed those whose enthusiasm for the

Three tides of westernization have flooded in upon our noble families. The first was after the Mutiny of 1857, in Sir Sayyid's day, when Qabil Jang and Mashur ul Mulk had changed their way of life. That westernization was something like that of the Turks and Egyptians today: that is European ways, European clothes, horse-riding, frocks for the girls, 'Darling' as the form of address for all the women of the family, dogs, English food, English drink, butlers, Christian nursemaids for the children – in short, a desire to be just like the sahibs.

The second tide sought to bring about a change from within. With it came nationalism, self-respect, a sense of dignity, and an enthusiasm for western literature, the western arts and sciences, and so on. This second wave has left little trace on the characters of our novels because, along with this inner westernization, the first tide of English clothes, English conversation, clubs and dances, was still flowing strong, and it carried these characters along with it. And the third and last tide – call it westernization or nationalism, socialism, free-thinking – this was a tide which flowed in, it is true, but which by the time it reached Kishanpalli had spent its force and was no more than an intellectual fashion. It may or may not have brought about a revolution among the Indian people, but the people of whom we are writing, were not and are not concerned with that. It may have won a few arm-chair victories on Malabar Hill, but it could not scale the heights of Kishanpalli.

Qabil Jang kissed his little daughter Khurshid Zamani on both cheeks. 'Papa, Papa,' she said.

'What is it, dear?'

'Why is Miss Crewe coming to teach us now?'

'So that you can stay at home for a few months.'

'Not in the convent school, Papa?'

'No.'

'Why, Papa?'

'Because I shall be at home on leave. Who will manage the house if you aren't here?'

'The butler can do it.'

'Don't you want to stay then?'

She put her arms round her father's neck and said, 'Papa, all my friends are at the convent.' Qabil Jang did not reply.

West led them not only to adopt its modern outlook, but also to imitate slavishly its manners and customs.

'Papa, Papa!'

'What is it, dear?'

'Why do you part your beard in two halves?'

'Why?'

'Nothing! I was only asking.'

'Because the Khan Hazrat parts his beard in two halves'; and Qabil Jang went on trimming his whiskers with the scissors.

'Papa, Papa. Why do you dye your beard black?'

'I don't know. I just do.'

'People do it to make themselves look younger, don't they?' She laughed and rubbed her face against her father's chest.

'You're getting very cheeky lately. I shall have to complain to your Matron about it.'

'Papa. When Matron sees your beard, it makes her laugh.'

Qabil Jang smiled and went on trimming his beard.

'Papa, Papa.'

'What?'

'Are you very old?'

'Go and do your homework and stop chattering.'

And Miss Crewe duly came to teach her. She was an Anglo-Indian, about twenty-five years old, and quite the lady, with her Victorian frills, her little parasol, her red lips and rouged cheeks, her ginger hair and her little green cat-like eyes. Khurshid Zamani did not like her at all, and whenever she saw her laughing and talking to her father, it made her furious. She would bite her lips and say to herself: 'Look at her making eyes at Papa! Cow!'

'Papa, Papa!'

'What, dear?'

'I don't want Miss Crewe to teach me.'

'Why not, dear?'

'She doesn't teach me properly.'

'Don't be silly.'

'But Papa, she doesn't like me.'

'Don't be silly.' And Qabil Jang kissed her on both cheeks and went out.

At night she thought of his forked beard tickling her cheeks and cried herself to sleep, muttering to herself again and again, 'She *shan't* teach me! She *shan't* teach me!'

After that she set up a constant refrain to her father, 'I *won't* be taught by Miss Crewe, I *won't*, I *won't*.'

Her father would scold her and smack her, but she still insisted stubbornly, and in the end she was sent off once more to the convent school. There, most of her school-fellows were *'chatte-kars'*, a comprehensive Kishanpalli term embracing at one extreme the English misses and at the other the coal-black Untouchables who had only yesterday declared their faith in Jesus the Messiah. There were a few Hindu girls as well, but Khurshid was the only Muslim girl in the school.

Twenty-five years later, Khurshid Zamani related the whole strange story to her own children. 'Papa had sent me to the convent school, but I used to come home every Sunday. Although Papa was so up to date, he was a good Muslim and a *maulvi* used to come every Sunday to teach me the Qur'ān. One Sunday I went into Mamma's room. I used to cry whenever I went into her room. It was five years since she had died, but I often used to think of her. Before I reached the door, I could smell perfume. I was taken aback and stood there for a moment before going in. The wardrobe doors were wide open and all kinds of English clothes were hanging there. I tell you, Khaqan, I can remember the shock it gave me as vividly as if someone had just struck me. . . .'

Her eldest son Khaqan nodded his head and Khurshid Zamani went on: 'Then I saw in front of the mirror – Khaqan do you remember that mirror? You remember the big dressing-table in Qabiliyat Manzil? You know, the one with the full-length mirror which Ihtisham ul Mulk gave Mamma as a wedding present – well, that hag Miss Crewe was standing in front of it, putting on her make-up – exactly where Mamma used to make up. I was so furious that – well, I can't tell you how furious I was. I went straight to Papa's room. Rahimuddin was there – you know, the old man – he was Papa's valet in those days. He was helping Papa to pull on his long boots. When Papa saw me, he lowered his eyes and I couldn't understand why. I threw my arms round his neck, kissed him on the forehead and said, "Papa, Papa, that Miss Crewe is making up in front of Mamma's mirror. Tell her not to. If you don't, I'll run away."

'Papa gave me a hug and said, "Listen dear, her name isn't Miss Crewe any more. Her name is Sikandar Begum. And now *she* is your Mamma, and you must respect her. She isn't going to hurt you." I left him and ran off to my room, and threw myself face down on the bed, and cried and cried until the pillow was wet. Dinner time came and Rahim came to fetch me; but I wouldn't go. Then Papa came. I still wouldn't go, but just kept on crying; then a bit later she came – Miss Crewe, or Sikandar Begum – call her what you like (Papa had persuaded her to become a Muslim and then married her with full Muslim rites). I pulled the bed-clothes over my face but she came over and cuddled me. She didn't say anything, but she began crying, too, and that made me cry all the more. I clung to her too. And both of us lay there crying together. Then Papa came, and when he saw us both crying together he began to laugh, and we told him to go away.'

Khaqan burst out laughing and said, 'Really, Mamma, you've always been funny.' Khurshid Zamani Begum said, 'Be quiet, you rogue. What about you? I suppose you're *never* funny? And don't interrupt when I am talking. Well, that's how my step-mother and I became friends, and after that as long as she lived she never made any distinction between me and her own children.'

Khaqan got up and went out. The middle girl, Sartaj, put her arms round her mother's neck and herself started crying. 'What's the matter, my dear?' Khurshid Zamani Begum said. 'What are *you* crying for?'

The day Qabil Jang married again, Sir Taj ul Muluk had visited Mashur ul Mulk in mufti. Mashur ul Mulk was so used to seeing him in uniform that he was rather surprised. Sir Taj ul Muluk was in good humour, and his face wore an ironical smile.

'Have you heard the news?' he asked.

'What news, General Sahib?'

'Don't you know? He has got married again.'

'Who has?'

'Qabil Jang.'

'No, General!'

'Oh yes, he was, I swear it to you.'

'Who to?'

'That Anglo-Indian woman – what's her name? – Grace, Grace Crewe. You know old Crewe in the Seventh Infantry? I've just recommended his promotion to Major. It's his sister. But what do you think of it? At his age, too!'

'Hee, hee, hee.'

'Hee, hee, hee.'

'At his age!'

'At his age! Hee, hee, hee!'

'They tell me that the Court Physician has sent him his best mercury aphrodisiac.'

'Hee, hee, hee.'

Qabil Jang is dead now, and so is his second wife Grace Crewe, or Sikandar Begum. She bore him five children, two boys, Nayazi and Mahmud Shaukat, and three girls, Nazli, Nazima and Kahkashan.

He was still living when an incident took place which initiated a revolution in the social life of Farkhundanagar. This was the wedding of Khurshid Zamani, and the incident which caused such a stir was that Khurshid Zamani entertained the guests at her own wedding. Even today throughout India, and in Farkhundanagar as in every other city, the bride sits with the hem of her saree drawn out over her face, and with her eyes closed. What with the fatiguing *manjha* ceremony and her mingled fear and longing for the married future, she cannot think properly. The *arsi mushaf* ceremony, and many others, too, are still performed. And even if they are not, at any rate, it is unknown for a bride, at her own wedding, smiling and dressed in a fashionable saree, to welcome the guests as they arrive. The old ladies could never have dreamed of such a thing, and they were deeply shocked. This was the revolutionary innovation of Grace Crewe or Sikandar Begum. Instead of making her step-daughter sit huddled and apprehensive in a wrapping of cloth of gold she made her the peri among the wedding guests. But then, that was the time when everything English was either unspeakably good or unspeakably bad, according to your point of view. If you adopted English ways you were either regarded as extremely cultured or were accused of 'turning Christian'. In those days culture meant Edwardian suits and frilly frocks, ox-tongue for dinner (and occasionally even wine and whisky), bearers, commodes and bungalows. No one could even dream that the day would come when the sahibs' ears would be affronted by the cry of 'Quit India!'

The comments of the old ladies were something to savour. 'These nawabs are turning their daughters into mem-sahibs. Just look at them! They can read and write; they wear frocks; they run after men, and write love-letters to them and have illegitimate brats – it's one thing after another. And now, if you please, it's come to this that they even arrange their own weddings, laughing and showing all their teeth, and talking quite shamelessly. It's all a sign that the end of the world is coming.'

But these signs of the end of the world did not worry either Qabil Jang or the bridegroom's father, Mashur ul Mulk. It was enough for them that no other Muslim family in Farkhundanagar could produce a girl who spoke English so fluently, called her parents Papa and Mamma, kissed her brothers on the cheek, and called everybody in the family 'darling'. No doubt their rival Sir Taj ul Muluk was making rapid progress, but both Mashur ul Mulk and Qabil Jang were certain that once their two families were united they could get the better of him. And this family alliance was the foundation of the present union. The Khan Hazrat was very fond of Sir Taj ul Muluk. All right, let him be. The British had conferred a knighthood on him. What of it? Mashur ul Mulk was quite certain that he, too, would get a knighthood within a year or two. He regularly sent presents to the British Resident, and he would not have hesitated to divulge the Khan Hazrat's secrets to him, too, but for the fact that he had seen what had happened to Munfarid Jang.

What had happened to Munfarid Jang was that he had come to grief through trying too hard to please both the British Resident and the Khan Hazrat at the same time. One day in his royal displeasure his august monarch had called him an idiot. At the time he had lowered his eyes and said nothing, and had bowed to the ground as he left. The incident had occurred in a place which he was not permitted to mention, and he writhed helplessly until in the end he had the idea of sending an anonymous letter to the British Resident. He folded his monographed note-paper, tore off the monographed part, and wrote what he had to say on the other half, including all manner of impudent references to the Khan Hazrat's private life. The British Resident took care to have a copy of this letter sent to the Political Department, but proposed also, as a mark of his sincere friendship, to send the original to the Khan Hazrat. However, the British Resident had in his service a favourite bearer who was also one of the Khan Hazrat's trusted spies. (It was customary in those days for the Khan Hazrat to have his spies amongst the British Resident's employees, and vice versa.) This bearer suggested to the Resident that there was no point in sending the letter yet, as the Khan Hazrat would have no means of recognizing the handwriting; it would be better to wait until Christmas. Christmas cards from all the nobles would come, and the handwriting could be compared and identified. So this was done, and the bearer identified the writing as that of Munfarid Jang. When he told the Resident whose the letter was, his reaction was to delay matters, reflecting that he could use the disgruntled nawab to get further useful information. He sent for him and found out all he could, secretly sending full reports to the Political Department. Meanwhile the favourite bearer, seeing that the Resident's intentions had now changed, stole both the letter and the Christmas card and took them to the royal palace where he laid them before the prince. The Khan Hazrat visited his most severe displeasure upon Munfarid Jang. He was dismissed and ordered into exile, and Taj ul Muluk (he had not yet been knighted) was promoted to fill his post. And when Munfarid Jang met the British Resident at the Viceroy's party in Calcutta, the Resident apologized to him profusely, but said that in the circumstances it would have been quite impossible to protect him.

This episode had inspired Mashur ul Mulk with a healthy fear, and he used to keep well away from the British Resident's bungalow, so that Sir Taj ul Muluk should have no opportunity of pinning anything on him. But now that his elder son Sanjar Beg was married to Qabil Jang's duaghter Khurshid Zamani, he began to feel more confident; the union of the two families would certainly weight the scales in their favour.

Nur Jahan was the youngest of their family. The truth of the matter is that her coming into the world had not been particularly desired. Sanjar Beg had not really wanted another child, though he had no real objection either. But Khurshid Zamani was not in the least prepared to welcome another newcomer. Her first son, Khaqan, had robbed her bosom of its beauty, the second, Asghar, had taken away the lustre of her complexion, and the third (Mashur un Nisa, a girl) had brought out her dark circles under the eyes. The fourth (another girl, Sartaj) had put wrinkles on her face.

This fifth child would be the forerunner of old age, and Khurshid Zamani Begum was not at all ready to welcome old age. It was only yesterday that she had welcomed her wedding guests, though that 'yesterday', it is true, was eighteen years ago. Sanjar Beg's hair had already turned grey and Khurshid Zamani Begum knew the whole history of the process. First, one or two grey hairs had appeared among the black; then came the day when there were as many grey hairs as black; then a grey line began to appear all along the temples. Then all his hair became grizzled; and finally one morning Khurshid Zamani Begum looked at him and saw so much grey hair that she took alarm for her own fate. She began to wear her most tightly fitting blouses and adopted the fashions of an eighteen-year-old. Not cloth of gold to be sure, but heavily embroidered sarees with Banarasi borders. In short, she used every weapon to resist the enemy's attack. But still the enemy came on, turning her hair whiter and whiter beneath the cover of her black dye, robbing her complexion of its colour, loading her with flesh and fat, and steadily increasing the number of her wrinkles. And now this young lady had made her entrance. Well, once she had made it, of course she had to be reared as the others had been.

3

Nur Jahan has vivid memories of her childhood. She can remember how when she could only just talk, and she and Sartaj used to play together with their dolls, Asghar had caught hold of her and Sartaj during a dance at their house and shut them in the big dirty linen-basket in the corridor. And there they were clinging to each other, yelling and shrieking, while Asghar went off to dance with his aunties Kahkashan and Nazima. The two little girls could see through the chinks in the basketwork, and the ayahs simply couldn't understand where the crying was coming from. In the end Khurshid Zamani Begum, gesticulating angrily, traced it to the linen-basket, and she went over and lifted up the lid and looked inside. But instead of getting angry with Asghar, she started laughing, which made them howl all the more. They were jumping up and down among the dirty clothes, wailing 'We can't get out!' until Khurshid Zamani Begum got hold of their arms and pulled them out. They went on crying for a long time until they saw Asghar offering some chocolate to Aunty Kahkashan and Aunty Nazima. Then they stopped crying and watched expectantly with mouths watering until Asghar at last condescended to give them some, too.

Nur Jahan well remembers the dancing in the big lounge – the slow foxtrot 'I love you sweetheart', and Asghar dancing with Anglo-Indian girls and holding them close. 'I don't like to see the boy holding his partners so close,' said Sanjar Beg to his wife, 'I don't like it at all.' But Grace Crewe or Sikandar Begum, the mother of Kahkashan and Nazima, saw nothing objectionable in it. 'Let the children enjoy themselves. What's wrong with it?' – it was 'What's wrong with it? . . . What's wrong with it?' until her dying day. Little Nur Jahan and Sartaj sat watching Asghar dancing with Aunty Nazima and Aunty Kahkashan. Both aunties had brown hair and blue eyes, red lips, and gleaming white teeth. Both of them looked very 'sweet'. Both of them teased Khaqan a great deal. Nur Jahan and Sartaj both liked them. They had decided that when they grew up Nur Jahan was going to marry Aunty Kahkashan and Sartaj Aunty Nazima. They were looking forward to bedtime, when Aunty Kahkashan and Aunty Nazima would come to kiss them good-night, and tell them, 'O how I love you, my little darlings!'

Nur Jahan can remember many other things – her first school in Farkhundanagar, the school at Panchgani, Saliha Begum's Persian class. (She still giggles when she thinks of it.) Little girls in tight trousers and long muslin shirts and waistcoats, embroidered caps on their heads, shrieking with laughter. And Saliha Begum's big teeth, red with betel, and her gums black with *missi* and her thick lips half red and half black, wiping the reddened spittle away with her hand and saying crossly, 'Hee, hee, hee – what are you laughing at? You naughty girls!' And the girls mimicking her behind her back, 'You naughty, naughty, naughty girls!'

She remembered the other mistresses, too, like Miss Queeny, who was fresh from Australia, and could not have been more than twenty years old. The girls used to rag her a lot, because she looked so nice when her white face went red with anger. But she was not as amusing as Saliha Begum, with her 'Naughty, naughty, naughty girls!'

Sartaj was a terribly naughty child. She and Nur Jahan were often sent out of the class. They would stand outside the door calling out repeatedly in chorus, 'Saliha Begum, can we come in now? . . . Saliha Begum, can we come in now?', and Saliha Begum would lose her temper and shout, 'No! I don't want naughty girls like you in my class.'

And then the two of them would run off and make the round of the whole school chanting in sing-song 'Naughty, naughty, naughty'. And if they met the headmistress, Miss Nelson, and she scolded them, they would wail to her, 'Saliha Begum has turned us out.' Once when Nur Jahan was wailing like this, her nose began to run and when Miss Nelson held out her handkerchief to wipe it, she blew so violently that the whole handkerchief was soiled. Miss Nelson gave her a gentle tap and said, 'Nuri, that is very rude.'

Sartaj replied like a shot, 'Miss Nelson, would you tell Saliha Begum, too? She is always eating betel in class and wiping the spit with her hand.'

A carriage used to come to fetch Sartaj and Nur Jahan from school. When it arrived they would hear Papa's voice calling, 'Taju! Nuri! Come along my dears!' And both of them would come running. Both wanted to be first to get on their father's knee. Then they would tell him all about what had happened at school

28

that day. 'Papa, you know Saliha Begum? Today she was horrid to us,' Sartaj would say in her most innocent and appealing way. 'Papa, Papa, you know Miss Nelson? Today she was saying "Sartaj is the prettiest girl in the whole school." I *am* pretty, aren't I, Papa?' Sometimes they would talk about the other girls. 'Papa, you know Zainab?' 'Papa, you know Mr Askari's little girl, Bilquis? Today she came to school in a Hyderabadi stole. We said we are too little to wear clothes like that. That's right, isn't it, Papa? Only big girls should wear a Hyderabadi stole, shouldn't they? We're too little, aren't we? That's right, isn't it, Papa?' 'Papa you promised to bring us chocolates didn't you?' 'Papa, Papa, Papa . . .'

Then Khurshid Zamani Begum's voice would thunder, 'Come along, Sartaj. Come along, Nuri. Wash your hands and face and change your clothes and come and get your tea.' Both of them would jump out of the carriage, and come running and leaping like young deer, and rush giggling to the bathroom.

In those days a little boy who lived nearby used to come at about five o'clock and practice riding his bike in their courtyard until it got dark. He was always teasing Nur Jahan. Once or twice he nearly ran her over with his bike. Several times he had hit her and she had pulled his hair and scratched his face and let out a string of curses which she had heard from the housemaid, 'May God strike you!', 'May you drop dead!', and so on, until her ayah got hold of her and dragged her inside to Khurshid Zamani Begum.

The boy's name was Athar, and he was Sir Taj ul Muluk's grandson. One day, after a battle royal, Nur Jahan was still going around pouting; and he gave her his whole share of chocolate.

At school Sartaj and Nur Jahan often used to have stand-up fights. 'Sartaj, you're always showing off,' and Sartaj would reply by giving her a hard slap and go on boasting to the other girls. 'You know what, Zainab? Yesterday evening the Khan Hazrat's car was passing our house. He told the driver to stop. I was playing near the gate. The Khan Hazrat said to me, "You are Sanjar Beg's daughter, aren't you?" I said, "Yes, your Highness." Then the Khan Hazrat called me over and sat me on his knee and kissed me and said, "What a pretty girl!" And the Khan Hazrat gave me a sovereign and went away.'

Zainab would listen to all this wide-eyed and gulping. But Nur Jahan would pipe up, 'It's all lies! It's all lies!' Sartaj would scold her, 'Shut up, you! What do you know about it? You weren't there.'

29

And Nur Jahan would say 'You shut up. Goodness, you don't half swank! The Khan Hazrat never came. He never spoke to you. It's all lies.'

The other girls would giggle at the spectacle of the two sisters quarrelling. Sartaj would get angry. 'Shut up, you! Look out or I'll hit you with my shoe.'

'You shut up!' Nur Jahan would get angry, too.

'You'll have a black mother-in-law.' (Sartaj's abuse showed a certain originality.)

'You'll have a black mother-in-law,' Nur Jahan would at once reply.

And then they would really set to. And so it went on all through primary and secondary school, until they were sent to Panchgani to prepare for their Junior Cambridge.

4

Mashur ul Mulk was very fond of his grandson Khaqan. It would be hard to say why. From start to finish Khaqan showed no signs of any considerable intelligence or alertness. Lank, lean and brown, and with less than his fair share of brains, he was the butt of all his relatives and friends. His own younger brother Asghar was always making fun of him and Mashur un Nisa used to say in his presence, 'My goodness, what a crazy brother I've got!' He never bothered much about school, and indeed in those days boys of good family were not expected to. Their parents were only concerned with seeing that somehow or other they passed their matric, and then got a commission in the army. In the families of Qabil Jang, Mashur ul Mulk and Sir Taj ul Muluk, this was standard practice.

Khaqan grew up with about as much understanding as a child. He was only a little younger than his uncles, Nayazi and Mahmud Shaukat, and it was thanks to them that he now landed in serious trouble. These two were thorough-paced rogues. They would ride their horses out of Farkhundanagar, and coming along at a gallop would carry off the young stone-hewer women, lifting them bodily into the saddle as they galloped past. Their menfolk would run after them, throwing stones until they were out of breath and the horses beyond their range, and an hour later the women would return weeping and straightening their clothes. Even in the city, it was an everyday thing for them to reach out for the breasts of a low-caste woman as she passed them in the street. And Nayazi was a heavy drinker, too. He was perhaps the handsomest youth in all Farkhundanagar, with his brown moustaches and red lips, his cat's eyes and his well-formed, slim body. These two, like everyone else, used to amuse themselves by ragging Khaqan. One of their favourite games was to keep slapping him on the head until he lost his temper – and then be especially nice to him, to make up for it. One day when they had been teasing him unmercifully they decided as a treat to take him 'hunting' with them to Chunnapalli Lake. This was one of their regular hunting grounds, for the embankment of the lake was under repair, and a large party of stone-hewer women was working on it. If they had wanted to, they could have had any of these women for eight annas or so. But then they would not have had the pleasure of hunting them. And then, again, they always boasted to their friends that they had never yet spent a penny on any woman.

But this time there was a hitch. The repair work at Chunnapalli came under the charge of Araish Husain, who was at that time head of the Irrigation Department. (He was always careful to keep on very good terms with his superiors and reaped his reward by always being appointed to projects in or near Farkhundanagar, while others were posted to outlying districts. In later years he was honoured with the title of Araish Jang, and during the days when Ala Kausar Navaz Jang was at the height of his power, he came to wield very considerable influence.) Araish Husain knew the two brothers well, and out of gratitude to their father, who had been a good friend to him during his lifetime, had always treated them with consideration. When his inspectors and over-seers first told him of their exploits he had sent for them and remonstrated with them. But though they had behaved very meekly in his presence, they were soon up to their old tricks again, and Araish Husain had decided it was time to teach them a lesson. He had wooden gates made ready at two points on the narrow path along the embankment, so that the next time they came 'hunting' they could be caught and brought to him.

So this time when Nayazi and Mahmud Shaukat, with Khaqan in train, came galloping along, the overseers and inspectors were ready for them. As soon as they entered the area of the embankment, the wooden gate behind them was closed. Nayazi and Mahmud Shaukat, as usual, each captured his woman, but then they saw the gate close in front of them. They threw the women down on to the soft, long grass, jumped their horses over the gate and were off, while poor Khaqan, who could neither hunt nor manage a horse well enough to jump gates, was trapped. Before the overseers could reach him, the stone-hewers had dragged him off his horse and beaten him soundly, while the women stood by with their hands on their hips, laughing and abusing him until the chief overseer came up and drove them away. 'I hope you aren't hurt, Sir?' he said to Khaqan.

But Khaqan was hurt, and humiliated, too. When he got home after his beating, Khurshid Zamani was like an angry tigress. She sent for her two half-brothers repeatedly, but for several days both of them lay low. 'God damn them, they are ruining my son. If their father had been alive he would have taught them a lesson – sons of an Anglo-Indian bitch.'

When after some days Nayazi at last came to see her Khurshid Zamani really let fly at him. He just let her go on and the more angry she got, the more often he interrupted her, 'Khurshid, I'm awfully hungry. . . . Have you got any carrot *halva* in the cupboard?', and so on, until in the end he cut her short with, 'All right! All right! Have it your way. But, Khurshid, there are no two ways about it. The boy's a great coward . . . more like a girl than a man. All right, so he took a beating. What do you want me to do about it?'

Meanwhile Khurshid Zamani Begum had been persuaded, largely by aristocratic ladies of the old school, that both Khaqan and Asghar were now of an age where steps would have to be taken to keep them out of trouble. The traditional way of meeting this situation among the aristocracy of Farkhundanagar was the institution of *chokris*. This was a variant of the harem. In the households of the nobility numbers of these girls would be kept. Some were bought cheap in times of famine; others were destitute orphans; and many were themselves the children of chokris who had been in the same family for several generations. When any of these girls took the fancy of the head of the house, she became his concubine – and the rival of the Begum Sahiba. Next in status came those whom the sons of the house fancied, and who became their concubines; while those who were too ugly, or too dirty, or too deformed to appeal either to the head of the house or to his sons, were married off to servants either within the household or elsewhere. As times changed, the chokris shed some of the restrictions to which they had been subjected. The usual pattern was for a chokri to warm the bed of one of the sons of the house for a while, and then when she got tired of him, to run off with a groom or a cook, though their ideal was always a chauffeur.

Qabil Jang, influenced partly by 'westernization' and still more by his Anglo-Indian wife, had never permitted chokris in his house, and Khurshid Zamani's own mother, too, had come from a 'westernized' family where the custom was unknown. Khurshid Zamani, too, had never kept chokris in her own household while her husband was young, for what was the point of cherishing a viper in one's bosom? But with every passing year, she put more and more trust in her incomparable husband's stainless character. He had never gone in for debauchery, out of loyalty not so much to his wife, as to his religious principles, which, as all his friends could testify, he had always scrupulously upheld. He had never permitted in his own home, or lent his support anywhere else, to entertainment by dancing girls. True, he did attend such gatherings at other people's houses, and would even exchange ribaldries with the dancing girls, but that was about all. In short, he was safe enough, and that was why, when Khurshid Zamani Begum finally decided to follow the example of the old nobility and introduce chokris into her house, she felt no apprehension on her husband's account.

In any case she was a woman whose one great aim in life was to vie with the older aristocracy, displaying her wealth as they did, and imitating all their ways. Unless one could establish one's position above that of one's fellows, what was the point of living? It was thanks to people like her that Farkhundanagar could work the miracle of linking the middle ages with the standards of the nineteenth and twentieth centuries.

So when famine broke out in Tasdiqnagar, Khurshid Zamani Begum had three fourteen-year-old girls purchased for her. She named one of them Sunbul, the second Gulnar and the third Sada Bahar. The three 'wretched, god-forsaken rustics' were taught Urdu and converted to Islam. It was explained to them that when they were told to bring water, they must pour it in a glass, cover it with a muslin cloth embroidered with beads and serve it on a little silver tray. She tried over and over again to get them to pronounce 'cup' properly but with as little success as she had had with the cooks and the bearers.

She had picked out Sunbul for Khaqan, but the wretched little slave made fun of the young master as everyone else did, while Khaqan on his side took no advantage of his opportunities, and when, eighteen months after coming to Farkhundanagar, Sunbul produced a child, it was certainly not Khaqan's. Khurshid Zamani Begum was very angry about it, and she was adamant that come what may, Sunbul should not marry Nadir Beg's chauffeur, who was the father of the child. She even quarrelled with her half-sister Nazli (that is Begum Nadir Beg) on this point. . . . At all events Khaqan never paid these chokris any attention, except for teasing them occasionally. And Asghar in those days was away at the Dehra Dun Military Academy.

Khaqan had got his commission, and Khurshid Zamani Begum now began to make plans for his marriage. The experiment with the chokris had not proved too successful. The problem now was to find a suitable girl.

Her whole aim was to arrange a match with a family of higher status than her own. In other circumstances she might have contemplated a marriage alliance with the house of Sir Taj ul Muluk, the traditional rival of her own and her husband's families. (Two of his grand-daughters had married the princes of two small Coromandel principalities, and though the other two were still too young to marry, distinguished matches were already arranged for them.) In this way she might have not only satisfied her ambition, but ended the rivalry between their houses. But this was out of the question. Mashur ul Mulk would never agree to a grandson of his marrying into Sir Taj ul Muluk's family, for he prided himself on his pure Mughal stock and could trace his family-tree back to Babar's time, and beyond that to the Chaghtai Turks of Badakhshan, Tirmiz and Andjan. In his eyes, Sir Taj ul Muluk was an upstart – an upstart who had attained to high office, but an upstart all the same.

So she turned her attention to the second most distinguished Mughal family in Farkhundanagar, that is, to the house of Zijah Jang.

Zijah Jang was a grand old man, and lived in imposing style. Though only Home Secretary, which in the Farkhundanagar administration was not a ministerial post, he gave himself all the airs of a minister, and except for the Prime Minister, Raja Shujaat Shamsher Singh (whose aristocratic modesty and lordly asceticism compelled universal homage) he cared for nobody. It was his misfortune that this attitude earned him the sustained enmity of one of the most powerful of the ministers, a man of great ambition and a master of suave diplomacy, Ala Kausar Nawaz Jang, the special friend of the British Resident and dictator in the financial affairs of the state. The Finance Minister at every turn found Zijah Jang a thorn in his side. He could not stomach his insolent pride, and moreover the man was close enough below him on the political ladder to be a potential source of danger to him. There were other things, too. Zijah Jang held estates that were twice as large as his, both in Farkhundanagar State and in British India. Zijah Jang was an aristocrat born and bred, while he had risen from the middle classes. Zijah Jang held himself somewhat aloof, but there was no duplicity in him, and once his support was promised to a man, then, in the old aristocratic tradition, it was a

35

point of honour with him to give it to the end. Whereas Ala Kausar Nawaz Jang was easy of access, courted the support of men of all parties and groupings and factions, and made his way to the top by bowing to the stronger and trampling the weaker underfoot. Zijah Jang was a man who liked his comforts. He was never in his office before eleven o'clock, and at one o'clock sharp broke for lunch. He would lunch in style with a few friends and protégés (and according to reports reaching Ala Kausar Nawaz Jang these 'lunches' were regular banquets, followed by rounds of the hookah until half-past three), returning to his office for a brief afternoon session before closing at four. Whereas Ala Kausar Nawaz Jang was industrious and hard-working. He thought it scandalous to conduct government business in this way and had more than once complained about it both to the Prime Minister and to the Khan Hazrat. Zijah Jang was a man of old-fashioned loyalties – to his religion and to his monarch. The modern conception of loyalty to one's country he rejected as likely to conflict with these. On the other hand, Ala Kausar Nawaz Jang was, in his own selfish, ostentatious way, something of a patriot. He faithfully served his religion, his ruler and his country – provided that no risk to his own position was involved – and it was his initiative that had adorned Farkhundanagar with a number of fine buildings and public works. Zijah Jang's initiative had produced only one public building. Between his own office and the offices of his department, there was a small dirty stream, and he had had an arched bridge constructed between the upper storeys of the two buildings. It was faced with marble, and when the file came before Ala Kausar Nawaz Jang for sanction in his capacity as Finance Minister he had entered a strong objection; and, as we have seen, Zijah Jang had gone to appeal to Rajah Shujaat Shamsher Singh. As a matter of fact Ala Kausar Nawaz Jang's real objection was not to the bridge, but to a black marble slab upon it, which bore the inscription 'By command of Zijah Jang'. How dare a man who was only Home Secretary inscribe 'By command of Zijah Jang' when he should have inscribed 'By command of the Khan Hazrat'?

In his preoccupation with his status and this constant friction with Ala Kausar Nawaz Jang, Zijah Jang had neglected his family, sons and daughters alike. The boys turned out all right to be sure. But all three of the girls went to the bad, and this was a great personal tragedy for the old man. Sarwari, the middle one, was the prettiest and the worst. If any woman in Farkhundanagar could be called a nymphomaniac it was she. Heaven knows what Khurshid Zamani Begum was about when she proposed for Sarwari's hand for Khaqan, simply to bring about an alliance with Zijah's family. What a match! A brazen, promiscuous woman like Sarwari, and a stupid, cowardly, idiotic boy like Khaqan. As she lay in the arms of her brave lovers, Sarwari herself would weep as she spoke of her engagement, but Zijah Jang and his wife both wanted to be rid of her as soon as possible, hoping that once she was married she might mend her ways.

No sooner had Khaqan brought his new bride home, than Khurshid Zamani Begum realized her mistake. She had made the alliance with Zijah Jang's house, but at what a price. In the first place Sarwari was contemptuous of her from the very start – and her tongue was ten times sharper than her mother-in-law's. And she also quarrelled all the time with her brothers- and sisters-in-law. Khurshid Zamani, in spite of her convent education, lived in dread of witchcraft, and in her eyes Sarwari became the queen of witches. She had completely enslaved Khaqan, and Khurshid Zamani would beat her head and say, 'This whore has bewitched my son. That's why he's so completely in her power.'

Finally things came to such a pitch that, in a battle royal with her mother-in-law, Sarwari slapped her, and went off taking Khaqan along with her. First they went to her father Zijah Jang, and then to a house of their own. Mashur ul Mulk, who had always been so fond of Khaqan, refused to see him again after this incident, and did not long survive it.

The young couple had not long been in their new house before Sarwari was up to her old tricks. One night Khaqan returned from the club at about ten o'clock to find her bedroom door locked. He knocked, but there was no reply. He began to bang on the door. The servants crept out to watch surreptitiously from the corners. Suddenly the door opened and Mahmud Shaukat came out. Before Khaqan could say or do anything, he brought his riding-whip down hard on Khaqan's back and was gone before he could comprehend the full force and full humilitaion of what had happened. He went into the room and began to beat Sarwari, and she began to scratch him and bite him. He called her a whore, and she called him a pimp, and Sarwari went home to her father's house. After a whole month during which Zijah had never ceased to press him, Khaqan too went to live there. There he made the new discovery that Sarwari drank toddy. He ran home to his mother, flung himself into her arms and burst into tears. Sanjar Beg said he should divorce her, and he was ready to do so; but Khurshid Zamani Begum would not hear of it, even though Sarwari had struck her. Was it a light matter to divorce a daughter of Zijah Jang? And besides, think of the scandal. At present some people believed the stories about her and others did not; but once he divorced her everybody would believe them. Think of the scandal and the disgrace. Sanjar Beg had never been able to get his way against Khurshid Zamani. In matters like these Mashur ul Mulk's decision would have been accepted as final, but he was dead. So there was no divorce and things went on as before. In the course of time most of Khaqan's friends and some of his relations had affairs with Sarwari. And these affairs were widely known, for the code of chivalry in Farkhundanagar was quite the opposite of that of medieval Europe. Here one betrayed the secret of a woman's love, and declared openly (truly or falsely) one's relationship with her; for this was the sign of one's manhood, a tribute to one's sex appeal, and evidence of one's fine indifference to all these things. In the end Zijah Jang got so disgusted with Sarwari's conduct that he turned her and her husband out of his house. The couple again set up house on their own, and so their life went on.

At all events Khaqan was married. But the girls are usually married off before the boys, and it was now urgent to find a match for Mashur un Nisa. Khurshid Zamani had always felt an abhorrence of go-betweens. Her own marriage had not been arranged in this way and she did not want any of her daughters' marriages so arranged, even though these were the normal procedures of Farkhundanagar.

Of all Khurshid Zamani's children only Mashur un Nisa lived a life about which there could be no two opinions. She was unique in inheriting both her father's popularity and his reputation for clean living. Modest and unaffected, she had even as a child hated her mother's pretensions. (Nur Jahan, too, had this dislike of pretension, but it was mainly the airs of Sartaj that were Nur Jahan's target, while Mashur un Nisa would even interrupt her mother to rebuke her – and get smacked for her pains.) Khurshid Zamani had numerous poor relations, who were office clerks, and superintendents, and people of that kind. In Farkhundanagar, as in every other part of India, the middle classes merged on the one side with the nobility and on the other with the working classes.

38

On one occasion Khurshid Zamani met a poor cousin of hers at a wedding. She had a handsome little boy, with a complexion as fair as that of a British tommy. Khurshid Zamani remarked, 'You haven't a penny to your name, but look at your boy. What a lovely child he is. God bless him! What lovely children God gives these poor women. And look at *our* children, each one uglier than the next. . . .' Mashur un Nisa was about twelve years old at the time. She saw that the poor woman's eyes were brimming with tears. She hated her mother for her callous pride, and piped up in front of everybody, 'Mamma, why do you say such nasty things? Aren't you afraid that God will punish you? Good times and bad come to all of us.' Preached at by her own daughter and that, too, before all the guests – Khurshid Zamani gave her a slap and said sharply, 'Be quiet you little preacher! No higher than my knee, and see how she talks!' Then she turned to the cousin and began to make up to her, 'Don't be offended, Amani, I didn't mean you. I meant it generally.'

Mashur un Nisa would often say to her father, 'Mamma's like all Qabil Jang's family – she's always boasting. Why should we despise anyone? That's right, isn't it Papa?'

Sanjar Beg was very fond of her, and this used to pique Khurshid Zamani. Most fashionable mothers do feel piqued at their eldest daughter. There she is, growing taller year by year as the bloom of youth comes to her face, and her figure fills out, while all the time the mother's own youth is passing away for ever. This over-all jealousy, in which without doubt love too was curiously compounded, coloured all the relationships between Khurshid and Mashur. She would often hold up her hands in despair and say to Sanjar Beg, 'God knows when we shall get this wretched girl off our hands.'

'This wretched girl' was in her fifteenth year and studying for her Senior Cambridge when she came to the notice of Abul Hashim, the consultant engineer. She very rarely observed purdah and on the day in question was returning from school in Miss Nelson's car. The car had broken down, and the chauffeur was trying to get the engine to start. Abul Hashim, who knew Miss Nelson well, happened to be passing and he got out of his car to help her. He noticed this blooming young girl, and asked Miss Nelson who she was. The old lady told her to 'say "Good morning" to Mr Abul Hashim'. She was not used to saying good morning to strange men, and when she said it, she blushed all over her face.

Miss Nelson continued the introduction and told Abul Hashim that she was the eldest daughter of Colonel Sanjar Beg. The next day Abul Hashim had his mother send a letter to Colonel Sanjar Beg with a proposal of marriage. He sent his family tree along with it, and awaited results. Abul Hashim was then thirty-five years old, twenty years older than the girl – and her parents hesitated. Besides, Sanjar Beg, at any rate, thought that Mashur was still young and there was no hurry to get her married. On the other hand they had to bear in mind that they had two more daughters growing up. The sooner they got the eldest daughter off their hands, the better. But still the difference in their age. . . .

Abul Hashim's age was not the only thing against him. He was also a very heavy drinker. No one in the city was such a connoisseur of wines. His appearance was very ordinary: brownish in complexion, with even, white teeth, large eyes and black hair. He had amassed a considerable fortune, for though his salary barely sufficed him for pocket-money, his income from the contractors in 'percentages' of doubtful legality ran into thousands of rupees a month. When Ahdi Husnkar Jang initiated his scheme for the settlement of Kishanpalli, Abul Hashim had bought himself three acres of level ground, not on the hillside, but at the very summit, and built himself a beautiful house there, as green as the garden around it. Along the front of the outside veranda, and at right angles to it, there was a pergola in Greek style, with bougainvilia of different colours trained to grow over it. Abul Hashim ordered his bougainvilia from Sylhet, from Japan, from Spain, from Texas, and God knows where else. His stock of bougainvilia was as famous as Dr Qurban Husain's stock of cacti. His house was built in the 'German', that is, the cubist style – tiles on the veranda, and black tiles in all the rooms and on the stairs. His drawing-room, quite contrary to the prevailing taste in Farkhundanagar, was very large, and furnished in the 'Spanish' style, meaning that the chairs and sofas had carved arm-rests and legs and were upholstered in Spanish brocade. On one wall hung two mirrors in white frames, while opposite them were two boxes of carved and inlaid wood like medieval treasure-chests. The other two walls were hung with pictures by some mediocre Spanish artist, depicting a serenade or a bullfight. The staircase was striking, winding up like a spiral of black tiles. On the upper storey was a fine open veranda, adorned with rococo furniture, cane chairs and glass-topped tables. It contained the most beautiful bar in Farkhundanagar, well stocked with the choicest wines. All this had been paid for out of the contractors' 'percentages' – which meant that the very cheapest materials had been used on public works. It meant that Abul Hashim's house was beautiful, while schools and hospitals had leaking roofs, that roads were often left half unmetalled, and that the labourers often received less than half of what the account books showed under the head of wages.

Sanjar Beg would not at first return any definite answer to the proposal. But when Abul Hashim's side began to insist, he refused it, on the grounds that the difference in age was too great.

But Abul Hashim could not get this little fifteen-year-old girl out of his mind. For thirty-five years he had stayed a bachelor. His family had received many proposals, but he had turned them down outright saying that he was not going to be caught in any such tomfoolery. Every year he had taken special leave, and he had been all over the world, collecting his varied specimens of bougainvilia. He had been to South America and to the forests of tropical Africa. He had sailed in a fishing boat, enduring all manner of hardships, to see the icebergs of Spitzbergen. And when his Farkhundanagar friends told stories of their stay in England or Germany he would cut them short to tell them of his adventures in Lapland. In all Farkhundanagar, except for Dr Qurban Husain, there was no one else who had travelled so much and seen so much of the world.

How was it that after seeing so many women in so many different countries he could be so taken up with a fifteen-year-old girl of quite ordinary appearance from his own city? The reason was that he had suddenly begun to feel his loneliness. Notwithstanding all his travels, and his numerous friends, and his Kishanpalli house 'Al-Khizra' with its unique bar, there had been no grey hairs on his head. But one or two were now appearing at the temples, proclaiming with beat of drum that the time had come to settle down and take life easy. He himself felt that the girl was rather young. But what of that? A woman grows old four times as fast as a man, and at that rate in ten years' time when Mashur was twenty-five and he forty-five, their ages would really be equal – or so he reasoned.

Sanjar Beg's refusal of his proposal made him all the more keen. He paid court to Sanjar Beg's younger brother Nadir Beg; and Nadir Beg strongly recommended his case. Then he began to visit

41

Miss Nelson more frequently. She could see no reason why he should not meet Mashur un Nisa more often. In the first place there was nothing objectionable about it, and in the second place Khurshid Zamani was, at least in one sense, quite an enlightened woman, who years ago had entertained the guests at her own wedding. So Miss Nelson started inviting Abul Hashim and Mashur un Nisa together to come to tea with her. Neither Sanjar Beg nor Khurshid Zamani knew about this.

At first Mashur un Nisa did not understand what all this was about. Abul Hashim would often tease her, and she, like all girls, would enjoy being teased. And then, all of a sudden, the spell worked, and the fifteen-year-old girl fell in love with a man more than twice her age.

She was by nature a very self-possessed, simple, straightforward girl, just like Sanjar Beg, and even now it was still possible that if it had been her parents' wish that she should marry another man, she would have gone quietly with him, and been true to him all her life. But the pleasure which she derived from these clandestine teas with Abul Hashim was a new and exciting experience for her. She was not used to being thought of as a grown-up woman. Abul Hashim nicknamed her Tom, and she liked it.

In the end, at her suitor's insistence she wrote a letter to her father telling him that with his permission she would like to marry Abul Hashim. Sanjar Beg was quite unprepared for his daughter to express any wish of this kind, though to Khurshid Zamani it was less surprising. In the end they gave their consent.

Accordingly the marriage took place with great pomp and ceremony. Rajah Shujaat Shamsher Singh in person graced the occasion, and it was a tribute to Sanjar Beg's popularity that Ala Kausar Nawaz Jang and Zijah Jang sat side by side on the same sofa, and talked together for a whole hour.

'Tom' was happy in her marriage. Abul Hashim drank as heavily as ever, but he never struck her or swore at her. When he was drunk he would relapse into silence – a grave-yard silence which frightened Mashur un Nisa until she gradually got used to it. She seldom visited her own family and felt less and less in common with her mother. And whenever her mother felt a surge of affection for her, now that she was gone, she would praise not her but Abul Hashim. 'God keep him!' she would say. 'He looks after her well, and keeps her happy.'

In Asghar's case matters were more complicated. He had got

42

his commission. Mashur had been married some years. His father had died. And still he did not marry.

Sanjar Beg's younger brother, Nadir Beg, had married Nazli, eldest daughter of Qabil Jang by his second wife. He was not at all like his elder brother: alcohol, beauty, youth, money – these were the things in life which interested him most. His marriage had strengthened his inherited taste for the superficially westernized life – that is, for tennis, mixed parties, hill-stations and Anglo-Indian society.

Their eldest daughter Dil Afroz was seventeen, and still at convent school. She liked horse-riding, and would often go riding with her father or her cousin Asghar out beyond Kishanpalli. In those days she was counted one of the most beautiful girls in Farkhundanagar. She was certainly a very healthy girl, broad-boned and firm-bodied, and she had a very pleasant disposition without any trace of the pride and pretensions of Sartaj. As for any deep affection – well, of course not much of that was to be found in any of her family. But she was well-mannered, courteous and kind. She was a year or two older than Sartaj, and had begun to be very friendly with Nur Jahan.

Asghar had always been very fond of her; and now in his own way he thought he loved her. But Asghar's conception of love was somewhat out of the ordinary. Granted, it should end in marriage, but love was not love unless there was an element of roguery in it. Love was not love unless you could boast about your conquest; even if you were going to marry the girl, it was not love unless you first seduced her. This kind of love was intimately connected with whisky. Asghar had begun to drink heavily after getting his commission, and when he was drunk there was only one thing he could think of – women.

Thus Asghar had much in common with his uncle, and Nadir Beg was very fond of him. By blood he was only a nephew, but spiritually he was his son. Alcohol, youth and money. He did not value beauty quite as much as Nadir Beg did; but when you are drunk, beauty, colour, well-proportioned limbs and everything else are diluted by the liquor. Again like Nadir Beg, he had never felt any need to ponder too deeply about life – he never felt politics, for example, to be any more important than cars; or religion or economics any more important than lipstick. Like Nadir Beg, he had always been careless of his life. He had been involved in numbers of road accidents, but had escaped with his life every time. Like Nadir Beg, life to him meant movement – movement with pleasure, and pleasure alone, for its object.

Asghar was an excellent dancer. In Farkhundanagar there were few to equal him. In those days very few Muslim girls had the courage to dance, but Dil Afroz was one of them. She had grown up among the Anglo-Indian girls who, with the British army officers, dominated the dance halls, and many of them were related to her, for nieces of her grandmother Sikandar Begum (*née* Grace Crewe), and the daughters of these nieces, were everywhere in Farkhundanagar. These Anglo-Indian girls were not only accepted, but positively sought after in the high society both of the British cantonment and of old, aristocratic Farkhundanagar; and for their sake their husbands and brothers and male relations were tolerated and invited to social occasions. It was these mem-sahibs who gave the sons of the nobility their early education, and who taught their daughters the feminine accomplishments.

Asghar began to take Dil Afroz dancing quite often, sometimes without the knowledge of his mother or of her parents, and in the course of time he won himself a place in her heart. True, he was nothing much to look at, but he had dash and gallantry, and a way with the women. In male company he was the typical army officer; most of his conversational equipment consisted of dirty jokes, and his only serious topic was women. But seat him next to a girl and he was transformed: he became eloquent, witty and entertaining, flirting with her and admiring everything she said as though he had been born to it.

In his love for Dil Afroz success would have been almost certain if only he had been a little more cautious. Nadir Beg had always favoured him, and Nazli's only objection to him was his excessive indulgence in alcohol. But Asghar failed to take into account that there was one way of courting girls of good family and another of making love to fast Anglo-Indian girls. And simply because of this lack of caution a rather ugly incident took place.

He had never got on well with his uncle, Nayazi. And Nayazi was a much more frequent visitor to the dance halls than he. The two of them had already quarrelled at a party given by an Anglo-Indian captain named Jones. Captain Jones had been drunk, and just to provoke Nayazi had several times said to him, 'Just look at your niece Dil Afroz – going around with Asghar all the time.' If Dil Afroz was Nayazi's niece, so was Asghar his nephew, but for some strange reason, Nayazi had got it into his drunken head

44

that he was an outsider, and that it might create a scandal if Dil Afroz was constantly seen going about in his company. During the break in the dancing while the Anglo-Indian girls were sitting on their partners' knees and Captain Jones was handing round the sandwiches, Nayazi, who was now completely drunk, staggered across to Asghar and hit him. Asghar took it without raising a hand against his uncle.

Only a few days after this incident a proposal was made for Dil Afroz's hand. One of the Coromandel nawabs who was visiting Farkhundanagar had seen Dil Afroz out riding one day with Nadir Beg and Asghar. He had been greatly struck by the way she sat her horse, and by her youth and womanly dignity; and he sent a proposal for her hand. Khurshid Zamani did everything she possibly could to get the proposal rejected, not because she wanted Dil Afroz married to Asghar – that was a relatively unimportant matter – but because she did not want any daughter of Nazli's to contract a more favourable match than her own daughters. Two of Sir Tajul Muluk's granddaughters had been married to the nawabs of Coromandel, but no daughter of Mashur ul Mulk's or Qabil Jang's family had ever attained the good fortune of marrying into a princely family. The poor woman spent sleepless nights over it; she just could not bear the thought of her niece marrying a nawab and riding around in a Rolls Royce, owning huge estates near Vizagapatam, and visiting Europe every second year. What were her own daughters' prospects compared with this? The oldest, it was true, was married to a prosperous consultant engineer, but the other two were still in the marriage market. . . . Well, she promised herself that come what may she would pull off such a brilliant match for Sartaj that everybody would be astounded.

Dil Afroz did get married to the Coromandel nawab. Asghar began to drink even more heavily and a new kind of love awoke in his heart, a kind of love which had nothing to do with roguery or physical possession, or even pleasant flirtation, but which told him that there was a vacuum in his life. Some years after Dil Afroz's marriage he was sitting with his friends in the Harbour Bar when he suddenly said, 'Such a healthy, modern, intelligent girl. . . . And she wasn't even in love with me. They married her off just for money. And look at her now.'

In spite of her convent education, and her familiarity with Anglo-Indian society, and her horse-riding, Dil Afroz went off submissively with the man to whom her parents had married her;

but she too always felt that there was something lacking in her life.

It was at this juncture that Sunbul again came into the picture. She was pert and quick, the most presentable of the three chokris, and had long been infatuated with Asghar. 'What a handsome man Asghar sahib is, God bless him! I could die for him!'

One day some months after Dil Afroz's marriage, Asghar had returned very late from the military club. He was very drunk, and in trying to garage the car, he had buckled the mudguard. He left it and went over to the house, but the door was locked. While he was still shouting obscenities at the watchman, Sunbul came and opened the door. It must have been about half-past twelve. There was a light burning in the courtyard and Khurshid Zamani and Asghar's two younger sisters were asleep on the veranda. Asghar was going to his room to get undressed when Sunbul again appeared coquettishly before him and asked, 'Shall I bring you something to eat?'

Asghar swore and said, 'Yes.'

Sunbul swung round alluringly. Her full breasts showed prominently beneath her bright red shirt. Her long plait swung round and came to rest on her shoulder. She had stolen some *kohl* from Sartaj's make-up box, and applied it lavishly to her eyes. Her hair was black and gleaming, plastered down with coconut oil. Asghar tickled her and said, 'All right, bring me a drink of water.' When he tickled her she giggled loudly and said, 'Be careful, Asghar sahib, what are you doing? The mistress will wake up and I shall get a beating.'

'Get on, get on, you bitch; bring me some water.'

She laughed again, and walked away swinging her hips. Khurshid Zamani raised her head to see what was happening, and then turned over. Her labour had not been wasted then after all. At any rate the boy had taken a fancy to one of the chokris, and now he would forget about Dil Afroz. Asghar had already gone to his room. When Sunbul returned with the water he got hold of her and gave her a drunken kiss. She pulled off his long military boots and socks, undressed him and massaged his feet. She slept with him until morning and from then on became his concubine.

After some time Asghar's friends noticed that when he was very drunk, though he sometimes spoke of Dil Afroz as he used to, sometimes he would say 'Sunbul' instead.

Now there were only Sartaj and Nur Jahan to worry about. Asghar was no longer a problem. 'He's a man,' Khurshid Zamani would say, 'and when he finds a girl he likes he'll marry her.' All her thought now was for the 'brilliant match' she was determined to arrange for Sartaj.

When Sartaj was only eight years old she had said one day, when she was playing with her dolls, 'I shall marry a nobleman when I grow up.' What better could Khurshid Zamani want? Granted that the nobles of Farkhundanagar could not compare with the nawabs of Coromandel; but at any rate Sartaj would not be far behind Dil Afroz.

She thought of a revolutionary plan. With Mashur ul Mulk and her husband dead, why should she not now end at a blow the long-standing rivalry between Sir Tal ul Muluk's family and her own? Besides, that would give Nadir Beg and his wife something to think about, and revenge her for her failure to win Dil Afroz for Asghar.

Sir Taj ul Muluk had a grandson, Haidar Muhiuddin, a man of very dark complexion, but very nice and good at heart. Sartaj was extremely beautiful, the beauty of the family. The two could hardly have been more different. A mere hint from Khurshid Zamani aroused Haidar Muhiuddin's passion and he sent a proposal for Sartaj. It was Sartaj herself in whom Khurshid Zamani first confided. 'He is rather dark, dear, and rather fat, but he will keep you in comfort. His estates bring him eight-hundred thousand a year.' And as her mother had expected, Sartaj at once agreed. 'Yes, Mamma. What does it matter if he is dark. Dark men take good care of their wives and put up with a lot from them. These fair-skinned fellows are always intolerably conceited. Who'd be saddled with one of them? Mamma, I want whatever you want. Besides, he is rich, isn't he? I hear he's got a Rolls Royce.'

'Yes, dear, he has; you'll be able to ride around in a Rolls Royce.'

Now there was only Nur Jahan to dispose of.

47

5

Sultan Husain, consultant engineer, had spent nearly twelve years since his return from the United States as a free man. His personality had not developed much during these years. Time left him untouched. It had brought one or two wrinkles to his face, and one or two grey hairs at the temples. But in general his youthful appearance had not changed.

The only new experiences which had entered his life during these years were of machines and construction materials. Every year without fail he spent a holiday in Mussoorie. As an old 'Mussoorian' he had a wide circle of friends and sweethearts, and had not felt any particular urge to marry. His mother and his widowed sister Zubaida looked after the house and saw to it that he was comfortable.

Then a small fissure appeared in the structure of his life, and, as time passed, it began to widen alarmingly. Year after year his price in Mussoorie fell, mainly because he was growing older every year, and younger girls chose younger men to flirt with. The two 'girl-producing' colleges of Delhi, Lady Irwin and Lady Hardinge, sent a fresh crop to Mussoorie every summer; and these young nymphs made eyes at boys of their own age, laughed and fooled around with them, and in the end married them and settled down. And Sultan Husain remained a bachelor. But then he was not prepared to marry any of the girls he flirted with. He divided love for a woman into two sharply defined stages. The first began with the first glance and continued through compliments, dating, friendship, correspondence, teasing and, if the girl was exceptionally pretty, reciting a verse or two of Dagh as one shaved; after which came the regular stage, petting, necking and occasionally sleeping together. The second stage lay beyond that, and involved things that Sultan Husain could not bear to contemplate – namely responsibilities, pregnancies, children and the dull, repetitive routine of married life.

He aimed every season to have a new affair at Mussoorie – an affair of the first stage. Then a season came – one of those unlucky ones – when he could not make a fresh conquest. Worse than that,

48

he found that slips of girls were beginning to make fun of him. And quite an ordinary event then occurred which changed the whole course of his life.

That season Mrs Sajid Ali was holding whist drives at her house every Thursday. Sultan Husain had always been one of her great social lions. She had always mothered him and once or twice had urged him to get married. One Thursday Sultan Husain noticed a very pretty Parsee girl at her party. There were eight tables; the players were the old regular visitors to Mussoorie whom he had met so often that he was sick of them – Mrs Mashhadi and her two daughters, Pandit Hawakhwah Narang with his wife and sister-in-law, the Ahuja family, the Batra family, the Krishnas, Professor Tochi and his three daughters, Surendar, and amongst all these this new girl whom he had not seen before, sitting some distance away at table No. 6. He looked in her direction and said to his partner, 'Narang, who's that?'

Mrs Sajid Ali announced that hearts were trumps. The rustle of sarees, stoles and playing cards continued. Narang was always slow to answer. 'Who? That? That Parsee girl? Mrs Sajid Ali has just introduced me to her. Miss Nusserwanji, Nargish Nusserwanji.'

'Say "Nargis", fellow. What's all this "Nargish", Nargish"?' said Sultan Husain as he threw down his card.

At the next table he was partnered with Kamala Tochi, his (and a hundred other men's) old flame.

'What's the score, Sultan?'

'Ninety.'

'What a shame, my love,' she said and sat down opposite him. Spades were declared trumps.

A young Panjabi named Prakash, sitting on Sultan's right, began talking sweetly to her. She was not the one to resist the temptation of flirting with two men at the same time. In unexceptionable Panjabi she encouraged him, while under the table her golden shoes slipped into Sultan's trouser-legs, and began gently rubbing his hairy calves. Prakash, completely unaware of what the lovely lady was up to beneath the table, and secure in the confidence that no one else would understand what he was saying, was making violent love in Panjabi and steadily losing the game. His partner, a solemn-looking, bald Madrasi, was suffering all this in silence.

Sultan Husain won the round, and went up to the next table, while Kamala, who had lost, went down. In the end he got to the Parsee beauty's table and was able to inspect more closely her round face, cream complexion, and big eyes, and her flowered silk saree worn in Parsee style.

He introduced himself and began to behave rather forwardly. She snubbed him with a faint smile. The round came to an end and there was an interval for tea and sandwiches.

'Your name's Nargis, isn't it?'

She nodded and looked away towards one of her Bombay friends who was escorting her.

'Do you know what Nargis means?' Sultan made his opening move. Nargis put down her cup with the utmost delicacy and with a venomous smile replied, 'Yes, I know what it means. And I also know what you are going to say next, namely that my eyes are as beautiful as the narcissus.[1] Then you will assume that I am flattered, and pay me another compliment. Then you will say that you love me. But I can tell you right away, it's all W.T.'

'What?' said Sultan Husain. He was entirely unprepared for this sudden counter-move.

'W.T.' she repeated with casual sarcasm.

'I am sorry, I don't understand.'

'You don't understand. Are you married?'

'No.'

'Oho! You must be about forty, aren't you? Oh well, you'll get married one day; then you must ask your wife what W.T. means.'

She again looked towards her Bombay friend and waved. He was a good-looking boy of about twenty-five. He got up from his table and came over and sat on the arm of her chair.

'There's a gentleman here who doesn't know what W.T. means.'

He burst out laughing, and with the unsophisticated informality of Bombay, he slapped Sultan on the back and explained, 'Waste of Time.'

So now Sultan knew exactly what W.T. meant. Now it at last dawned upon him that he had been wasting his time with the girls – his time and theirs. And it was revealed to him that now that the days of his youth were passing, pretty young girls would no longer allow him even that small privilege – the privilege of wasting their time.

And there and then he realized that outside marriage there was no hope for him.

[1] Nargis means narcissus.

6

Next came the problem of selection. Sultan Husain began to romanticize it all. Marriage – a leap in the dark! What a dramatic situation! A girl becomes your wife, not after a prolonged court-ship, as in the West, but suddenly, all at once. Yesterday, a stranger, unseen, unknown: today your wife, your lifelong partner. He found this Oriental concept of the stages of life very attractive. In the first stage, the future husband and wife, complete strangers, unaware not only of each other's lives but of each other's very existence. Then the second stage, when they are each other's life-companions. This was real, dramatic romance. The lame, dragging, long-drawn-out 'romance' of Western courtship could not compare with it. What a ridiculous process that is! Some girl catches your eye, or you have seen her about ever since you were a child; you spend years trying to get to know her; she flirts both with you and with others, and you must enter into competition with them like entering for the civil service examination. You cast your net for her, and so do others. What usually happens is that someone more handsome or more wealthy than you carries her off and leaves you standing. But suppose you do win, and the girl agrees to marry you, you have to put up with all her whims; you must not interfere with her freedom; you must not show the slightest jealousy. If you do she will at once tell you, 'How possessive you Orientals are! Do you think you've bought me?' (This was why Sultan had not married in Europe or America.)

The dramatic Oriental marriage is quite the opposite of all that. This is real romance. A girl who is a complete stranger to you, about whose appearance, character and temperament you know nothing, enters your life by a secret door and comes into your heart. All her life she worships you. This is real romance. Your first tryst with the girl is your wedding day. First sight, first kiss, first embrace, all in one night. And in his romantic day-dreaming Sultan quite forgot that in the brothel, too, first encounter imme-diately precedes the night of love, and that all this 'romance' of marriage, too, can be, at bottom, a matter of sale and purchase. In one the contract is for a night; in the other, for a lifetime.

In the romance of Oriental marriage it does not matter who the girl is. What does matter is first, that she should be of good family, and second, that she should be a virgin, so that the husband's property rights in her may be absolute.

Sultan's widowed sister Zubaida was now employed night and day in searching for a suitable girl for her brother. At the club, the cinemas, at the exhibitions, wherever she went, she would weigh up every girl she saw as a potential sister-in-law.

Zubaida had been widowed in the prime of her youth but her experience of marriage had not been a happy one, and she would not contemplate marrying again. The third of her father's property which was hers in her own right gave her a comfortable living and she was content, so long as Sultan was a bachelor, to run his house for him.

Khurshid Zamani about this time was going through a period of great anxiety. Some Rohillas[1] had recently been arrested and charged with a series of burglaries and armed robberies. This was a new experience for Farkhundanagar, for although petty theft had always been common enough, burglary in North Indian style had hitherto been unknown there. Nayazi had related a highly embellished version of these events to Khurshid and told her that it was really the cunning Bengalis who were behind it all. Then one day a notice appeared on the gate of Khurshid Zamani's house. It purported to be a warning from a 'Bengali Babu' who announced to Khurshid Zamani that one of his men would be waiting by the railway bridge on the far side of Shahid Sagar, and that the sum of one thousand rupees must be sent to him at once. Otherwise her house would be raided and her daughter kidnapped and carried off. Khurshid Zamani in great agitation at once informed the police and prevailed upon Asghar (who ridiculed the whole thing) to bring two rifles from his regiment. The police searched the bridge, but there was nobody there. Then when a second notice appeared, everyone realized that this was Nayazi's handiwork. Khurshid Zamani sent for him and abused him roundly for scaring her so badly. Then she handed him a letter and said, 'This is in Persian; I can't understand a word of it.'

Nayazi began to read it: ' "Part One: in the praise of those Sayyids who are the essence of Light. . . . But the pedigree of their father extends through Imam Ali Naqi to Imam Husain, on whom be peace. Their forefather, Amir Kabir Khwaja Khatir who

[1] People of Afghan stock from northern India.

52

was born in Nakhshab in Turkestan which is four days' journey from Herat, came by the turn of fortune to India. The Sultans of the time were gracious to him. In the days of King Muizz uddin Kaiqobad and King Ghayas uddin Balban he was rewarded with the high office of minister. . . . The pedigree of Sultan Husain, son of Jafar Husain, son of Tahawwur Husain, son of Mir Muhammad Ahsan, son of Mir Muhammad Muhsin, son of Qazi Abdus Shakur the martyr, son of Khwaja Ata Ullah, son of Khwaja Sayyid Miran Shah, son of . . ." so and so . . . Khurshid, this is that idiot Sultan Husain's pedigree . . . "son of Sayyid Mahmud Khatir the first, the prime minister of King Jalal uddin Firoz Shah . . ." then son of, son of, son of until he gets to. . . . And Nayazi kissed the fingers of both hands, turned over a few more pages and said, 'Khurshid, Sultan Husain has sent his pedigree and asked for Nuri's hand.'

It is Indian tradition for the womenfolk of the prospective bridegroom's party to come and inspect the prospective bride, who sits with a solemn face and with eyes closed, dressed in all her finery. But when Sultan Husain's mother and sister came to inspect her, Nur Jahan could not restrain her smiles. She smiled when Sultan's mother raised her chin to get a good look at her face. She smiled again when Zubaida asked Mashur's little nine-year-old daughter, 'Who is this?', and the child said, 'Aunty', and Sultan Husain's mother said, 'Your aunty is very nice, isn't she?' Sultan's mother went on smilingly, 'We are going to take your aunty away.' The child said, 'I won't let her go!' and began to cry. Zubaida said, 'We shall take her away, you'll see!' And the child began to stare anxiously at the strange women who were threatening to take her aunty away. Nur Jahan's eyes were closed, but she felt like hugging her little niece and telling her, 'No they won't, little one; I am not going to leave you.'

History had turned a somersault. The first tide of progress had ebbed and the second tide, on which Nur Jahan was being carried along, was not yet running strong. Khurshid Zamani had entertained the guests at her wedding. And now her daughter, even before her engagement, was sitting like an owl with her eyes closed being inspected by the prospective bridegroom's relatives. She had had a modern education at convent school and then at Panchgani, but the family of the bridegroom-to-be were of the old school, and Khurshid Zamani thought she must suit her ways to her customer.

53

Zubaida tickled her to try to make her laugh. And she wanted to burst out laughing, but managed only to smile. Then they took their leave and went.

When Sultan's mother and Zubaida got back home, he was waiting for them. He gravely took off his *sherwani*[1] and hung it on the coat-hanger. Then he took off his socks and went into his mother's room, where he sat down on the floor. As he had expected, it was Zubaida who spoke first, launching into a torrent of words, 'Sultan, we've seen your bride, and we like her very much. She's very good-looking.'

He looked at his mother who was still breathing hard from the exertion of getting out of the car and climbing the steps into the house. There was perspiration on the wrinkles under her lips in which the redness of betel was discernible. She took off her spectacles with their small lenses, and put them in their case. Then she put the case in her betel-box, and began to fan herself. In the end Sultan, for all his restraint, could not bear it any longer. 'Mother, have you seen the girl?' he asked. 'What does she look like?'

'She is not bad-looking, son. Not beautiful and not ugly. Quite slim, fair complexion, rather a long face, medium height – I didn't think that she was all that good-looking, but still, not bad. She's all right.'

Zubaida smiled and said, 'She was smiling all the time.'

His mother laughed. 'Yes', she said, and the redness of the betel again spilt over her lips into the creases round her mouth.

Zubaida said, 'I liked the way she smiled.'

Sultan was secretly glad, but he said, 'Oh? Why?'

Zubaida smiled, 'I don't know, I just liked her smile.'

'What was she smiling about?'

'Nothing. She was just smiling.'

His mother said, 'There are some girls who cannot conceal their happiness at getting married.'

Zubaida held up her hand, 'Oh, no Mummy! She smiled because I was tickling her. That doesn't mean she was dying to get married.'

Sultan secretly agreed with her.

After that the two women began a detailed commentary. On Nur Jahan's clothes, on her mother, her mother's appearance and clothes and voice, on Mashur un Nisa. 'She seems a very nice girl.'

[1] A long, close-fitting coat, buttoned to the neck.

54

On Kahkashan and Nazima. 'Awful creatures, with their short hair and their arms bare to the shoulder, just like mem-sahibs . . .' and so on and so forth, until it was time to eat.

Zubaida kept on saying, 'Take my advice, brother, and finalize the engagement. She is certainly the prettiest of all the girls that I've seen.'

His mother was grumbling, 'The cook's put too much salt in the food; it tastes like poison.'

7

It all seemed like a dream to Nur Jahan, a dream of hitherto forbidden, and now untrammelled, sexual indulgence; and she felt it as an experience in itself, independent of its relation to the particular individual who was her husband. Sultan was just a male, short in stature, broadly built, with brown moustaches and black hair, only greying slightly at the temples. Her sexual attachment to him was to her a freedom and not yet a limitation, and in this state of mind, she was travelling to Delhi, *en route* to Mussoorie in a first-class compartment on the Panjab Express, sitting by the side of a male, and wanting to stare at all the other males she could see out of the window. Well-dressed men in suits, here and there in close-fitting sherwanis and tight paijamas. Tall, well-built men. She wanted to stare at every well-dressed young man and catch his eye for a moment as he passed. Her intoxication with her new-found sexual freedom was still overwhelming, and she could not yet realize that it was to one male alone – her husband – that her attention had to be confined, his eyes alone that she could look into, his manly beauty alone that she could admire. It was when they were halted at Agra Station that she noticed for the first time that her husband disapproved of her behaviour. She was staring out of the window at a young man, and he was staring back at her when Sultan got up and let down the shutter. Her first feeling was one of surprise. It had not occurred to her that she was doing anything improper. But she said nothing, for though she was not yet conscious of the full range of a husband's pre-rogatives, it had been impressed on her from her childhood that a husband's wishes must always be respected.

They were staying at the Hotel Marina in Delhi. At lunch she suddenly asked her husband, 'Why did you let down the shutter at Agra Station?'

Sultan was buttering his toast with solemn dignity. The dining-room was filling up with men and women, British and Indians, women with bobbed hair and short sleeves and men in shirts. The ceiling fans whirred in the heat. Sultan did not reply.

She did not repeat her question.

56

Two minutes later he remarked, 'Isn't it hot in here? I'd no idea it could be so hot in Delhi even in April.'

Now it was her turn to be silent. Sultan looked at her intently. She was toying with her stew. Sultan laid his hand on her arm and said softly, 'Nur Jahan.'

She was sitting with her eyes lowered. She did occasionally raise her head and look around her, but the reality had now dawned upon her that she had become the property of a single, individual male. She answered him quietly, 'Yes?'

'Are you all right?' asked the short-moustached consultant engineer, again laying his hand on her arm.

She wanted to shake it off, to get away, to laugh like a child, to throw her Irish stew and all those half-cooked vegetables on to the floor and run to her mother's knee and cry. It was so hot. And, oh!, the incessant whirr of those wretched fans! In a faint voice she replied, 'It's nothing. I must be tired after the journey.'

'Don't you like the food?'

'No, not much.'

'Let's have Indian food tonight, then. Darling, you must tell me what you want. After all, I am your husband.'

'Yes,' she said. She felt like crying. She was depressed, she did not know why. She put her knife and fork straight and sat there waiting for him to finish. An Englishman was joking with two mem-sahibs, and flirting with both of them at once. She sat there listening to them, and suddenly her husband answered the question that she had asked him. 'Darling, I closed the shutter because a man was standing there staring at you all the time.'

'I see,' she said slowly, and made up her mind that she would discuss it no further.

Now they were eating fruit salad and cream. Her husband again laid his hand on her wrist, where her wrist watch on its thin golden strap showed that it was twenty past two. Suddenly she felt sleepy. She heard her husband say between mouthfuls, 'It's rude to stare at a woman like that. That's why I closed the shutter.'

Suddenly a feeling of amusement prevailed over her fatigue and sleepiness and boredom, and she began to giggle mischievously. 'And if a woman stares at a man, then?'

Her lord and master's reply came in a tone somewhere between the hiss of a snake and the command of a king, 'Then she is not a woman but a whore, and not fit to be accepted in any decent family.'

The amused smile died on her lips. She felt as though he had slapped her face. She bit her lip and stared at the table-cloth, as if it held all the secrets of the universe. And it was as though electric fans began to whirr in her head. She wanted to get up and go. But where to? All roads of escape were closed and she felt nearly suffocated. She again bit her lip, and tried to reconcile herself to the fact that she was now the sole property of one man.

She raised her head and looked into his eyes with the passion of youth and thought, 'Very well, if it is to be one man, then let it be you.'

The day they reached Mussorrie it was cloudy. There was mist on the mountains, and a wind so strong that it threatened to uproot the pines on the slopes. Coolies were carrying their luggage on their backs towards the office of the Savoy Hotel. It was three o'clock and the hotel seemed still and deserted. Two girls and a young man were sitting on the lawn under a sunshade, playing cards. One of the girls was wearing Panjabi dress with a muslin stole; her hair was tinted, and a regular routine of powdering and rouging had conferred a synthetic beauty on her face. She noticed Sultan Husain and waved to him. Turning to her companion she said, 'You know him, Sultana; it's Sultan Husain from Farkhundanagar. This year there's a girl with him. It looks as though he's got married after all. He comes here every year. You know him, don't you?'

Sultana nodded and said, 'Yes.' The young man who was playing with them picked up a card as though he was about to declare rummy. Kamala (the pretty girl in the white Panjabi dress), held her breath and frowned, 'Ha . . . my dear Surendar, you're going rummy.'

The man could have been anywhere between thirty and forty. His complexion was a dark brown, his face longish, and though his yellow protruding teeth gave him an appearance faintly reminiscent of Frankenstein's monster, yet on the whole he seemed human enough. He was wearing grey flannels, a double-breasted jacket and an open-necked shirt. 'No fear, Kamala,' he replied, laughing, 'I'm nowhere near rummy.'

Sultan smiled and waved back at Kamala, and Nur Jahan asked him, 'Who is that?'

'Oh, someone I met here last year.'

'But who is she?'

'You're very inquisitive. If you must know, her name is Kamala Paresh. She is one of three sisters. She was married last year, and her husband owns a lock factory in Ludhiana.'

'Who are the others?'

'I don't know. I'll get a notebook if you like and note down everyone's name in it.'

Nur Jahan did not reply.

She went and had a bath, and joined Sultan for tea. She had dried her hair, which now hung down on her shoulders. Looking out of the window of their room from where she stood you could not see the steep slope below – only the hotel parapet and, beyond it, the sky. Nur Jahan felt as though she were on a magic carpet soaring up towards the sky with a strange man at her side. Over to the right there was a view of the mountain path and the green trees, just visible through the mist, clinging to the hillsides; above them the pines, and among the pines cottages with red roofs and open windows. She pulled a sweater on over her net saree and sat down by the fire. She began to feel drowsy. Her husband was wearing a gaudy tie with a pattern of purple flutes. She watched him putting on his jacket, and as he came and stood in front of her she felt like getting up and giving him a hug.

'Sultan, you really do look handsome,' she said smilingly, looking at him with adoring eyes.

At the peahen's praise the peacock spread his plumage. He gave a slight twirl to his moustaches, threw out his chest, and taking Nur Jahan by both hands pulled her to him. 'Darling, you look beautiful, like a mountain nymph.' He took her into his arms and gave her a long kiss, letting her go when he began to feel excited. 'I am going for a walk,' he said. 'Do you want to come, too?'

'Not just yet. There's plenty of time, and I am feeling very sleepy.'

'All right, you have a snooze then.'

The woman's instinct in Nur Jahan sensed something in his tone which meant that he was glad she was not coming.

She plucked up the courage to ask him where he was going.

'Nowhere, just for a short walk, as far as Hackman's. I'll be back within an hour. You get ready and then we'll go out together.'

Nur Jahan was really sleepy now. She went and lay down on her bed.

Sultan went downstairs, and over to the sunshade. The sunshade was so unnecessary in that pleasant sun. He looked round to make

59

sure that his wife was not watching him from the window. He lit a cigarette. Kamala Paresh saw him coming and again waved to him. But the three of them were so engrossed in their rummy that even when he drew up a chair and sat down beside Kamala she did not introduce him to the other girl.

'What's the score, Surendar? Are you winning?' Surendar pushed the paper towards him with the score written on it.

'Kamala, you're winning.' Sultan put his hand lightly on Kamala's shoulder. Her shapely, experienced shoulders, shoulders which had felt the pleasing caress of hundreds of men's hands in the dance halls, slowly shrugged. 'Sultan dear, you've just arrived, haven't you? Excuse my rudeness. This is Sultana, Sultana Mirza. Sultana, this is Mr Sultan Husain.'

'Pleased to meet you.'

Sultana laughed and shouted, 'Gigli.'

'What on earth is "gigli"?' Sultan asked.

'Gigli? Gigli is a great secret.'

Surendar took Sultan's proffered cigarette, thanked him, and said, 'Gigli is a card which your opponent wants and which you shouldn't play.'

Kamala Paresh declared rummy and got up. She began to talk rapidly to Sultan. 'Darling, forgive my rudeness. Tony was telling me that you were married. I simply couldn't believe it. Darling, you were a confirmed bachelor. How old are you now? Forty? Who's the lucky girl? . . . Must be the one who came with you. She looks very nice. Congratulations, darling!'

Surendar was saying to Sultana, 'Never mind, I'd put a hundred-rupee note aside knowing that Kamala was going to win. Let her win as much of it as she can.'

'What are you doing this evening?' Sultan asked softly.

'Nothing,' said Kamala with a polished, sophisticated laugh. 'Everyone will have her husband this week-end – Sultana her Jahangir, Savitri her Romeo and I shall be all alone.'

'Tut, tut,' Sultan clicked his tongue sympathetically.

'No thanks, I don't need the sympathy of any newly-married husband.' And she laughed aloud – the kind of laugh to make every man within a hundred yards' radius feel at home.

He slipped his arm around her waist, 'Will you come to the pictures?'

'When?' she asked with a naughty gleam in her eye.

'Now.'

'No.'

'Why not?'

Kamala again gave her intimate laugh. 'Two's company, three's a crowd,' she said translating the English saying into Hindi. And she burst out laughing.

'But Nur Jahan's not coming. She's asleep.'

'Nur Jahan? Is that your wife's name?'

'Yes.'

'How sweet!'

'Thanks. Are you coming?'

'I promised Tony not to go out too much.'

'Going to the cinema isn't "going out". You sit there and watch the film.'

'Oh, is that what you do there?'

'Yes.'

'Oh, yes.'

She laughed again. 'With your arms round each other's necks. You should be ashamed of yourself, Sultan darling. I'm a married woman and you're a married man. Let's behave like grown up people. . . .'

'Hurry up, Kamala, it's nearly six. What time does the first showing begin?'

'Six.'

'Come on then.'

'Let me just go and wash my face. . . .'

Sultan glanced stealthily up at the window of his room. Nur Jahan was not there. He lit another cigarette and waited for Kamala to come down.

As Nur Jahan drowsed off she felt as though the cool wind from the mountain peaks was singing her a lullaby, and she gave herself up to its caress. As she slept she floated among the clouds. She dreamed that her father's fingers were combing her dishevelled hair. Even in the dream she was aware that this was Mussoorie, not Farkhundanagar. Her body felt elated, her soul no longer confined within it, but all around her. She was lying on a bed of flowers. 'Sartaj, stop showing off.' Her sister's hand was raised to hit her. A girl in a paper hat, covered with flowers, soared higher and higher into the air. Sartaj's face was red with anger. But the icy wind cooled it, and wafted Nur Jahan higher and higher, up where the pines were fanning her. Far, far below were the fans of the dining-room in the Marina Hotel in Delhi; and the harsh voice of her husband died away somewhere in the depths, '. . . then she's not a woman, she's a whore. . . .' Then a short, well-knit man wearing a purple tie was embracing her. She began to breathe more quickly. Her breath was the wind that sang her a lullaby. Kahkashan's red lips, Nazima's teeth, Mamma's tightly-fitting blouse, all floated in the air with the gaudy purple tie. The air was full of colours; red, mauve and green; green above all, the green of the tree-tops shining in the sun, the dark green of the same trees in the deep shade; the green of the pines. There was another gust of wind. Drowsy, drowsy, restful sleep. She had no worries. She slept soundly. She was climbing the hill to the Savoy. What a funny building! She slipped, started in her sleep and woke up.

The shadows of the trees had lengthened. Only a hint of daylight was left. The pines emanated coolness. She got up and went to wash her face. She did not want to look out of the window. She got out her grey georgette saree and began to dress. Her husband liked that colour. He would be back any moment now, and they would go out for a walk.

When she was dressed she went over to the window and saw her husband; just a glimpse of his back. With him was the girl who had been playing cards that afternoon. Both were going down the steps, at the point where the hotel terrace met the sky.

She stood there stunned.

A few minutes later, the usual visitors to the world of consternation came: suspicion, jealousy, tears, and a new kind of distress which she had never yet known, and which wrung her heart. Her head ached and the tears flooded up and coursed down her cheeks.

She sat down, quiet and still on her chair. Now the pine trees were lost in the darkness. From the hillside cottages on her right, lights were gleaming. The wind had become unpleasantly cold, and in the Savoy Hotel lights were being switched on in several of the rooms.

She sat there quite still, as though someone had stabbed her to the heart. And gradually a feeling began to prevail over her jealousy and anger, a feeling which was to change her whole life. A feeling that it was all so unfair. If she had no right to look out of the carriage window, then her husband had no right either to take a girl out on the first evening of their honeymoon at Mussoorie. Either they should be each other's property, or else neither was the other's property. She felt a new resolve arising in her heart, a new sense of self-respect pervading her whole being, and with lips compressed she awaited her husband's return.

It was growing dark. People passed to and fro by the tennis court. Finally Sultan came in. She compressed her lips, looked at him once, and then went over to a chair in the corner and started to knit.

'Sorry I'm late, darling.'

She did not answer.

'Shall we go down to dinner or shall I order it here.'

Again, no answer.

He came across to her and bent over her with his hand on her shoulder. Nur Jahan shook it off and stood up.

'Take that whore who went out with you.'

'Darling! Darling! That's no way to talk. . . . That was Mrs Paresh. I have known her for years. You were asleep and I didn't want to wake you. We went to the cinema together.'

Nur Jahan knew he was wronging her. But she did not know how to answer him. She wanted to quarrel with him; and yet at the same time she was reluctant to. But to say nothing would be to admit defeat. In the end she could only say, 'Why did you bring me here?'

'Darling! What are you saying? This is our honeymoon. Should I have come alone?'

Now she knew how to start. Yes, that was it. On the first day of their honeymoon he had deceived her. Sultan was thinking how pretty she looked in her anger, her teeth gleaming, and her lip curled sarcastically. 'On the first evening of our honeymoon you take another woman to the pictures. Tomorrow, you'll bring her back here to sleep with you. Why did you marry me?'

Sultan Husain again tried to soothe her. He thought if only he could get her to go down to dinner, that would at least postpone the quarrel for a while.

'We shall be late for dinner,' he said.

Nur Jahan replied belligerently, 'Then let's go down.'

The newly-married couple were sitting at dinner. The gold powder in the parting of the bride's hair had not yet faded. She was eating her soup with head bent forward. Mr Nanda, who could sum up every young woman at a single glance, looked at her, but did not see the tears in her lowered eyes, which it took all the force of her will to hold in check. Mr Desai looked at her and mumbled to his mutton chop an acknowledgement of her simple beauty. This Mr Desai was a strange man. He was bald, with a perpetual smile on his lips, half pleasant, half sensual. He spent all his time running around trying to get introductions to girls, and whenever he was introduced to one his first words were always, 'We shall all of us have to become your pupils, and you must teach us how to appreciate beautiful things.' Some girls could not stand him; others felt that on the whole, with his white hair and bald top, and half-pleasant, half-sensual smile he was 'rather sweet'; and all were agreed that he was 'quite harmless'.

Mr Nanda's sharp eyes at once weighed up the situation. During the meal husband and wife had not once spoken to each other, and they left as silently as they had come. Mr Nanda got up, lit a cigar and asked Mr Ahuja to join him at bridge.

At one o'clock in the morning Sultan Husain awoke. The body of the woman lying next to him was shaking with sobs. He strained his ears to listen. But he could barely hear her, for she was lying with her face pressed to the pillow. Sultan Husain laid his hand gently on her heaving shoulders and said, 'Darling.' The shoulders shook off his hand, and for the first time his conscience began to trouble him. He held his breath and listened, until at last she was quiet. She sighed deeply and turned over. She opened her lustre-less eyes in the darkness and closed them again. And then sleep, like a treacherous enemy, stole upon her tired heart and eyes. Sultan lay there watching her.

The three sisters, Savitri, Kamala and Chandralekha, had been coming to Mussoorie for a good many years. Year by year the Camel's Back had felt the tread of their feet, and had seen the growing charm of their youth. Hackman's Hotel had witnessed their plump shoulders filling out. The old colonels at Charleville Hotel had watched their eyes grow brighter year by year. And as the old colonels' hair grew white, so did the long forked beard of the girls' old father, Professor Tochi. He was a very remarkable, kindly old Sikh, meticulous in the observance of the standards he set himself – and in constantly changing them. Like a true Sikh he had never trimmed his beard and never smoked. Since their mother's death he had kept the three girls in cotton wool. But they grew up, and all at once he found they were no longer little dolls, but grown women – and women of Mussoorie at that, who danced at Hackman's and the Standard. Savitri was the first to start plucking her eyebrows and having her hair waved and

wearing blouses and sarees of the latest fashion. There are large
notices in the Camel's Back warning riders to keep their horses
well into the hillside, away from the outside edge of the mountain
road; but rash novices often gallop along on the wrong side jostling
the pedestrians perilously near to the edge. So did Savitri begin
to jostle men's hearts, and still more their pockets, until in the
end a rich consumptive Sikh, finding that he could not get her in
any other way, married her. In this way she sold herself to
tuberculosis, with her charming smile, her sparkling eyes and
gleaming teeth, her pretty oval face, her blouse bursting to fullness
and her bright-red saree and golden sandals. And year after year
her painted lips and rouged cheeks fought a losing battle against
the wasting disease.

Surendar with his protruding, uneven yellow teeth – the prehistoric gift of the aboriginals to the Dravidians, and of the
Dravidians to the Aryans – finished his eighth glass of whisky,
and said drunkenly to Sultan Husain, 'Let me tell you, Sultan;
do you know who is responsible for the state Kamala and
Chandralekha are in today? Savitri is.'

Bult Sultan was preoccupied with the problem of why Surendar
never wore a tie, and why he was so proud of the fact that on gala
nights when everyone at the Charleville wore tails, or at least
dinner jackets, he would walk in in his grey flannels and sports
jacket, and nobody would venture to stop him.

On the counter of the Savoy bar two whiskies gleamed with the
froth of soda still on them.

'All the best.'

'All the best.'

Surendar pushed the cigarette tin towards his friend. Sultan
struck a match, took a pull at his cigarette and said, 'It's funny,
Kamala won't even look at you when Paresh is around, let alone
sit and talk to you. Yesterday I was in Kulhri bazaar when they
passed me in a rickshaw; I waved to them and Paresh waved back,
but she looked the other way.'

'That's the first sign of a whore, not to know her old boy-friends
when her husband is around.'

'Not to know her old boy-friends,' Sultan laughed drunkenly.

'Not to know them.'

'Not to know them at all.'

'Not to know them at all. Two small whiskies, please.'

'All the best.'

'All the best. Here's to Catherine the Great, to Kamala the Great.'

'Yes,' said Surendar, 'Great Catherine whom glory still adores . . .' and his prehistoric teeth flashed with reminiscences of irrelevant history, as he gazed at the light in the ceiling.

'Who said that?' asked Sultan, making a ring on the counter with his whisky glass.

'Byron,' said Surendar. 'My boy, all this engineering makes a man an ass. All that you can think of is girders and iron bars and lengths and breadths and depths. What's Byron to you?'

'Depths! You've hit the nail on the head there!' he said and slapped Surendar on the shoulder.

'My friend, you're finished with all that now. You're married and out of the running. You've heard about the wrestler, haven't you?' and his yellow teeth again flashed. 'One day an old friend saw this wrestler lying flat out in the ring, with all his old fighting spirit gone, and flies buzzing around his dirty face. His friend asked him, "What's happened to the champ?" and the Champ replied, "My boy (Sultan liked the way Surendar kept saying 'My boy') . . . I don't like to admit it, but I'm married now, and my wife can throw me every time." '

'Waiter, two small whiskies, please.'

'All the best.'

'Here's to marriage,' Surendar said. 'Come on, let's finish this glass and go. My friend, why are you hiding your wife? Doesn't she go to Hackman's or anywhere?'

'It's not that,' Sultan replied quickly. 'She's not feeling well. She's having her meals brought up to our room.'

'Why, what's the matter? Is there going to be an increase in the population?'

'No, no,' Sultan said, and then to change the subject, 'Come on, let's be off. It's late night at Hackman's tonight. Has that cabaret girl arrived yet?'

'What cabaret girl?'

'The one who does the snake dance.'

'Greta?'

'Yes, Gretchen.'

'Remarkable girl. You'd think that she hadn't a bone in her body; she's like a snake herself.'

'Sultan, my boy, have you ever had her?' and Surendar's mouth watered.

'All that belongs to the Dark Ages now.'

Kamala's husband had returned to Ambala to look after his lock factory. For two days her gold-embroidered black velvet coat was not to be seen at Hackman's or the Standard. At Hackman's, the Rumanian, Hungarian, and Austrian cabaret artistes went on waggling their hips, and flashing their white thighs in the air like so many mouth-watering slices of melon. The castanets rattled for the rumba. But Kamala Paresh visited only her tailor, accompanied at the most by her Alsatian, or her servant or her ayah; or from lunch to half-past six she would sit under the sunshade on the Savoy lawn playing rummy in her tight-fitting blouse which left her midriff bare, and emphasized her pointed breasts. The fascinated eyes of Surendar and Beg kept glancing at them stealthily and then modestly taking shelter behind their cards. Suddenly Surendar remarked:

'It's strange, Kamala. Have you noticed? Sultan's just married, isn't he?'

Kamala's happy and healthy laughter resounded in the mountain air: 'Yes, yes, they're on their honeymoon.'

'But it's a strange thing . . .' Surendar said throwing down his nine of spades.

'Oh, thank you!' With the same pleasant laugh, Kamala picked it up.

'Gigli?' Surendar's uneven yellow teeth flashed. 'I'd forgotten all about it.'

'Rummy,' said Beg, spreading out all his cards on the table.

'Oh, no! Look! Look, Mr Beg, how cruel you are! I was only one card short.'

Surendar totted up the score and began to deal. Then he again said, 'It's a strange thing. That wife of Sultan's Nur Jahan. She seems a very nice girl. But I've never seen them out together. And she doesn't observe purdah either. I asked Sultan about it all, but he was very evasive.'

'I told Sultan myself not to go out with me on the first day of their honeymoon; but he wouldn't listen.'

'So it was you, Kamala!'

'Well! What was wrong with that?'

'Nothing. But you ought to go and see her. . . . Seven of hearts. Whose turn is it? Mine?'

'Yes, sir,' and peals of Kamala's laughter danced in the sun like glowing butterflies.

Nur Jahan plaited the small white *juhi* flowers into her hair, swathed herself in a white georgette saree with a Banarasi border, put on her silver sandals, touched up the powder on her cheeks and took a final glance at herself in the mirror. The woman who faced her in the mirror – not a woman but a slender young girl – had black circles under her eyes. With her feet in chains she had prepared herself for the long journey across the barren desert of life ahead; and today at her husband's repeated insistence she had changed her dress ready to walk with him along the Mall, and was now waiting for him.

There was a knock at the door, and she told the ayah to go and see who it was. A girl came into the room, fragrant with the perfume of jasmine, wearing a Panjabi suit of white silk, with her stole resting fashionably across her forearms. Between her eyebrows shone the vermilion mark, bright and cheerful, and on her lips was an engaging, friendly smile

Nur Jahan greeted her with a smile, and the newcomer introduced herself: 'My name is Kamala . . . Kamala Paresh.'

'How are you Mrs Paresh? I am very pleased to meet you. My husband was telling me about you.'

Kamala looked Nur Jahan over from head to foot and exclaimed: 'Darling, you are beautiful! Let me look at you. Why have you been hiding from us?'

'Mrs Paresh I have not been feeling. . . .'

'Cut it out, darling. Call me Kamala. And I like your name. Nur Jahan! What a lovely name!'

'Won't you sit down?'

Kamala at once made herself comfortable. 'Thank you, darling,' she said. She was staring at Nur Jahan with sincere pleasure, not unmixed with feminine jealousy.

As Sultan Husain came out of the bedroom he was amazed to hear Kamala's voice. 'This is a surprise,' he said, and then turning to Nur Jahan, 'Darling, I have known Mrs Paresh for some years, ever since I started coming to Mussoorie. . . .'

When a little later Nur Jahan went out with him, he noticed that for the first time since the evening they had quarrelled she was talking freely with him. As they watched the cabaret at Hackman's he asked, 'Darling, shall we eat here tonight?' Without taking her eyes off the cabaret she nodded. Sultan Husain found the movement of her neck most attractive, and he laid his hand lightly on hers, and whispered to her, 'Nur Jahan darling, I love you very much.' She did not pull her hand away, and went on watching the cabaret; the colour of her cheeks neither lessened nor heightened. Her heart was still flat and featureless and unrelieved as the great desert she had begun to cross.

At about half-past ten when they were on their way back after dinner, they could see a forest fire beneath them, in the plains towards Dehra Dun. In the darkness of the night the fire seemed to kindle a silent, remote, terrible beauty.

'Look, darling! The Burning Bush!'

Both of them watched entranced the majestic blaze of the forest fire. To one side of it the lights of Dehra Dun were burning dimly through the summer haze. In front of them were the summer palaces of the rajahs of Rampur and Kapurthala. Beyond them on the mountain roads were rows of electric lights. Where they stood the Mall was unusually quiet, without even a rickshaw man in sight. The whole scene was silent, majestic. Nur Jahan could faintly hear the tinkling of the bells and the songs of the camel-drivers as though a caravan were coming towards her across the desert, from the burning bush. Just then Sultan took her in his arms and said again, 'My dear, I love you!'

For a second the desert and the burning bush became confused and intermingled. Her young heart beat more rapidly. The beauty of the scene around her was suddenly enhanced a thousandfold. It was so beautiful that she closed her eyes. Her lips thrilled to the touch of her husband's kiss. Then the footfall of a running rickshaw man came from the bend of the road; and hand in hand they walked slowly towards the Savoy.

As the night advanced, Surendar quietly closed his book. With his hard toothbrush in his monkey jowl he scrubbed his yellow teeth. Then he lay down on his bed, and wrapped his quilt around him. Before he put out the light, he lit a Black and White cigarette. He did his smoking to a definite timetable; 555 before breakfast, Players No. 5 between breakfast and afternoon tea, Three Castles from tea to dinner time, and Black and White after that. Cigarettes accounted for a sizeable slice of his monthly salary.

Viewed from his open window the lights in the valley below were an attractive sight. Far beneath him was the scorching valley of Dehra Dun. Tonight he had had twelve whiskies before dinner and he was still a little drunk. On his meagre salary of six hundred rupees a month he gambled with millionaires, and lost and won with equal dignity. Tonight he had had so much to drink that winning was out of the question. And now in the haze of the cigarette smoke when he began to chew over the events of the day, the first thing he thought about was the games he had lost. That wretched fellow Khanna has never read a word of Culbertson; on the strength of one and a half tricks he calls no trumps. Bloody fool . . . and in that second hand he really excelled himself. There am I calling diamonds, and the silly b—— goes on calling spades – and I only had one solitary spade. Dr Ghate's better half plays well. She's fat and ugly and looks pretty stupid, but she's a good player.

As he ruminated, his mind took a leap from Mrs Ghate to other things – Lucknow, Banaras, Delhi, the Dehra Dun valley below. And women. Women in their dripping sarees, bathing at dawn in the river at Banaras; women for sale in enticing perfumes in the red-light quarter at Lucknow. My boy, that was the traditional voluptuousness of the past. Nowadays you take a long, healthy walk at dawn in the Lawrence Garden in Lahore, where you may count as many varieties of sarees as of flowers. And in the evening one walks along Anarkali and the Mall. But I don't like Panjabis. They're a lot of boors. A fine sight it was when I was out in Srinagar that day with Mr and Mrs Jugal Kishore and their daughters. We were walking along the Jhelum embankment. Mr Puri's daughters were with us, too. All at once Mr Jugal Kishore clambered down the embankment towards the river. He was lucky not to slip over in the mud. The next moment, there he was, without so much as a thought of the ladies, pissing in the river. Meanwhile Mrs Jugal Kishore for no apparent reason had undone the girdle of her silk trousers and was re-tying it. As for Miss Jugal Kishore – Sheila – well, she'd been educated in Delhi at Lady Irwin College, and picked up a little culture; she looked a bit ashamed of her parents and wouldn't look at me. Poor girl. Nice place, that Srinagar embankment, not like this lousy Mall at Mussoorie. You see women walking there, too, but not like here, just to show off their sarees and silk trousers. This evening – My God! That wretched fellow Daud practically killed me. Twice we walked down from the Library to Kulhri Bazaar – and God save us from the ups and downs of Kulhri Bazaar. But that Anglo-Indian girl was good to look at, a sort of cross between Joan Crawford and Constance Bennett. Her brown fluffy hair-do was like the trees at Schönbrunn; the trees there always reminded me of the mem-sahibs' hair styles.

Those were the days! Vienna in springtime. Now Hitler's got it. There must be swastikas all over it.

The cigarette in his hand was practically finished, and was beginning to burn his fingers. He took it dexterously in his left hand between the nails of his finger and thumb, took another Black and White out of the tin and lit it from the stub. Cigarette metempsychosis. The soul of the dying cigarette takes fresh birth in the burning of the new. Now he was reflecting on his own ruminations. Where the Dehra Dun Valley had been, an unfathomed sea now raged. The road they now called the Mall was a kind of Promenade des Anglais, or the road at Monte Carlo skirting the bay, or at least Walkeskwar Road or some other seaside road in Bombay, and he, sitting at the Mall in Mussoorie, was counting the sea-shells he had stored in his mind. All kinds of gleaming, glittering shells. Ah failure,[1] I can only collect shells on the shores. Ah failure . . . but all the same what idiot would want to cross this ocean of failure? Mr Surendar, what girl could fall in love with you? . . . You with your dark skin and monkey jowl and yellow teeth. You were always the one to fall in love, and you thought that Amrit Shergil and Farkhunda were in love with you. One of them succumbed to T.B., the other bagged a Muslim I.C.S.[2] 'Ah failure' my foot. To hell with 'Ah failure'. What games I have played with my life! I had two enemies, poverty and illness. As I fought against one I succumbed to the other; until in the end All-India Radio saved me from the one, and my own indifference from the other. Now I belong to all the clubs in Delhi – the Chelmsford, the Roshan Ara, the Imperial Gymkhana. I come to Mussoorie every year. I have been to Europe twice. In All-India Radio I have no one to fear except the Director-General. To blazes with 'Ah failure'. I didn't marry. So what? Paresh and Kamala Paresh – the bitch who doesn't even greet you when her husband is there, but as soon as he is gone will sit on your lap drinking *crème de menthe* and kissing you. Or Sultan and his wife Nur Jahan. Bloody fool, he has a brand-new wife, and everyday he flirts with Kamala at the Savoy and with Gretchen at Hackman's. Marriage? Marriage be damned!

Surendar stubbed out his cigarette in the ash tray and did not light another. The flavour, smoke and flame of the cigarette transmigrated to the World of Ideals. He tried to close his eyes.

[1] A reference to a line of Iqbal.
[2] Indian Civil Servant.

Six hundred a month from All-India Radio. A win of fifty thousand on the Stock Exchange. Losing and winning. Clubs. All the clubs in Delhi. Regular bridge. One heart, two diamonds, three no trumps, four spades, finis, little slam, grand slam, Salam-alaikum, Namaste. Good-bye. Good-bye darling. Goo'bye sweetheart. Sweet Lady. Western poetry is mostly Good-bye, and Eastern poetry is mostly Welcome. Welcome, auspicious bird, harbinger of good tidings.[1] That idiot Sultan tries to explain Persian verses to me. He thinks because I am a Hindu, I can't know any Persian. It makes me laugh. Welcome auspicious bird, harbinger of good tidings. Welcome! What news? Where is my beloved? Where is my love? All the birds have flown. My hair is thinning and turning white. I am nearly thirty-seven. In three years' time I shall be a sedate forty. I conscientiously read all the communist publications, but I still go on with my three trumps and four hearts in the Chelmsford and the Roshan Ara. Tonight I lost some seventy-five rupees. The Stock Exchange, gambling; rubbing shoulders with millionaires; watching the wily smiles on their daughters' lips, and occasionally touching their painted nails across the card table. (To touch their lips costs more than I can afford.) In short, Surendar Babu, nearly forty and sedate, and sitting by the Mall at Mussoorie, or on the promenade by the sea, you gather shells and your life passes by. Birth, copulation and death.

He felt a craving for another cigarette. Cigarette smoke. The flame. The chain of metempsychosis of the flame which was in the World of Ideals, that is, the world of fancy, that is, the world of fancifulness. That is 'no spark can fly from so damp a fire'. The poet, that is, the reactionary, says, 'My master! call me to Medina'. By all means let their master call them to Medina. About the spark; Iqbal only meant that when the matches are damp you can't strike a light. But see here, it burns. And that other line. 'O, drop of falling dew, where is the oyster? Where the pearl?' O, well, Mussoorie's Mall has again become the promenade by the sea and I am sitting there gathering shells. Oysters. Empty shells. What shall I do? What can I do? The Mall, where Begum Mashhadi wears out half a dozen pairs of shoes a season dancing with youngsters half her age; billowing along like a threatening cloud with her two daughters; and both of them like a chorus, either repeating or affirming their mother's dicta. And where the erstwhile Kamala Tochi, now Kamala Paresh, and her sister in

[1] A line from the Persian poet Hafiz.

72

their boats – I mean in their rickshaws, showing all their teeth, displaying their bosoms – these bosoms, they've dropped out of the popular songs these days. . . . In short, your humble servant, sitting at the Mall, at the edge of the sea, watching the lights of Dehra Dun beneath the water, and the underwater fish and fireflies and lights, listens to the songs of the mermaids who come swimming from Patna and Allahabad and Lucknow and Lahore and Ambala Cantonment and New Delhi.

> I hear the mermaids singing each to each
> I do not think that they will speak to me.

Your age is forty minus three. But anyway, a song-bird sings to me in German – Gretchen dancing the cobra dance at Hackman's. The Viennese cobra; queen of snakes. 'Allein die Nacht ist nicht mir schön.' Alone the night is not beautiful for me. From what poem has this Viennese cobra-bird come flying? From twig to twig, from branch to branch. Behind her hovers the eagle of the swastika; and this poor Jewess, Gretchen – Mussoorie is far from Vienna, Kahlenberg from the Camel's Back, Himmelstrasse from Kulhri Bazaar, Mizsko's goulash from the ice-cream at the Kwality (with a 'ĸw' please). I told her, 'Alone the night is not beautiful for me.' She smiled, and shook her long golden hair. She doesn't take any lunch, to save for her old age; she just drinks her glasses of tomato juice. She won't go outside Hackman's. But in Hackman's she sits close to you, so that you will pay for the tomato juice and the packet of Three Castles. Then she goes off to her room. And if the traveller wishes to spread his wings and fly away, she stops him and tries to tell him her story. And if he won't stay, and edges towards the door, then unlike the bird in the poem, she does not curse him to travel on for ever. And the traveller, unlike the traveller in the poem, does not fall dead to the ground. No, he goes out and calls a rickshaw, and goes straight to the Savoy where he takes his wife Nur Jahan in his arms and she, poor girl, loves him so blindly that it doesn't even occur to her to wonder where the foreign perfume comes from. . . . I, 'Mr Eugenides, the Smyrna merchant', the employee of All-India Radio, the hunter and the hunted at the bridge table, see and understand all this, which I have seen and known and experienced before.

This time he stubbed out his cigarette and pulled the quilt up

73

over his head, and by a supreme effort stopped his ruminating and concentrated on getting to sleep – sleep which was on the other side of the ocean. On this side came the dance music from Hackman's and the Standard, and at the Capitol a Joan Crawford film was showing; and that Anglo-Indian woman who looks like her is wearing her red georgette saree with the silver border and calling to her handsome moustached companion Prem – and this Prem doesn't know how to dance.

Then, as usual over the past twelve years, in the middle of May, the bottles of Livogen and Osto-calcium again appeared on the round table in the centre of the Savoy dining hall and along with them all kinds of vitamins, A, B¹, B², C, and several varieties of pickles. And Ahuja, Surendar, Sultan Husain and all the other regulars of Mussoorie knew that Begum Kazim Mashhadi and her two daughters had arrived.

A little later the Begum Sahiba sailed into the dining-room. She was forty, and wore a French coiffure prepared with meticulous care; dark-red lipstick which she wore like a film star, not confined to her lips, but spread across her face like a moustache with a Cupid's bow; jewellery in profusion, traditional and modern mixed – a brooch of the newest fashion copied from some advertisement in *Vogue* and large Indian ear-rings; round her neck the latest in fashionable necklaces from Nauratan Das Bhau, and along with it an Indian *champakalli*, a saree of painted georgette and a sleeveless blouse. Her two daughters were equally resplendent. Fatima had a milk-white complexion that even the mem-sahibs might envy, a face like a full moon, and short, frizzy hair hanging down to her shoulders. Although Nature had given her all this beauty, she had also committed one blunder: Fatima's teeth were very beautiful – all of them – but the two front teeth were bigger and longer than the rest, like the tusks of an elephant or the fangs of a snake; and seeing her Sultan thought once again, 'God knows what persuaded Rashid to marry her; those teeth must get in the way when he kisses her'. The other girl was tall, and of darker complexion than her sister – not at all like a wax doll. She, too, wore her hair short and frizzy; and she, too, wore a sleeveless blouse; and she, too, like her mother and her sister had the same lipstick-moustache; but you could see at a glance that she was a different kind of creature from them.

On their way to their table, Sultan and Nur Jahan paused, and Sultan introduced the three ladies to his wife. They responded with anglicized effusiveness. The two girls did not say a single word in Urdu, speaking in English all the time.

When they got to their table Nur Jahan said, as she unfolded her napkin. 'They are very anglicized, aren't they?'

'Yes, darling,' said Sultan, 'Begum Mashhadi married her cousin, the son of Sir Ali Mashhadi the famous judge. She herself is Mr Hasan Mashhadi's daughter. Both she and her husband had lived in England since they were about four years old, and Begum Mashhadi stayed there until she was seventeen. It was there that she was engaged to her cousin Kazim. When she came back to India she couldn't speak a word of Urdu. She's learnt a bit now, but she talks it just like a mem-sahib.'

'But what about the two girls? They don't speak Urdu either,' said Nur Jahan, and began to laugh.

'Yes, I know. Begum Mashhadi is very fond of dancing and likes to have a good time. Her husband never stood in her way – he seems to be very much under her thumb – but the two girls were a problem. So she packed them off to Mussoorie, to St Margaret's Convent School. That gave her an excuse to spend the whole season here – "so as to be near the girls" – and go dancing all night. By the time the girls came out of the convent school they, too, were completely anglicized.'

'That's the kind of girl you should have married.'

'Well, I'm married to you now.'

'What of it? You can take a second wife.' She laughed, the fish fork between her teeth.

'Wouldn't you be jealous?' asked Sultan laughing.

'Not at all, sir, provided that I can hold the purse-strings.'

'Agreed,' said Sultan. 'Now, you choose the girl.'

'The young one's quite nice, isn't she?' said Nur Jahan playfully pointing to Jalis Mashhadi with her fork. 'She isn't married yet.'

'No, not yet.'

'Well, there you are then.' And Nur Jahan laughed.

Nur Jahan very soon made friends with Begum Mashhadi and her daughters. Generally speaking Begum Mashhadi's coquetries were reserved for young men. Generally she disliked women. But Nur Jahan was such a nice, shy girl that she quickly took a fancy to her.

It happened on the day after their first meeting. Begum Mashhadi was sitting with Jalis under a tree watching the tennis. A bald, dark-complexioned Panjabi businessman from Calcutta

75

was playing with the marker, and every time he hit the ball, it shot up in the air as high as the second storey of the neighbouring block. All his friends were laughing at him. His beautiful wife was standing watching with Surendar by the tennis court. Surendar, exhibiting all his yellow teeth, remarked, 'Bimla, Jagdesh seems to think the net is very high.'

'It's not that. He's playing cricket. See, he is just going to make a run.' Bimla laughed. She had a pretty oval face, a fair complexion, red lips, and long Ajanta-like eyes.

Surendar turned to Begum Mashhadi and whispered, 'These girls make a fortune out of their faces; they all marry rich men – rich and ugly and stupid.'

Begum Mashhadi laughed, 'You wicked man!'

'You wicked, wicked man!' Jalis echoed.

At this point Sultan Husain came up with Nur Jahan. 'Good morning, Aunty', he said to Begum Mashhadi. 'How are you?'

Jalis made room on the bench for Nur Jahan, and within a matter of minutes she was besieged by Begum Mashhadi's attentions. God had bestowed on Begum Mashhadi a wonderful descriptive power. Whenever she told a story, she could highlight every significant detail with a skill that a novelist might envy. She was talking about Fatima's marriage, and how she herself had met Rashid first. He had assumed she was a barrister and had asked her from which of the Inns of Court she had qualified.

Her laughter flowed like a torrent within the torrent of words. ' "Which of the Inns of Court? The Middle Temple? Lincoln's Inn?" Then he asked me, "Weren't you at Cambridge? Haven't I seen you at Girton? . . ." ' And the torrents of laughter and of words flowed on together. There had been a case in progress at the time of an English woman married to an Indian. She owned a house in Mussoorie, and her livelihood and that of her children depended on it. Begum Mashhadi had taken her under her wing, and gathered together all the barristers she could, and talked law to them on the strength of being a judge's daughter and a judge's wife. Her barristers pulled Rashid's leg and told him that she was a barrister herself. But none of them would tell him her name. For three days they had made a proper fool of him. So much so, that one day, late at night, he was walking alongside her rickshaw seeing her home when she said, 'Look here, sir, I don't need anybody to protect me. I can take care of myself. But if you are going anywhere near the Savoy you can jump in.' She went on

'And I squeezed myself into one corner. In spite of all his persuasion I wouldn't tell him my name. He was staying in the
Kashmir Hotel. But he asked the manager at the Savoy who I was,
and the next day what do I see, but Rashid standing before me at
Hackman's and asking me "Mrs Mashhadi will you do me the
honour of dancing with me?" I said, "Certainly not, I don't dance
with strangers." Rashid protested, "For three days I have been
fighting your protégée's battle, and you call me a stranger?" I
replied, "Anyway, I don't dance with anyone who isn't in my own
party." "No, Mrs Mashhadi," he said, "this time you will have
to make an exception." So I danced with him. I admit that after
the dance I said to Fatima, "He is the best dancer on the floor."
Then he asked if he might dance with Fatima. She looked at me
and I gave my permission. Then he danced with Jalis. . . .'

She paused, and Sultan said quickly to Nur Jahan, 'We can go
if you like; the sun's getting rather hot . . .'

'No, wait a bit,' said Nur Jahan, 'Aunty's story is so interesting.'

Begum Mashhadi beamed with happiness. 'I can see you like me.
And I like you very much, my dear. You are like my own daughters
to me. You go away, Sultan. Your young bride won't melt in the
sun. Leave her with me.'

Sultan laughed and Surendar chuckled, 'You see, you have lost
your newly-wedded wife. May I offer you the pleasure of my
company?'

'Yes, go away both of you. . . . Get out,' commanded Begum
Mashhadi.

'Men can go out in the hot sun, but if Nur Jahan or I were to
go we'd get sunstroke,' Jalis expanded her mother's line of
argument.

As the two men went away, Fatima came up. 'Fatima, I was
just telling them about your marriage. I was telling Nur Jahan. . . .
But do you know, Nur Jahan, when he sent his proposal, I was
astonished. All the season he had danced with me; he took Jalis
out occasionally, but treated her as a child and called her "baby".
He had never even looked at Fatima. . . . When the time came for
him to leave Mussoorie, he was like a man possessed. I thought he
had fallen in love with me.' Again the torrent of laughter mingled
with the torrent of words. 'But the letter of proposal was for
Fatima. I was amazed. But I advised Kazim to accept him at once.
I told him there were few barristers in the province to equal
him. . . .'

And that was how Nur Jahan's friendship with Begum Mashhadi and her daughters began. Whenever Sultan was occupied at rummy or bridge or, on that pretext, with Kamala Paresh or Hackman's Gretchen, Nur Jahan spent the time with Begum Mashhadi and her daughters. She liked the girls because they were so different from herself. The redness of betel had never touched their lips. Jalis knew even less Urdu than the mem-sahibs and the Anglo-Indian girls. And mother and daughters had such beautiful eyes and foreheads that when they were talking Nur Jahan could not take her eyes off them. She never went with them to the dances at Hackman's or the Standard unless Sultan was with her; but the effect of seeing the freedom which the two girls enjoyed was awakening in the depths of her womanhood an unconscious longing for the same freedom for herself.

Some weeks later Begum Mashhadi fell ill. The night before all of them had gone to a restaurant at Kulhri Bazaar, where you could get the best *roghan josh* in India. On the way home in the rickshaw Begum Mashhadi began to feel giddy. Jalis took her hand and began to stroke it solicitously. Sultan rushed in his rickshaw to the Kwality and brought her some lemonade. When they got to the Savoy she wished them an affectionate goodnight and put her arm round Nur Jahan's neck and kissed her on the forehead. Kamala Paresh and Chandralekha Tochi were approaching, and she made a sarcastic remark about the way they had been clinging to Jagat Narain, who was flirting outrageously with both of them, at the ice rink that morning. They all said good night again and went off to their rooms. But the following morning neither Begum Mashhadi nor Jalis appeared at breakfast. Fatima told them, 'Mummy is really very ill.' After breakfast Nur Jahan went up to see her in her room.

Begum Mashhadi told her something of her illness, while Jalis ran a full commentary on it. Doctor Dube had been to see her and had diagnosed an ordinary chill. But Begum Mashhadi took hold of Nur Jahan's hand and said, 'If it was an ordinary chill, why did my lungs hurt so much that I could hardly bear it?' Jalis, in her beautiful white silk dressing-gown, turned as she sat at the dressing table, rouging her cheeks, and said, 'Nuri, if you'd been here, you'd have seen for yourself. Mums was in such terrible pain that she turned quite white. You know, Mums never complains until she is in real pain.' Begum Mashhadi continued, 'I was not at all satisfied with Dr Dube's diagnosis, so Jalis telephoned

Dr Said Khan.' Jalis, who was putting on her lipstick, again turned round to confirm this: 'Yes,' she said, 'I telephoned Dr Said Khan at seven a.m.'

For the sake of saying something Nur Jahan asked, 'Is he a good doctor?'

'Very good,' said Begum Mashhadi. Poor Begum Mashhadi! Lying there in bed, stripped of her artificial youth, which lay encased in the little round boxes arrayed on her dressing-table. Her lips were blackish and dry, and there were circles under her eyes. Nur Jahan felt very sorry for her and began to listen to her attentively. She was saying, 'Dr Said Khan has always treated me, and he at once told me that it was my old illness, pleurisy. But this is dry pleurisy. It doesn't weep. Nuri darling, my lungs are very weak, and for the last eighteen months I have had T.B. as well.'

In this way Nur Jahan saw for the first time the other side of the picture, the misery and the fatal sickness of this smiling, dancing, forty-year-old westernized lady.

Jalis got up from the dressing-table with an air letter in her hand. The sender's address was written on the back in such large letters that Nur Jahan could not help seeing it. Frederick Samuel, and a New York address. At the time Nur Jahan did not give it a thought.

Begum Mashhadi lay ill for several days. Then she began to feel better. Nur Jahan regularly went up after breakfast to ask how she was and to talk to her for a while. One day she found Jalis dressed in her saree instead of the usual dressing-gown, swinging her bag. Fatima, too, with a ton of paint plastered on her round face was just off shopping. They asked Nur Jahan to go with them, but Begum Mashhadi stopped her and said: 'You're both going out and I shall be left all alone. Let Nuri stay here with me. She'll talk to me and keep me company, won't you Nuri?'

Nur Jahan smiled. Jalis in her special style said, 'Cheerio, then,' and she and Fatima went off. Begum Mashhadi in a confidential tone told Nur Jahan to come and sit on the bed beside her.

Nur Jahan was rather surprised, and not a little flattered. 'What is Aunty going to confide to me?' she wondered.

'Nuri darling, as you know, our family is known all over India. The Muslims of India used to revere my uncle and my father. Of course, we have all had an English education and as you see we lead a very free, Europeanized kind of life, but it was my wish, and your uncle's wish, too, that our son and our two daughters should marry Muslims. . . .'

'Of course,' responded Nur Jahan quickly.

'We are Sayyids.[1] But we don't insist that the boy should also be a Sayyid. Rashid is a very nice boy, and Fatima is very happy with him, and he is not a Sayyid. We want the other girl Jalis, too, to marry a Muslim.'

Nur Jahan's eyes opened wide. She swallowed and asked, 'Why, Aunty? Is Jalis going to marry a non-Muslim?'

'She is in love with an Indian Christian. His name is Frederick Samuel. Just think of it, the granddaughter of Sir Ali Mashhadi marrying a non-Muslim! Of course, Nuri darling, you know I have no prejudices. I have always mixed with Hindus and Sikhs and Parsees, invited them to our house and gone to their parties, but I have always told all the young men who come to my house, "You can talk to Fatima and Jalis and laugh and sing with them, but they will marry Muslim boys. . . ." ' Begum Mashhadi put her hand on her aching chest and paused for breath.

'But how did it happen?' asked Nur Jahan in the interval.

'This boy Samuel often used to visit us. It was I who got him sent to America, to Columbia Technical Institute. It was not until he had been gone a year that we found out the girl was in love with him.'

'How strange!' said Nur Jahan, for the sake of saying something.

'Now there is only one hope. If we can find some nice Muslim boy of good family drawing about seven or eight hundred rupees a month – never mind whether he is a Sayyid or not – and if we can somehow persuade him to take an interest in Jalis . . . do you know any such boy in Farkhundanagar?'

Nur Jahan raised her head and, as she reflected, she looked intently at Begum Mashhadi. 'Aunty,' she said, 'of course there are plenty of boys in Farkhundanagar, but they tend to be rather shy. It wouldn't be easy to find one who could win the heart of a girl already in love with someone else. Panjabi boys are more dashing, I hear. . . .'

'The moment Jalis finds out she is being married off to somebody else, she will flare up. There was a boy called Ahsan Ali. He had a Government of India job at about a thousand rupees, and he was very good-looking. I suggested that she might marry him. At first she said she would think about it and tell me later. Then she told

[1] Those Muslims who claim direct descent from Muhammad.

80

your uncle and me: "Papa, Mums, I will marry anyone you want me to." And we began to get her trousseau ready. And then only the night before Ahsan Ali was coming to stay with us she ran off.'

'No, Aunty!' Nur Jahan said incredulously. 'Surely not! Anyway Samuel was in America, wasn't he?'

'She went to stay with some people who had been inciting her not to marry anyone but Samuel. They lent her money – two thousand rupees. She spent the lot within three months. Then I told your uncle, "Kazim, if you don't get the girl back, she won't even keep her virginity." And we decided that we would keep her with us until Sanuel came back, but that if she married him she would not get a penny of our property. We told her, "Miss Jalis Mashhandi will be free to go to her friends, and to marry whoever she likes, and to live wherever she likes; but for us from that moment she will be dead." Nuri darling, it is worrying about this that has ruined my health. You can see what a state I am in. This consumption. . .'

And poor Begum Mashhadi burst into tears. Nur Jahan felt very sorry for her. After a little while Begum Mashhadi told her in the same confiding tone, 'An astrologer told me that at the end of May a great change will take place in Jalis, that the boy will refuse to marry her, and that a few days later he will be killed in an accident. Yesterday she had a letter from Samuel. When she read it she cried a lot. Her eyes were quite swollen right up till tea-time. Now perhaps she will change.'

By this time Nur Jahan, too, had acquired great faith in the astrologer. She said with deep feeling, 'Yes, God grant that she changes. . . .' And then she asked, 'Aunty, shall I talk to Jalis about it?'

'No darling, that wouldn't do any good. At one time she refused to speak to Fatima and Rashid just because they tried to discuss it with her. You know how fond of me she is. But when this question comes up, she forgets all her love for me. And I myself am afraid to speak of it, in case she runs away again. Yesterday she went to the matinée, and didn't come back until eight o'clock. I thought she had left me again . . .' and the tears again welled up in her eyes.

In the end she lay back on her pillow and said, 'That's the only hope; that she falls in love with a Muslim boy. But in our province there aren't many nice, cultured Muslim young men.'

Nur Jahan said nothing. But she said to herself, 'That is where Begum Mashhadi's made her mistake. When you give a girl her freedom you should be ready to put up with the consequences.' But she felt vividly for the first time how real were other people's troubles, and how they feel them as keenly as she felt her own. For Jalis the choice between her parents and the man she loved; and for her gay mother worry for the honour of her family, and consumption.

A few days later she and Jalis were sitting outside on the lawn under the sunshade, drinking lemonade. Jalis seemed very dejected, and Nur Jahan thought to herself that perhaps the astrologer was right.

'What's the matter, Jalis?' she asked. 'You seem very depressed these days?'

'Who, me? Depressed? No fear!'

'Oh yes you are,' Nur Jahan said, and trying to be very clever – so much so that she surprised herself – she said, 'Jalis, ever since we met, I've felt that you had a secret that troubles you. I am sure something is worrying you. Why don't you tell me? I won't tell anyone. Not even Sultan.'

Jalis laughed drily, and put her glass down on the table. Then she stretched and closed her eyes and said with a smile, 'Everything's all right now. But a little while ago I was in a terrible state. I am in love with a boy who isn't a Muslim.'

Nur Jahan said nothing; she was anxious to hear her version of the story. Jalis, with her eyes still closed, continued wearily, 'Papa and Mums were dead against it. But in the end Sir Ghulam Ali persuaded them and they gave their consent.'

This was a new revelation. Begum Mashhadi had not made this clear, that she and Kazim Mashhadi had given their formal consent to her marriage with this Indian Christian. Her tone betrayed some curiosity as she asked, 'And what happened then, Jalis? Tell me.'

'What happened? I've told you what happened. I fell in love with a non-Muslim, a Christian, and he fell in love with me; and I made up my mind that no matter what happened I would marry no one but him. That's all.'

How do you know you are in love with him?' Nur Jahan half-jokingly asked her.

'Because I am; that's how I know.' She looked very pretty as she said this.

'What is love like?' asked Nur Jahan; 'I don't believe in it myself. It's all a hoax put over by American films. You get married, and you're happy with your husband, and that's all there is to it. This love business is a lot of nonsense.'

'All right! Don't believe in it, if you don't want to. But I tell you, I am in love with Samuel.'

'Tell me, then; what is love like?'

'How can I tell you, Nuri darling?'

Nur Jahan thought of a new manoeuvre. 'Jalis darling! People say that young girls take a fancy to a young man, and only think that they're in love. Perhaps that's what's happened to you. After all you're still very young. Perhaps this isn't real love at all?'

'In the first place I'm not all that young. I'm eighteen, only three years younger than you. Do you hear me, Granny? In the second place I've always been big for my age. Even when I was fifteen I looked quite grown-up. People used to think me quite a young woman. I'm not a baby any more.'

Nur Jahan continued what she conceived to be her mission of reform. 'Then you should have fallen in love with a Muslim boy.'

'That's something you can't control.'

The woman in Nur Jahan's blood could not answer this, so she said, 'It must have been a blow to your parents.'

'Yes, it is, but it can't be helped.' Jalis spoke shortly, and to atone for her shortness she picked up her glass of lemonade, took a large gulp and went on, 'Nuri darling, whose fault is it? I'm eighteen and I can't speak Urdu. At this moment I'm talking to you in English. I envy you your Urdu. I can't recite the Muslim profession of faith. I've never said my prayers. Tell me, whose fault is it? Mine, or Mums and Papa's? I'm what they've made me. And now they expect me to marry whoever they want me to, and to give up the man I love for some Muslim stranger of their choosing. I ask you, isn't that unfair?'

Nur Jahan did not know what to say. 'Yes,' she said, 'Aunty is certainly at fault, too.'

'At fault?' Now Jalis became serious. 'She herself is on familiar terms with Hindus, Parsees and Sikhs, and makes us be nice to them. Do you know, Nuri darling, last year I didn't dance once during the whole season in Mussoorie. If you don't believe me, you can ask Sultan. And do you know why? Because Mums had a favourite protégé called Hirday Nath. He was so ill-mannered that I didn't want to dance with him. And since he always managed

83

to get himself included in our party, Mums told me that I'd better not dance with anybody; I couldn't very well dance with others and not with him; it would look very rude. So I pretended to be unwell, and didn't dance with anyone the whole season. I ask you, when I've been brought up like this, don't you think it is too much to expect me to behave like a girl in purdah, and go meekly to any man they want to marry me to? Well, darling?'

Her eyes filled with tears. Nur Jahan, to change the subject for a little while, said, 'Was Hirday Nath all that unpleasant, then?'

'Nuri darling, he was awful; a really repulsive man.'

'Why, what happened? Did he try to make love to you?'

Jalis laughed. 'No, no, I'll tell you what happened. We met him for the first time last year at the beginning of the season. Mums fell for him right away, and invited him to our very first party. He asked me to dance with him. I looked at Mums, and she nodded; so I got up to dance. The first question he asked me was "What is your name?" I said, "Miss Mashhadi." "I know that," he said, "but what is your first name?" I again said, "My name is Miss Mashhadi." And he again asked what was my first name. I said, "My first name doesn't concern anyone except my relations and my close friends, and I don't want any one else to call me by it." Even then he kept on and on. And in the end he said, "All right, then, I promise you not to call you by your first name; but at any rate tell me what it is." I said, "If it's just that you are curious to know my name, and you promise not to call me by it, I'll tell you. My name is Jalis." Then he said, "Jalis, now I know your name, and if I call you by it, what can you do about it?" "Just call me by it," I said, "and you'll see what I can do about it." Then he began to mimic me, "You'll go crying to your mother," he said. "Mummy, Mummy, Hirday calls me Jalis." I was extremely angry, and stopped dancing. He got hold of my hand and said, "Jalis, why are you cross with me?" I pulled my hand free and went straight back to my place and sat down.'

'Well done!' said Nur Jahan laughing, 'but when he got hold of your hand, you should have given him a good kick.'

Jalis laughed, 'After that he came to apologize. I didn't answer him. The next day he greeted me, "Good evening, Jalis." But I looked straight through him. After that Mums and I were always quarrelling about him.'

After a little while Nur Jahan came back to the old topic. 'Jalis, you haven't told me all your secret.'

84

'No, I didn't tell you that I ran away from home,' said Jalis in a sarcastic tone.

'What?'

'Yes, I ran away from home. Mums must have told you that. That's why you are taking such an interest in my future.'

'Jalis!'

'Mums gets hold of everybody and tells them all about me. She must have told you, too.'

'Jalis, I am your friend. Otherwise I would never have asked you about it. Are you cross with me for talking like that?'

'No, Nuri darling.'

In the end Nur Jahan, the great reformer, decided to strike her final blow. 'Jalis, darling, let me ask you one more question.'

'Well?'

'Do you love your mother?'

'Yes, very much.'

'More than anyone except Samuel?'

'Yes, more than anyone except Samuel.'

'And you know that aunty is very ill? That she has had T.B. for nearly two years, and at the most she can't last more than another two or three years?'

Jalis's eyes filled with tears. She looked helplessly at Nur Jahan.

'Jalis darling, in a month I shall be going back to Farkhundanagar, and I don't know whether I shall ever seen you again. But promise me one thing. Promise that you won't kill aunty before her time.'

The tears overflowed from Jalis's eyes.

Nur Jahan continued, 'Marry the man you love – it doesn't matter whether he is a Christian or what he is. But wait for three years and let aunty die in peace.'

Jalis laid her hand in Nur Jahan's and stood up. 'Nuri darling, I have already promised myself that a long time ago. You can rest assured. I'll see you at lunch. Bye-bye darling . . . and thanks.'

Nur Jahan cried after she left. But she was smiling amid her tears. She was feeling for the first time the sorrow, the joy, the love and the pull of conflicting ties – emotions in which she was not directly involved. For the first time she felt that there was an outside world, peopled by human beings like herself; women who bore their trials as she did; and her heart brimmed over with sympathy for them.

Sultan was coming down the slope towards the Savoy with

Surendar. After his whiskies Surendar was so obsessed with the necessity of keeping fit that he was determined to walk twice to Kulhri Bazaar and back. The fashionable crowd was strolling back and forth from the library to Hackman's, but Surendar was bent on a serious discussion.

'I am proud of my class, the middle class. In Russia, so they tell us, they have a classless society. Well, we haven't been there, so we don't know. But where there are classes, no class can compare with ours. The upper classes try to copy us, just as the lower classes do.' Surendar was making a regular speech.

'How do you make that out?' Sultan asked. He was looking at a group of U.P. girls, and concluding that their silver braid was a good deal more attractive than they were.

'Because we set the pace in all the arts and sciences. We are the inventors and the authors, and the artists. We design the buildings in which your Maharajahs live . . .'

'But the middle classes don't build them.'

'Maybe not, but the brain behind them is ours, you can't deny it. And if you do deny it, my engineering friend, then you are not making an honest living.'

'Of course, its only in All-India Radio that you make an honest living.'

'Look at the radio, for instance! What a boon it is! That's a gift from the middle classes, too. It's relieved the upper classes of the trouble of reading the papers, and their P.R.O.s of the task of preparing news summaries. Do you think your fashionable princesses read the *Statesman* or the *Hindustan Times*? Not on your life! They only look at the advertisements for the creams and powders and rouge and lipsticks which the middle-class fashion experts have invented; and when they've plastered their faces with them, in imitation of the middle-class women, they switch on the radio to hear the music and incidentally pick up some bits and pieces of news – quite enough for drawing-room conversation. And look what we've provided for the lower classes. Before the advent of the radio they only had their toddy. . . . Now they sit in their dirty cafés with the radio on and listen to the girl singing "Today I went to find my love". And the worker, on his eight annas a day, is quite happy imagining that at any moment the girl from the radio may come into the café to look for him.'

Below them towards Dehra Dun, in the evening haze, lights were beginning to show, and before them a light grey mist was

86

stealing over the mountain side. Surendar held out his cigarette-case to Sultan, and baring his yellow fangs in a mocking smile, went on, 'It's the same with politics, with the brains behind politics, I mean. Political theory has all come from the middle classes, from Machiavelli to Marx, and from Plato's *Republic* to Hitler's *Mein Kampf*. Who constructed all these systems? We did, my friend. . . .'

Sultan did not answer. He was looking at the pretty girls from Banaras, their skin like butter, shopping at Lila Ram's, and had to get out of the way of an approaching rickshaw.

Surendar noticed that he was not paying attention. 'Sultan, my friend,' he said, 'you're married now. But you still look at a woman as if you'd never seen one before.'

Sultan only laughed.

It was getting late now and the mermaids had departed from the Mall, except for an occasional one hurrying back to dinner with her husband or her lover. Now the rickshaw-wallahs, the butlers and domestic servants dominated the scene. The middle classes were either watching the last reel in the cinemas or dancing at Hackman's, or drinking or flirting, or seated around the dinner-tables gossiping about other people's morals. Amongst these last was Nur Jahan, who was listening to Begum Mashhadi. Jalis had a headache and had not come down to dinner. Sultan was not yet back from his walk. And Begum Mashhadi and Fatima were discussing Jalis.

Fatima was saying, 'Ever since she was little, Jalis has always been a flirt. (I never liked being with the boys too much.) You remember Roy? When she ran away, he was the one who put her up to it. But she was supposed to be running away for the love of Samuel. So why did she have to flirt with Roy?'

'Who is Roy?' asked Nur Jahan open-eyed. She was learning something new about Jalis all the time.

'He was a Bengali Brahmo Samaj boy, who lived with us for two years,' Begum Mashhadi explained. 'I was great friends with his mother. He, too, fell in love with Jalis; and it was he who advised her to run away. His game was that once Jalis left home, he could marry her himself. But she went off to Samuel's people; and it wasn't long before she realized what Roy was up to.'

'But Mums, Dr Mujtaba's daughters told me that when she was with them, Jalis would kiss Roy, and sit on his knee and cuddle him.'

Nur Jahan was all ears. She was enlarging her experience, and doing her best to be completely neutral between Begum Mashhadi and Jalis. Kamala Paresh passed by their table. 'Look at her,' said Fatima; 'her blouse is so thin that you can even see the hairs on her body. . . .'

Begum Mashhadi coughed and said, 'She doesn't wear such clothes when her husband is around.'

Six weeks passed like this on the magic mountain. The Mall was resplendent with light. Below in the valley shone the dim lights of Dehra Dun. Cars crawled like lice along the flowing black tress of the tarmac road which wound down the mountain-side. The hunters took their quarries in rickshaws to the Municipal Park. On the lawns of the Savoy, in the twilight, fashionable wives clung to other women's husbands. Twice the moon waxed and waned, lighting up the white walls, sharpening the outlines of the crags, putting to shame the lights on the road to the Charleville, and casting a magic spell over the Dehra Dun valley. Everyday at the Savoy, and at God knows how many other places, from breakfast to lunch, from lunch to afternoon tea, and from dinner to midnight or the small hours of the morning, the bridge-warriors set up their tables, winning and losing. Easy money, easily lost. At Lila Ram's and Ghani's the season's stock of fashionable clothes rapidly diminished. At the bars before dinner fast young men and faster young women gathered to drink aperitifs (except for the occasional girl more experienced in innocence, who would insist on tomato juice). The corks flew, and the froth foamed. Marriages were wrecked. Businessmen ran off with other people's wives and divorced their own. The dancing went on. Tea dances, cocktail dances, dinner dances, exotic evenings. Paris Night, Vienna Night, Soho Night. Starving India had sent its bloodsuckers to the hills for a rest during the summer, while she went on spitting blood, enduring the hot wind, and dying, and rotting.

In the early days the blood-suckers had all been white. It was they who opened the big hotels where dinner-jackets were obligatory in the evenings. Then the Central European Jews who follow in the wake of the conquerors opened the dance halls. But then the natives went one better than their masters. First they took over the dance halls. And soon they completely out-distanced their masters, swinging their sticks as they walked into the hotels, attired in their elegant English suits, dancing the rumba, flirting with women in the hill stations and teaching their own womenfolk to dance and to flirt. In short, their own *Plain Tales from the Hills*.

Nur Jahan knew nothing of Kipling's *Plain Tales from the Hills*, nor of the complexities of life on the magic mountain of Mussoorie. Content with her husband's embraces and with the entertaining talk of Begum Mashhadi, she was absorbing quite unconsciously the poison of the place. She no longer had any worries of her own. Her only worries were about Jalis, and they would probably have remained so as long as Sultan's leave lasted. But all of a sudden Mussoorie overwhelmed her like a terrible ogre.

One evening she had gone out for a walk with Jalis and Fatima along the Camel's Back. When she returned to the Savoy, Sultan was not there. Usually he told her where he was going before he went out. Instead of going straight up to Begum Mashhadi's room, she went round first by the hotel office to ask whether her husband had phoned any message for her. As she walked along the veranda towards Begum Mashhadi's room, she could hear through the open window Begum Mashhadi saying to Fatima, 'Fatima darling, I can't bear to see him deceiving that simple girl to run after a whore like Kamala Paresh. . . .'

Nur Jahan did not realize they were talking about her. She knocked at the door and went in. Begum Mashhadi was sitting with a shawl round her shoulders. She was having dinner brought up to her room. As Nur Jahan went down to the dining-room with Fatima she asked inquisitively, 'Who's running after Kamala Paresh? Who were you talking about?'

Fatima gave her such an embarrassed look that she suddenly realized and trembled. Hastily Fatima replied, 'We were talking about an old acquaintance of ours, Balmukand.'

Three or four days later she was straining her eyes into the darkness, trying to see beyond the squash courts – where the sunshades were. She had no reason to feel suspicious. Sultan had said that he was going with Surendar to Hackman's and had asked her to come, too. She had not gone, because nowadays she felt sick all the time, and a little tired. The lady doctor had advised her to go for walks, but not to stay up too late at nights or to exert herself unduly. It was now half-past ten. Mr Desai, who had booked a trunk call to his wife in Bombay, had cancelled it and gone. The front lawn was deserted. But beyond the squash courts where flirting couples usually lingered on, there – she did not know why – she suspected Sultan would be, with someone else, perhaps with Kamala Paresh. She did not have the courage to go there alone and see for herself. She had turned off the light in her room and sat there tense and waiting. She knew that as they came towards the hotel the light would fall on their faces. She sat there waiting. Eleven o'clock. Lovers do not notice the passing of time, particularly when they are making love to other people's wives. Half-past eleven. One couple came slowly towards the hotel, still arm in arm. It was Kishore and Chandra. They were engaged anyway. Probably no one else would come now. Twelve o'clock. Lovers' Corner, beyond the squash court, seemed deserted. And Nur Jahan, thinking that it would be a good two hours yet before the cabaret was over, and that Sultan and Surendar would not be back before that, had got up to come away from the window, when a rickshaw stopped below, and the happy laughter of a young woman rang out. 'Yes, sir.' The stillness of the night flung these words towards her window. A young man got out of the rickshaw. Who was it? Her heart missed a beat. A young woman adjusting her saree, put her hand on the young man's shoulder and jumped to the ground. It was Kamala Paresh. Suddenly Begum Mashhadi's words flashed across her mind.

Her first mad, jealous impulse was to throw herself out of the window. She felt a chill shudder run down her spine. Her head began to spin as she stared at the departing rickshaw. Kamala Paresh climbed the stairs opposite her room, and her companion, reassured at seeing there was no light at the window, approached on tiptoe, whistling softly, up the stairs towards her own, Nur Jahan's room. Monsieur and Madame Alé's Alsatian barked at his footfall for a second, and then all was still again. Nur Jahan heard him coming. She thought of getting into bed and pretending to be asleep, as though she had seen nothing. But she felt a strange nervous paralysis come over her. Sultan opened the door and put on the light. He saw Nur Jahan standing motionless by the window, and stopped dead. It was late. His own head was swimming. He sat down on the sofa and began to take off his shoes. 'Nur Jahan, darling,' he said, 'you're still awake? . . . Kamala was coming this way and I offered her a lift. . . . It's not safe for women to go about late at night, alone. . . . What's the matter, darling? You look quite white. Don't you feel well?'

She did not answer him. She knew only that if Sultan as much as touched her she would lose her self-control. She was stifling her feelings, determined not to let him see that she suspected him.

One thing alone restrained her, the self-respect which she had inherited from her grandfather and her mother.

Next morning she asked Fatima outright: 'Fatima, you were hiding something from me, weren't you? The name of the man who is running after Kamala Paresh isn't Balmukand. It's Sultan Husain, isn't it?'

All Fatima could say in reply was, 'Darling. . . .'

Nur Jahan had lain awake all night, tossing and turning. And now suddenly the storm broke. Fatima hastily closed the door, and Nur Jahan laying her head on her shoulder burst into sobs of helpless misery.

At last Fatima said, 'Darling, Mussoorie is a wicked place. God knows why men find such women attractive. A woman smiles at them, and they fall for her head over heels. There are plenty of women like that here.'

Nur Jahan was still crying. She heard someone else come into the room, and made an effort to control herself. Someone else put her arm around her; she felt her head taken gently onto someone else's shoulder. And she clung to Begum Mashhadi, feeling for a brief moment that it was her own mother, two thousand miles away. She sobbed violently, and Begum Mashhadi stroked her head. At last the sobs died away. Then Begum Mashhadi said, 'Nuri darling, that is the way of the world. A woman must never admit defeat. You must not be afraid. Fight back. And above all, get Sultan back to Farkhundanagar as soon as you can. The whole atmosphere here is poison. Get back as soon as you can.'

That day after lunch Sultan and Nur Jahan had a violent quarrel. She heaped on him all the curses she knew. She wept. She screamed. Sultan could not shout back in case the neighbours might hear. And in the end, still swearing his innocence, he promised her that they should go back to Farkhundanagar immediately.

Nur Jahan's eyes were bloodshot, and she had a splitting headache. She felt even more sick than usual and could not eat any lunch. She thought of Jalis, and then of herself, and then of Mussoorie with its walls burning in the moonlight, its blistered Mall, and beneath it near Dehra Dun the forest on fire; and all this wreckage, these falling rocks, this avalanche descending upon her head.

8

Sultan Husain watched the houses going up in the foothills of Kishanpalli. Everywhere were heaps of cement, mortar and stone, and stacks of iron bars. Hundreds of stone-hewers were converting the hanging rocks into building stone. Their muscular arms swung their heavy picks and the stones shattered in fragments. Foundations were being dug. Stone was being bonded to stone and brick to brick. Timber was being sawed and planed. Behind all this building were the well-proportioned limbs of the stone-hewer women, human muscles, human sweat and blood, human hearts beating beneath the heavy loads, and occasionally an unborn baby turning in the womb.

The houses were going up – foundations, walls, roofs of concrete, supported by scaffolding like spiders with innumerable legs. Here a house was being plastered, there a floor of polished limestone or of tiles was being laid. Lorries were coming and going, and hundreds of bullock-carts crawled up and down the narrow hillside tracks.

Besides the stone-hewers there were women of other sub-castes in costumes reminiscent of Central Asia, with their profusion of glass bangles and their long skirts studded with pieces of crystal or stone. Some of them still retained their hereditary Mongoloid features. In short, Ahdi Husnkar Jang's dream was being realized on an ambitious scale.

There had been many changes in Farkhundanagar. The age of Maharajah Sir Shujaat Shamsher Singh Bahadur had passed away. Thirty years ago he still rode to the Palace on an elephant, showering silver coins among the bystanders. Later in his reign when he drove to the Council Chamber in his Cadillac, it was only four-anna and two-anna pieces – a less abundant shower – and towards the end of his time it had come down to copper pice. But to the end he kept up the tradition that any petitioner who wished might lie down on the road and bar his progress. The Rajah of Rajahs would order the chauffeur to stop; the suppliant would tell his tale of woe, melt the Rajah's heart and receive words of comfort; and his petition would be handed to the Rajah of Rajah's

Secretary-in-Waiting, Ahdi Husnkar Jang. The other ministers were kept waiting in the Council Chamber and the opening of the session delayed. Now those days were gone. Ala Kausar Nawaz Jang had succeeded the Rajah of Rajahs as Prime Minister and all Farkhundanagar trembled at his name. He did not like Ahdi Husnkar Jang, and his influence had diminished. But the Kishanpalli project had captured the imagination of the aristocracy and the highly-placed officials, and the houses were going up all the time. Strange houses. One like a dreadnought, one like a prehistoric cave, one in Japanese style, one displaying Sassanian arches. Most popular of all was the 'German' design, the 'cubist' house; and here and there one might see half-circles, and arcs, and roofs of tile and concrete. Nearly all the houses were mortgaged to money-lenders, who in their Marwari turbans, and with the long caste-marks on their foreheads, came in their tongas to collect their dues. They would stand respectfully with folded hands before the high officials who were their debtors, and address them as 'Ji Huzoor, Ji Huzoor'. But their arrangements were foolproof, and meekly and methodically they sucked the blood of their fashionable clientele. At worst they drew their compound interest, and at best foreclosed on the houses. Either way they could not lose. And so the Kishanpalli estate was coming into being – so high, so low.

Sultan Husain, too, was having a house built. He had lived carefully, and before his marriage had already saved quite a bit of money. He had taken a house loan from the Government; but this was just a convention, a standard part of the façade of honesty.

A big hotel proprietor in the capital's twin city, Tabindanagar, had conceived the idea of opening a luxury hotel on Kishanpalli. To be more precise, the idea came not from him, but from his daughter, Sheila, or perhaps from her lover Balmukand, a smart, unscrupulous steel contractor. Anyway, it was at her suggestion that her father had rented the house known as 'The Abode of Spring' and fitted it out in the style of an English North country inn. He had called it 'Ye Olde Ale House', and provided it with everything requisite to the entertainment of the British army officers in Tabindanagar cantonment.

Ye Olde Ale House rapidly became the centre for Kishanpalli's fashionable parties. Every week Britons and Americans travelling by American Express came to stay there. Aristocrats' sons and fashionable young women gave parties on the roof, parties of various grades with refreshments ranging all the way between ice-cream and gin and brandy; some were very decorous, others more flashy, and yet others made a show of daring depravity. Balmukand, the beloved of the proprietor's daughter, equally expert in matters of sex and in matters of building-steel, would sit on the hotel lawn in wait, like a spider weaving his web, for the mem-sahibs passing through on their travels. It puzzled everyone that he could openly carry on with them in Sheila's presence without her seeming to mind at all. She remained his slave just the same, although there was nothing prepossessing about his appearance. God knows what women found attractive in him, with his big, full, sensual mouth and his little cunning eyes.

Ye Olde Ale House had already opened before Sultan's house was completed, and it was here that Surendar stayed when he came to Farkhundanagar. It was evening at the very end of the rains when the last expected showers had already put out the Dipavali lamps.

Surendar and Sultan were sitting in the Old Ale House garden. A party was in progress on the roof. Most of the guests were relations of Mahtab Jang's, including Athar, the boy who had teased Nur Jahan so much when they were children together. He was back in Farkhundanagar now, after an absence of several years.

Surendar watched them amusedly, listening to their laughter descending in cascades from the roof. He had rather wanted to be introduced to these people, but Sultan was in a retiring mood.

Surendar turned to watch the antics of Balmukand, who was sitting at a nearby table. He was staring at two Englishwomen, who were presumably stopping off on their way from Madras to Bombay by air. They must have been between thirty and thirty-five, and both of them seemed pucka mem-sahibs. But Balmukand was an old hand, and thought nothing of such obstacles. He consumed one glass of beer after another, leering and staring at them all the time. Surendar could not take his eyes off him. In the end Balmukand found some pretext to speak to them. Out of politeness, they both answered him, and then resumed their conversation. Balmukand again forced himself upon them. This time they snubbed him. He pestered them again. They said something about feeling tired and got up to go. He wished them a loud 'Good night'. They ignored him.

94

Balmukand signed his bill and got up. As he passed Surendar's table, Surendar leaned forward and flashing his teeth in a drunken grin said, 'Cheer up! Better luck next time.'

Balmukand clenched his teeth and made no reply.

Surendar had been out with Sultan to see the building on Kishanpalli and the other sights of Farkhundanagar.

Plot for sale. Final auction. A hotel overlooking the blue water of Shahid Sagar – as blue as a frozen lake – surrounded by beautiful houses. . . . How amusing that the Farkhundanagar policemen all smoked and cracked jokes with the passers-by. One had been swaying his hips effeminately as he directed the traffic. . . . Dinner at Sultan's. Husband and wife quarrelling at the dinner table, quarrelling violently, in front of him. And Nur Jahan getting up and going out of the room. In short, it made one laugh, just as the policeman's swaying hips made one laugh. Nur Jahan's eyes, red and challenging . . . Sultan doesn't know the meaning of respect for a woman. In short, the black-haired beauty, reclining in her chair, attacking him with withering sarcasm. In short, Kamala Paresh. In short, as Hasrat puts it:

> First the eyes succumb enchanted;
> Then they teach the heart to love.

The heart imitates the eyes. In short, love is born of eyes and heart and hands. But then the opposite currents. Between the hands that reach out, and yet do not reach; and the eyes which see, but see no further than the body's hunger. In short, boredom, monotony. Like the menu of Ye Olde Ale House: 'Clear Soup, Cold Meat and Salad, Mutton Curry and Rice, Golden Pudding, Savoury and Coffee'. Flatulence; but belching is not allowed. Once, Sultan tells me, Nayazi in his cups gave a majestic belch just to annoy the two Englishmen at the next table; and then, when they glared at him, he said gravely in a childish voice, 'Excuse me, I am a damn fool, hee, hee, hee. . . .'

Ought I to laugh at that? Hee, hee, hee. . . . Farkhundanagar. Medieval arches and twentieth-century cubism. Cars and bullock-carts. Concrete roads and filthy side-streets. Along the concrete road comes a bullock-cart. In Farkhundanagar we call it 'bundi'. All right, bundi then; you win, I lose. One of the bundi bullocks is gravely observing to the other, 'I believe in the progressive policy of the mules, and in their even more progressive patriotism. And

95

if I am elected to the Bullocks' Assembly, then I promise to shed the last drop of my blood in the service of my country, and to rob the country of its last farthing. I believe that in the national interest our incomes must keep ahead of rising prices. I swear to obey the laws of the land, as I have done hitherto during every massacre in Delhi.' Then locking his horns with the other bullock he swore, 'I believe in complete equality between all bullocks. We are equal to horses and far superior to men. Here comes a car.' Hearing it sound its horn the driver pulled the bullock-cart over to the side of the road; and Surendar in conversation with Sultan, flashed by. I believe. . . .

. . . That the centuries are not dead. They are alive. Alive to keep on dying, and yet not completely die. Alive for Genghis Khan, and for Hitler and for Churchill and for Sardar Vallabh Bhai Patel and for Sir Firoz Khan Noon. I believe, I believe, I believe . . . in the League of Nations which is dead, and in the United Nations, not yet in being. I believe in the great religions of the world, which preach peace and tolerance, and whose followers preach mutual bloodshed. I believe in Aristotle, who teaches that life is ethics and ethics is static. I believe in Hegel's philosophy of history. I believe in Nietzsche, and the Superman and in syphilis which inspired the concept of the Superman. I believe in Hitler and Mussolini who regard mankind as material for a vast biological experiment. I believe in Churchill and Roosevelt and General de Gaulle who are fighting to make the world safe for democracy. I believe in Marx, Engels, Lenin and Stalin who declare class war to be the great fact of life. I believe in the policeman with the swaying hips. Look out, Sultan, there's a bus coming, and the policeman's signalling you to stop. Stop, stop, go. Why is he saluting you? Aha! I see! Every policeman in Farkhundanagar must salute everyone, even the clerk and the peon, in case one day he has to serve under one of them. . . . What was I saying? I believe in your marriage to Nur Jahan. The high and holy bond. . . . What did you say? Shut up? Right Sultan, I'll shut up. Give me a cigarette. I say, your hand is never steady on the steering-wheel. Look, the policeman's signalling you to stop. Stop. No. Go. Go.

That year Sartaj, with her fat black railway engine of a husband had gone to Ooty. They had deliberately chosen not to go to Mussoorie so that Nur Jahan and Sultan should be free to enjoy themselves on their own. Besides, Azim Jang and his daughters were going to Ooty that year, and Azim Jang's wife was her 'aunty'. In fact, the wife of every titled noble – Jang or Daula – was her 'aunty', and their daughters were her 'sisters'. Her own relatives were either as good as dead, or no more than servants. Except for her own brothers and sisters, she hardly ever mixed with them, and whenever she met them, she emphasized all the time her own superiority. 'Allah! Sarwari, what a sweet man the Prime Minister is. What a sweet little beard he has. How sweetly he talks to you.' – 'Allah, Aisha, what a handsome man Wali Chalak Jang is. Allah, I have never seen such a handsome man. I don't know why girls go crazy about Tyrone Power or Clark Gable. I tell you, Aisha, there is no more handsome man – not in Farkhundanagar at any rate.' At every wedding, at every meeting of the Ladies' Club, at every family ceremony, at every special occasion, Sartaj would be there, wearing an expensive brand-new saree of the most up-to-date fashion, with one wrist bare and the other adorned by a jewelled bracelet or loaded with bangles. And then God had done everything to make Sartaj a beauty. True, if you took her features one by one you could find fault with all of them, but her high forehead, her small but lustrous eyes, her long finely-chiselled nose and her full lips, taken together made her a very beautiful woman. Besides which she took infinite care with her make-up. 'Allah, Aisha,' she would say, 'why don't you come out into society? You think that everyone has to speak English there, but it's not so. Plenty of people speak Urdu. The other day I went to Mutmain Jang's party. The old hunchback ought to be ashamed of himself. He keeps his own wife and daughters in purdah, and invites other people's wives to his mixed parties. But Allah, Aisha, what an able man he is; French, history, Islam, how well he talks about all of them. I can't praise him enough. Wali Chalak Jang, Afaq and Dr Qurban Husain wanted to play bridge, but they couldn't find a fourth. They asked me to play. Allah, Aisha, what charming silly ways Dr Qurban Husain has. He's very sweet. He must be past middle age. I said, "Of course, I'll play." I always say there's no harm in women playing bridge with the men. There's no sense in a mixed party if all the men sit on one side and all the women on the other. The old-style purdah women's parties are better than that. For you girls who observe purdah they're quite all right. Anyway, what was I saying, Aisha? Yes, at the bridge table we spoke Urdu all the time – all of us, I, Wali Chalak Jang and Qurban Husain. Do you know why?

Nowadays one talks Urdu a lot, because of nationalism. It's regarded as the right thing to do. Do you know, when I came back from Panchgani finishing school, I had practically forgotten my Urdu. . . .'

Nur Jahan always tried to stop her. 'Oh, that'll do, Sartaj. Stop showing off. Whoever forgets his own language?'

And with Nur Jahan's objections in mind, Sartaj would say to her poor cousin Aisha who observed purdah and bore patiently the scoldings of an ill-tempered husband, 'Allah, Aisha, what a sweet language Urdu is.' Then turning to her ayah she would say, 'Rahim Bi, tell the chauffeur to bring round my Rolls Royce.' At which Aisha and all the other women would burst out laughing. Sarwari especially. But then everybody knew how envious Sarwari was. When Sartaj mentioned her Rolls Royce they would all laugh, and Nur Jahan would tell her, 'Sartaj, everybody laughs at your swank. Even my old Ford is better than your ancient, ramshackle Rolls.'

Sartaj's husband, Haidar Muhiuddin (the Black Railway Engine) did indeed possess a Rolls, but it must have been the first that ever came out of the Rolls Royce factory. White, shining like silver, ugly, proportionless – but anyway it was a Rolls. It had been presented by the late Khan Hazrat to the late Sir Taj ul Muluk on his victorious return from the Tibetan War; and the late Sir Taj ul Muluk had given it away with the dowry of his daughter, Haidar Muhiuddin's mother.

Anyway, when Sartaj returned from Ooty, and met Nur Jahan for the first time after her return from Mussoorie, she noticed at once the difference between Nur Jahan's marriage and her own. Sartaj, on the strength of her 'aunties' and her 'sisters' and with Max Factor's help was pulling her Black Railway Engine with her towards the heights of snobbery, ostentation and success; while Nur Jahan's engineer was pulling her in the opposite direction, towards a gulf which he was making no effort to bridge.

'Nur Jahan, my baby, my love! What has happened to you?' And Sartaj hugged her close, as Nur Jahan burst into tears.

Nur Jahan had told her mother, Khurshid Zamani, what had happened at Mussoorie. Her reaction had been different from Sartaj's and full of worldly wisdom. 'My dear, men are like that; you just have to put up with it. It won't be long before he gives up all that. Look at your Uncle Nadir Beg. You know how he went on sowing his wild oats with the Anglo-Indian girls, even

98

after he'd married your Aunty Nazli. And you see how he changed after the children came along. You'll see, when the baby's born, he'll come round of his own accord. . . .'

Her eldest sister Mashur had said the same thing. She was rather like Nur Jahan in her ways, but was much older than her, and not very close to her. On the other hand, Sartaj, although temperamentally quite the reverse of herself, was not only her sister, but her childhood playmate and her closest friend. True, everybody said that Nur Jahan took after her father's father Mashur ul Mulk, while Sartaj took after her mother's father Qabil Jang, especially in the airs she gave herself. But when Sartaj called her 'My baby, my love' and hugged her, she could only say 'Oh, Sartaj!' and burst into tears.

When she had heard the whole story, Sartaj felt very sorry for her. But with all her sympathy, she was at a loss to know how to advise her. As far as she herself was concerned a situation of this kind was inconceivable. After all, what girl would feel attracted to dear old Haidar Muhiuddin, the Black Railway Engine? Besides, she kept the reins firmly in her own hands and gave him only such freedom as she thought fit. She herself was unswervingly loyal to her husband. And although she was a great socialite her chastity was unimpeachable, and her husband had full confidence in her. And then she had another advantage over Nur Jahan in that her in-laws, Sir Taj al Muluk's people – after whom she herself had been named by her grandfather, despite their official rivalries – were very broadminded. They had been one of the first of the big families of Farkhundanagar to abandon purdah. Sultan, on the other hand, came from a purely 'old city' background. His forebears had grown up in the dark alleys of the old city, and even the measure of freedom which Sultan had given Nur Jahan at Mussoorie was the product of an artificial tolerance.

But the biggest difference between the sisters was that even if Haidar Muhiuddin had had an occasional fling like Sultan, Sartaj would not have bothered about it greatly. She was chiefly interested in the proceeds of the estate, in glamorous clothes, jewellery, her Rolls Royce, comfort and show and style. She would not have worried even if her husband had wallowed in the dirt of the district headquarters wherever he served. (She never accompanied him, and after all, he was a man . . . .) When he returned to the city, she would have been just the same, and would have given herself to him like a dutiful wife, without passion, but without aversion.

Love was an emotion which she had never experienced intensely, and never would; for this was an ingredient which nature had not included in her make-up. She was merely conscious of her duty as a wife. The estate and her husband formed a single unity to which she was devoted. So every three years she produced a child, and in between times she renewed the stock of her sarees, her bracelets and her beauty. And all this she managed so well, that though other women called her stuck-up, no one could question her good name. There was no place for scandal in the way she organized her life. In her, her mother Khurshid Zamani had taken re-birth during her own lifetime; and so had the celebrated pride and splendour of the Qabil Jang family. And Sartaj would do nothing to jeopardize all that.

She gave Nur Jahan the same advice as her mother and elder sister had given her; but she did not lecture her like them. 'Listen, Nur Jahan, my love! Don't upset yourself. You must give men a bit of rope if you want to control them. See how I've straightened out Haidar.' (This was not exactly true, but she had to exaggerate a little, even when she was talking to her own sister.) 'You must go carefully. Be considerate to him and he'll be considerate to you. Don't torture yourself. The more you do, the more you'll hurt yourself. He won't mind. He'll eat well and grow fat on it. Look, there's a dance at the Airport the day after tomorrow. Let's all go together. You can at least sit and watch.'

'Old ugly mug won't let me go to dances here. Mussoorie was different. There we were strangers, and he used to let me go with Begum Mashhadi. Here he won't.'

Sartaj tapped her teeth with her manicured nails and said, 'Is he going to shut you up in purdah then? If that's what he wanted, he should have married a girl from the old city.'

'No, he doesn't want me to go into purdah either.' And she laughed. 'He is a funny man, sometimes quite enlightened, sometimes quite strict. On our way to Mussoorie he saw someone staring at me, and at once lowered the shutter – and then quarrelled with *me* about it.'

After that the two sisters went on gossiping about this and that, reviewing new marriages, commenting on the bridegrooms' appearance, and so on.

When Sultan came in and greeted Sartaj, she covered her head and bosom modestly with her saree and began to take him to task. 'What's this I hear, Sultan? You go around from party to party and won't let Nur Jahan go out anywhere. If that's how you wanted it, why did you marry into our family?'

'I'm not stopping her.'

' "I'm not stopping her," he says. My dear Sultan, I hear that you want to follow city ways. But city girls are quite different from us. We went to Panchgani finishing school. Do you think we can be like them? Don't you know who Nur Jahan is? The granddaughter of Mashur ul Mulk and Qabil Jang, the daughter of Sanjar Beg, the niece of Nadir Beg, and the sister of Sir Taj al Mulk's granddaughter-in-law. . . .'

Nur Jahan could not stand this any longer. She felt herself glowing with shame from head to foot.

'Oh really, Sartaj! That'll do.'

Sultan Husain laughed out loud, 'Yes, that's her real claim to greatness, isn't it? She's your sister, Sir Taj al Mulk's granddaughter-in-law's sister. . . . Yes, I grant you that.'

Sartaj forgot all her social charm. 'Well, what about it? Do you take us for city loafers like your people? Who was the grandfather of your grandfather? Nobody ever heard of him! But the whole city knows us. Understand?' And she laughed triumphantly.

Again Nur Jahan could not restrain herself. She felt herself humiliated on Sartaj's account. 'Oh that's enough, Sartaj, that's enough. The way you boast! You're a real chip off the old block.'

Now Sartaj turned on her, 'A fine one you are, my lady! I'm taking your part, and you side with your husband against me. All right, Sultan, you keep her in a chicken-coop. That's all she's fit for.'

'Stop it, Sartaj,' said Nur Jahan, angrily.

'I won't stop it.'

Sultan began to laugh. 'I'll leave you two to fight it out; I'm going out for a while.'

'No, I'm going,' said Sartaj getting up. 'Here am I taking this creature's part, and then she rounds on me.'

Sultan said, 'No, Sartaj, you must stay to dinner.'

Nur Jahan softened. 'Forget about it, Sartaj. I apologize. Don't be angry.'

Sultan, too, said, 'Yes, let's forget about it.'

All Sartaj's charm at once returned – the charm which made her so popular in Farkhundanagar society. She sat down on the arm of the sofa where Nur Jahan was sitting, and put her arm around her and said smilingly, 'Allah! Sultan, what a flashy tie! I can't stand these American ties.'

'Then you must get my ties for me.'

'Why? Do you think I'm a pedlar-woman? Get them yourself. All you need is to cultivate a bit of taste. What's "taste" in Urdu? *Mazaq.* Cultivate some *mazaq.* Go and choose your own ties from K. A. Rahim's. Is that clear?'

'Yes, quite clear.'

'And listen, Sultan. The day after tomorrow there is a dance at the Airport. You and Nur Jahan are to come to dinner with us, and then go with us to the Airport. Is that clear?'

'But . . .', began Sultan, twisting the flashy American tie around his fingers.

'But me no buts,' said Sartaj – with mock imperiousness. 'Dinner with us at seven-thirty. Haidar will be back from district headquarters. And then we shall all go together to the Airport for an hour or two.'

'Hasn't your Black Railway Engine come back from his headquarters yet?'

'My Black Railway Engine is a damn sight better than you. What if you *have* been to America? What's that Persian proverb? Allah, what a sweet proverb! "Jesus' ass may go to Mecca, but he's still an ass." You follow me, sir? Mr Sultan Husain, Consultant Engineer? Come with us to the Airport. Meet people. Get civilized. Otherwise you'll make Nur Jahan a dead loss like yourself.'

9

Two days ago it had rained and tonight it was ususually cool. The clouds had vanished in the growing darkness of the evening, and the heavy mist in which the dark green of the leaves and the light green of the grass look so intensely beautiful, had lifted. It was dark. Up the rough track which wound between the piles of sand and stone, came Sartaj's ancient Rolls with its enormous lights shining. They were switched off as it came to a stop, and the chauffeur, his dishevelled hair half hidden beneath his dirty fez, and the collar and half the buttons of his khaki uniform undone, got out and stood holding the door open. Haidar Muhiuddin was the first to get out, and Sultan, who had come to the steps to greet him, said, 'This is a twentieth-century miracle. A Black Railway Engine contained in a Rolls Royce.' The Black Railway Engine only tittered good-naturedly, showing his big teeth stained with betel. It was Sartaj who as she got out retorted on his behalf: 'O, yes Sultan. You're very handsome, of course – with your caterpillar eyebrows and your great bugle of a nose. And you have the cheek to pass remarks about my husband!'

'Don't be cross,' said Sultan. Sartaj's shoes clacked as she walked up the steps, holding up the hem of her gorgeous Banarasi saree. 'Just look at it!' she said. 'Is this the way you build a house? It looks as if you've collected all the rubbish of the city here. I take my hat off to you, Nur Jahan. It takes some pluck to live in a place like this.'

Nur Jahan ran her eyes over the brilliant figure of her sister. What a lucky woman she was. Everything about her from head to foot was beautiful. Her long black hair, which fell to her knees when she let it down, was now gathered up English style, in a huge bun with jasmine flowers plaited into it. And how tastefully she made up, so that her soft skin seemed even softer and more delicate, and as clear as waxed silk. A dark lipstick emphasized her full lips, and against all the rules of fashion she was eating betel; but the red of the betel blended perfectly with her lipstick. And her clothes . . . 'Allah, Sartaj, where did you get the material for your blouse?'

'He bought it for me in Bombay. Why? Do you like it? I've got some left at home. If you like I'll send you it.'

And her saree! Nur Jahan had never liked heavy, embroidered sarees, and herself rarely wore anything but georgette. This one was turquoise alternating with grey, painted with large tulips, and she carried an embroidered Banarasi handbag to match.

They were about to leave when, lurching dangerously over the heaps of cement and stone, came Nayazi's dark-blue Ford at about fifty miles an hour. For a moment it looked as though he was going to crash into Haidar Muhiuddin's Rolls, but he pulled up four inches short. Sartaj had already let out a scream, 'My Rolls!'

Even on this cold night Nayazi was wearing only a thin muslin shirt and close-fitting *paijama* with the ends of the girdle hanging down practically to his ankles. Sartaj shouted at him as he came up the steps: 'Uncle Nayazi, a fine one you are! What would I have done if you'd crashed into my Rolls? Do you think it's a joke to buy a new model?'

Haidar Muhiuddin felt rather embarrassed and tried to stop her. 'Oh, never mind, Sartaj.'

'Never mind? Why shouldn't I mind? You shut up!'

Nayazi was drunk, but he climbed the steps quite steadily. 'Good evening, Uncle Nayazi,' said Sartaj and Nur Jahan together. Sultan politely offered him a seat. He did not like Nayazi and was a little afraid of him. Sartaj went on at him, 'A fine driver you are, Uncle Nayazi! You only just missed my Rolls.'

'Stop bleating about your Rolls, girl!' he said, 'It's not worth twopence. Put it up for sale next market-day and if you get a penny more than five hundred, I'll double it.'

'Won't you come to the Airport with us, Uncle Nayazi?' asked Haidar.

'F—— the Airport,' said Nayazi under his breath, confident that his nieces would not know what that meant. 'Nuri, Sartaj, are you off to the Airport, too?'

'Yes, why don't you come?'

'What, in those clothes?' laughed Haidar.

'I'm not going to the bloody dance. Listen Sartaj, Baby. You know that whore Hilda, Dr Roy's wife? Tell her His Lordship isn't coming.'

'You won't come then?'

'Stop pestering me girl,' said Nayazi, and turning to Haidar he

104

said, 'What a stupid girl you've got yourself hitched to. You should give her a damn good hiding now and then.'

'Enough of that, Uncle Nayazi,' said Sartaj. 'How about you giving Aunty a good hiding first? You've got too much to say for yourself, and if you weren't my Uncle I'd have something to say to you.'

'All right, girl, all right. No need to get angry.' He turned to Sultan. 'And how are you Mr Engineer?' he said. 'When will your house be ready? Look at it! Isn't it a wonderful sight? I told Khurshid not to marry Nuri to an engineer. I told her, 'All those bloody fools know about is measurements – yards and feet and inches." All right, I'm off. Goodnight.'

And off he went. In a matter of moments his Ford was out of sight. The other four went down the steps. Haidar showed them into the antique Rolls, and seated himself in front beside the chauffeur.

The Airport was floodlit. All of fashionable Farkhundanagar society was there. In the centre were the smooth boards of the temporary dance floor, occupied mainly by Anglo-Indian girls dancing with English R.A.F. officers.

Haidar ordered tomato cocktails all round. He very rarely drank; and Sultan did not fancy drinking alone.

Dr Roy and his wife Hilda were there, sitting together like a pair of doves. She never danced with anyone else. Haidar gave her Nayazi's message and told her what a state he had been in. She laughed. 'Mark my words, one of these days he is going to break his neck in that Ford of his.'

Nur Jahan watched the dancing couples pensively. She was feeling rather sick. How different this scene was from Mussoorie. She could imagine what Begum Mashhadi would have said if she had been there. 'Buddy,' she would have told her young dancing partner, 'we seem to have come to the wrong place. What a stuffy crowd!' Nur Jahan watched Sartaj and Haidar as they danced. What an oddly-matched couple, he ponderous and awkward, and she standing out from the crowd in her beauty. At that moment she felt a great admiration for her sister. She was not a slave of pleasure; pleasure was her slave. 'She decks herself out so that the whole city falls in love with her; while she herself has eyes for no one but her Black Railway Engine.'

Nur Jahan glanced stealthily at Sultan. He was looking at a pretty Parsee girl sitting with her family nearby, talking in

Gujarati and looking very glamorous in the atmosphere of laughter and *crème de menthe*. She felt a stab in her heart, not because of the pretty Parsee – Nur Jahan was herself attracting plenty of male attention – but because she was so different from Sartaj, and Sultan was so different from Haidar. Even if she had wanted to be a glamour girl, she could not have done it. In the first place she was not as beautiful as Sartaj; she had usurped the whole family's share of beauty, and no *coiffure* she might choose, no new fashion she might adopt could make up for that. Besides, her wretched consultant engineer had not the means to keep such a golden butterfly; any one of Sartaj's sarees cost more than he earned in a month. And then to tell the truth she didn't care about clothes all that much. She liked them, but not as much as Sartaj. Beneath the skin Sartaj did not exist, while it was there that her own existence began.

And there, in the open atmosphere of the Airport, watching couples dancing in the cool evening, amid the coloured lanterns, and the unpleasant buzz of fashionable talk and fashionable laughter, and the equally unpleasant swing music of the band, Nur Jahan discovered a little more of herself. She was not used to intellectual self-analysis, because she had never given herself so much importance. But now she began to discover herself, to discern the woman in her, that was so different from the butterfly Sartaj. Sartaj was incapable of love. Married to anyone else, she would have been an equally happy, dutiful, faithful wife, provided that her husband had large estates. She would have managed her life just as correctly, maintained a reputation just as spotless, and her life would have been just as complete. But Nur Jahan felt her own life incomplete. Something was missing. Something was still to come. And she realized now that this something was love. She knew now that she had never been really in love, and that until she was, the vacuum in her life would remain. She glanced at her husband, who had turned to ask her casually, 'What are you thinking about, Nuri?' and then gone on looking at the Parsee girl. In love with this man? She sized him up from head to foot. He was not really bad-looking. Perhaps she could have come to love him. But she remembered the sleepless nights and the anguished days at Mussoorie. Kamala Paresh. She sighed deeply and wished that they had never gone to Mussoorie for their honeymoon. Then perhaps she might have come to love him. Now it would be difficult, very difficult.

She felt a wave of nausea overcome her. At last this dance was over, and Haidar and Sartaj returned. She whispered something to Sartaj, and the two of them picked up their handbags and got up to go to the Ladies. Sultan yawned, 'Haidar, I'm bored stiff. What a joint! It beats me why people come to these dances.'

When they returned, Nur Jahan saw that Sultan was dancing the rumba with the pretty Parsee, his little moustaches bristling with pleasure. With a glance of ironic indulgence she sat down.

More people had arrived. At one table she noticed her Anglo-Indian aunty, Kahkashan, with a British army officer who sat grinning, with a pipe between his teeth. Her hand was laid on his knee and she was chattering continuously at him. Sartaj glanced at her and then turned away in disgust. She had disgraced the name of Qabil Jang, so much so that even Khurshid Zamani had ceased to associate with her. There had been a time when everyone felt sorry for her, the time when her husband had been shot dead by his orderly. But since then she had overstepped the mark. Nur Jahan and Sartaj could plainly hear Begum Ahdi Husnkar's comment, 'Allah, what a merry widow! She has no sense of shame at all. What glory she's brought to the house of Qabil Jang!'

The 'Merry widow' was still very handsome, though she was past her middle thirties now and had grown-up sons and daughters. Her eldest son had already gone to the dogs, but all that had made no difference to her stylishness. Her brothers Nayazi and Mahmud Shaukat had more than once threatened to kill her, but her tongue was sharper than their threats. 'Let's see you put your own house in order first!'

Now as she came towards the two sisters their faces fell. It was impossible to run away. It was as though a whore had joined the ladies, claimed one or two of them as her sisters, and embraced them.

'Hallo, darlings,' she said to them, and adding insult to injury, kissed them on the forehead. They had to be polite, and Sartaj said hastily, 'Allah, Aunty, won't you join us? We haven't seen you for ages. I was going to call on you myself – honestly I was. But our chauffeur was away on holiday. And then something went wrong with the car. It's a Rolls, but it's rather an old one now. Haidar is going to get a new Packard, and then I shall certainly come to see you.'

Kahkashan settled herself comfortably in the chair. Haidar

107

asked her what she was drinking. Without turning a hair, she said, 'Sherry.' The sherry came, and she began sipping it slowly, and talking nineteen to the dozen. All about clothes – 'Chandi Das has got in a new stock of georgette. The stock of coloured sharkskin was gone in two days. Mrs So and So was wearing such and such a saree at that party. I don't like that horrid Panjabi-style dress at all. I think it's a peculiar fashion. No, it looks all right on a tall girl, but. . . .'

When the dance was over, Sultan escorted the Parsee beauty back to her table, and then joined the others.

'Who was that girl?' whispered Nur Jahan.

'The one I was dancing with?'

'Yes.'

'Miss Kanoonwala.'

'Who introduced you to her?'

'Why?'

'Oh! I just wanted to know.'

'Saghir did.'

'I see.'

Opposite them on the other side of the floor another large group was sitting. Presiding over it was Mahtab Jang with his thin pale face and shining eyes, his distinguished, greying hair and his thin red lips parted in a charming smile to show his regular teeth. Under his wing sat practically the whole of his clan; his fat, elderly sisters, including Haidar's mother and the nieces who had married the real or self-styled princelings of Coromandel; his nephews, some of them in military uniforms, others in immaculate dinner-jackets. The atmosphere was free and informal and gay, and was reflected in their faces. Haidar out of courtesy did not move from his table, but Sartaj now left poor Nur Jahan in Kahkashan's clutches and went over to say hello to them. Young men turned to look at her admiringly as she made her way between the tables, and she greeted those whom she knew with a smile. 'Uncle Mahtab,' she said, 'why have you come so late? The dance is practically over. Good heavens, if we'd known you were coming, we would have all come together.'

'Sit down, girl,' said Mahtab Jang, and Nazir offered her his seat. But she said, 'No, I mustn't stay. Sultan and Nur Jahan are with us.'

'Nur Jahan? Is Nur Jahan married then?' Everybody laughed and the questioner looked embarrassed.

'Good heavens, Athar, what world are you living in?' said Haidar's mother.

'How should I know?' answered Athar, 'I was in Dehra Dun. I didn't even get an invitation to the wedding.'

Sartaj gave him a puzzled look. He was a funny boy – always had been. Smart . . . and rather fast. Faster than all the other grandsons of Sir Taj ul Muluk. His hair was still as curly as ever, and he had the same mischievous gleam in his eye. He was short, but sturdy and well-built. He was mostly out of Farkhundanagar, and unlike her husband's other cousins, Sartaj had seen very little of him. In his childhood, he had been her and Nur Jahan's playmate. In those days his father Talha Jang had lived quite near their house, but when he died Athar was sent away to boarding school. He had never managed to get further than Intermediate. And then he joined the army, not in Farkhundanagar, but in British India. He was a funny boy, with a 'widow' or an 'adopted wife' in every city where he had been stationed.

'Where is Nur Jahan?' he asked Sartaj. 'I'd heard that Aunty had put her into purdah.'

Sartaj ignored his question. 'Allah, Uncle Mahtab,' she was saying, 'I hear you were playing bridge again yesterday at the Army and Navy Club. You told me you'd given it up. I don't play much bridge these days. Nowadays rummy is more in fashion. The day before yesterday I was playing for four annas a point. . . .'

Athar looked across the runway towards the hangar, where an old aircraft was standing. His eyes began to seek out Nur Jahan, and when they found her, the old mischievous gleam returned to them.

At the same moment, by the workings of an inexorable fate her eyes met his. It was sheer coincidence. But it seemed as though an electric current flowed between them. There was Nur Jahan, his old playmate, whom he used to tease so much in her Panchgani days. And now she was a woman, and another man's wife. How strange – and how ridiculous!

Sultan Husain with a last glance at the pretty Parsee, knocked out his pipe and said, 'Come on, let's make a move. It's getting late. Sartaj seems to have got stuck there.'

Haidar, the obedient husband, went over to call Sartaj and to say hello to Mahtab Jang. Sultan looked across admiringly. Nawab Mahtab Jang, whom nature had made so handsome and endowed with such social charm. God knows how many maharanis' hearts he had conquered. The maharajahs' friend and their consorts' paramour. To Sultan he was the luckiest man, the gayest man in India. Everybody's friend. A warm handshake for one, a familiar slap on the back for another. What charming manners! What style! What polished conversation! – superficial, but that was another matter. What a curious blunder of destiny to have created this man, this perfect courtier, in twentieth-century India.

And this Athar. Nur Jahan had told him they used to be great friends when they were children together. Used to be. Used to be. Suspiciously, he glanced at his wife, and saw that she was looking at him, and he at her. He whispered angrily to her, 'Who are you staring at?'

'Nobody.' She glared angrily at him.

'Yes you were,' he hissed back.

'Oh leave me alone!' she said.

'Whore!' he muttered between his teeth. Outraged, she looked at him in helpless anger. She suddenly felt the weight in her womb, and felt sick. The child of this hateful man in her womb. She felt that her body was no longer clean, no longer her own. For the 'promise' of bride-money she had been sold to him, just as if she really were a whore.

But now Sartaj and Haidar came up, and she controlled herself and smiled.

'Look, your lovers have come to see you again,' Sultan said to her as he went to his room. During the last two or three weeks he had often used this expression for the Chinese cloth-pedlars who came to the door. She glanced out of the window at them. A poverty-stricken Chinaman selling cheap silk, and with him a grubby boy with a bundle of cloth on his head. 'And what lovers!' she said, 'I would give my life for them.' She smiled bitterly and called out to the servant, 'Tell the Chinaman I don't want anything today.'

As he left for the office Sultan again asked her, 'Well, have your lovers gone?'

'Yes, they've gone.'

'Why?' He smiled sarcastically.

'They'll come back when you've gone to the office,' she said. She felt her temper rising.

'So that's how it is.'

'Yes, yes, that's how it is.'

'I was only joking, but you're getting cross.' Sultan saw the warning signs and tried to pacify her.

'Really? All this time you've been joking?'

'Why? Did you think I was serious? I didn't think you'd sink so low as to fall for cloth-pedlars. . . . Now if it had been Athar, that would have been different.'

'Stop it! Stop it! I'm sick to death of it. Anyone else would have gone off and left you long ago – or else taken poison.'

'Why not poison *me*, then? Women like you often do.'

'O God! What shall I do? Where can I go? What have I done to deserve a man like this?' Nur Jahan burst into tears.

'Nuri! Nuri! I was only joking.' He sat down beside her on the bed.

'To hell with your joking! You've made my life a misery. You taunt me and insult me day and night. What have I done wrong? I've been a faithful wife to you. Yet didn't I see you with my own eyes kissing Kamala Paresh? Did I, or didn't I? I've heard all sorts of tales about you. Everybody despises you. And on top of all that you make my life hell. If you don't like me, why don't you leave me? Leave me, for God's sake.'

'Nuri! Nuri, my darling! . . .' Sultan put his arm round her waist.

'To hell with your darling! I wish I was dead!' She was crying. Her face was all flushed and her lips were parted in anguish. Sultan thought how beautiful she looked, and deep down he felt a sort of intoxication.

After he had gone, the lady doctor came to give Nur Jahan her glucose injection. The same evening Khurshid Zamani came to see her. Nur Jahan clung weeping to her for a long time, and when Sultan Husain returned she took him sharply to task. 'Is this any way to treat my daughter? See what a state she's in!' Sultan felt rather abashed. There were not many people who could stand up to Khurshid Zamani.

Tonight Nur Jahan was going to Major and Mrs Nazir's party. Sultan was away at Durgapur, conducting an important survey, and had told her that it would be at least a week before he could get back. She had never been to a party without him before, and in spite of Sartaj's insistence was not at all keen to go. But Mrs Kulsum Nazir had come personally to invite her. There were personal politics behind the invitation. Araish Jang, the Minister of Works, did not like Major Nazir. Whereas Sultan, as everyone knew, was one of his favourites. Just as Araish Jang went everywhere with the Prime Minister Ala Kausar Nawaz Jang, so did Sultan everywhere accompany Araish Jang, at every inspection, and on every tour. True, Major Nazir had no direct official connection with Araish Jang, but he was after the post of A.D.C. to the Prime Minister, and the Minister of Works had great influence with him. And so he was keen to have Sultan, or at least his wife, at his party. He wanted to demonstrate to fashionable society that there were signs of reconciliation between him and Araish Jang. Besides Nazir liked display regardless of whether there was anything to be gained by it. Biting his red lips and finely trimmed moustaches with his great teeth, he made up his mind that come what may at least Nur Jahan must attend his party, and he persuaded his wife Kulsum to call on her and to press the invitation upon her. It was on her account that he had invited Sartaj and her husband, though both he and his wife detested Sartaj. (What if she had married into a branch of his family? It was a branch he did not particularly like.) So Kulsum, who had suddenly blossomed out after her marriage, made up to look her most striking and descended upon Nur Jahan.

A buffalo was plodding round and round in the forecourt grinding the lime. The walls of the forecourt were still not finished. In the three or four rooms that were ready for occupation, furniture of 'German' design – all octagons, cubes, triangles and circles – had been installed, and Nur Jahan had settled in. In two or three rooms the ceilings were still being plastered. The garage doors were still being painted. When Kulsum arrived Nur Jahan was resting, reclining weakly on a divan. She was eight months pregnant, and in any case had always been rather delicate. She tried to excuse herself, but Kulsum would not hear of it. If she did not feel up to it, she need not stay long, but come she must. If Sultan had taken the car with him on his tour, then she would have a car sent to fetch her. In short, Nur Jahan had to accept.

Carefully avoiding the heaps of lime and crashing through the heaps of pebbles, the car arrived to fetch her at about eight o'clock. She was ready, gorgeously dressed, but still feeling weak and miserable. Kulsum came out personally to receive her and to help her to the car.

Three rooms and two verandas were crowded with guests. In one of the ante-rooms stood three Government Secretaries surrounded by lesser mortals. Major Nazir, with the waiter in tow, approached one of them, Shahtir Jang. The whisky gleamed in the glasses on the tray. Shahtir Jang, a tall, dark-complexioned, but not at all bad-looking man, dressed in a stylish Saville Row dinner-jacket, was talking to Dr Tarif Mirza, who was already a little drunk. 'Yes, it was my draft. I pointed out that because of the war, prices were rising sharply and that the salaries of Government employees should therefore be increased.' Tarif Mirza helped himself to another glass and said, 'But I hear that those whose income is more than twelve-hundred are not to get any increase?'

Shahtir Jang took his handkerchief from his sleeve, shook it and tucked it into his breast-pocket, and said with great dignity, 'No, I shall not allow any such discrimination. What have the higher officers done that they should be penalized?'

Dr Tarif Mirza whose reputation for courtesy greatly exceeded his experience as a doctor, held up his glass to the light, and said, 'I was not thinking of myself. My salary hasn't reached that level. No. I, too, was wondering what you higher-ups had done to be penalized.'

'I see,' laughed Shahtir Jang and then turned to his fellow-secretary Nuruddin Zangi and said, 'Yes, Nuruddin you know best about the legal arguments for your decision, but in my view, as a layman . . .'

Dr. Tarif Mirza again held his glass up to the light and went on muttering, 'What have you higher-ups done. . . ? What have you higher-ups done. . . ?

The third secretary, Ahdi Husnkar Jang, was puffing elegantly at a cigarette which stood at right angles to the holder which held it. He was a man who could not enjoy anything which was not artistic. Nazir, in his meticulously ironed, spotless uniform came up to him and said, 'Sitting all alone, Nawab Sahib? Come and join the ladies at cards in the other room.'

Abdi Husnkar indicated with an aristocratic gesture that he was quite happy where he was, and added, 'No, I am talking to Shahtir Jang.'

'Another whisky?' asked the host.

'No thanks,' he said with an elegant pull at his cigarette, and leaning back against the wall behind the divan where he was sitting, he continued, 'Nazir, you asked me for a plot on Kishanpalli. There are not many left. Better phone Sultan Husain about it.'

'I shall certainly do that. . . . I hear you have sold your house "Kuhsar"?'

' "Kuhsar"? No, not "Kuhsar"; I've let "Kuhsar" to Asir i Zulf Jang. It was "Peacock Mansion" that I sold.'

'But Nawab Sahib, it's a beautiful house. Why did you sell it?'

'What can I do, my good sir? Even now I owe nearly two hundred and fifty thousand rupees, and practically all my houses are mortgaged. I got a good price for it – ninety thousand.'

'Nawab Sahib, do have another whisky . . . it's the best Scotch. Before long it'll disappear into the black market. Even now you can't get White Horse anywhere in Farkhundanagar.'

'All right then,' said Ahdi Husnkar Jang as he took another glass. The reference to 'Peacock Mansion' had rather depressed him. What a wonderful house he had designed and built, and what a blow it was that he had had to sell it. Its general appearance was exactly like that of a half-egg; absolutely white; on the inside walls were dancing peacocks executed in 'German' style – a feather here, a crest there. There were two bedrooms, one single, one double. The beds in both were of peacock design, and so were the dressing-tables. The backs of the chairs in the dining-room were shaped like a peacock's tail. The house had now been bought by a *banya* money-lender and he had installed his mistress, the famous cinema actress Zarina.

In the other room the ladies had finished playing cards. Kulsum, in deference to her husband's order and against her own will, was being especially nice to her cousin Haidar Muhiuddin, the Black Railway Engine. Athar was sitting next to Nur Jahan and talking to her.

'You shouldn't drink,' she said to him.

'May I know why?'

'Just that I don't like it,' she said. She had almost forgotten her tiredness.

'And why not, my dear young lady?' Athar put down his glass on the stool in front of him.

Nur Jahan, too, put down her glass of lemon squash and began to laugh. 'Now how am I going to answer that? I just don't like it.'

Her eyes met Athar's sharp mischievous glance, and she felt that his eyes – his clever, mischievous, wicked eyes – looked deep into her heart.

Athar called out to a passing waiter. 'Bring me a small tomato juice.'

'What? Not even a tomato cocktail?' Nur Jahan asked him laughing.

'Cocktail suggests alcohol. There's probably none in it, but just to please you I won't drink even that.'

'You're very kind, sir,' she said mockingly.

In general Athar couldn't stand pregnant women; in fact, he ran a mile from all married women. God knows what attraction this old playmate had for him, that he sat there sipping tomato juice with her.

Near them, Rajah Bajpai was carrying on an interesting conversation with Sarvari while Nawab Mutmain Jang, half recumbent on a nearby chair, put in an occasional thrust. Rajah Bajpai was telling Sarvari, 'Our Nawab Sahib here is a dark horse. We were both at the Governor's party in Bombay, and I was talking to the Governor's daughter. She's a racing enthusiast, and I was giving her a few tips about the coming week's race meeting. Our Nawab Sahib sidled up. Miss Cholmondleigh – May Cholmondleigh. You've never met her, have you? She is a very beautiful woman. . . .'

The Nawab interrupted him with a laugh. 'Beautiful! . . . If May Cholmondleigh's beautiful then you're the most handsome man in the world!'

'Go on,' said Sarvari, 'What happened then?'

'Then our Nawab Sahib came up and said, "It's not right for a young Rajah to detain a young lady so long in conversation. After all we old fellows, too, have some rights." I replied, "By all means talk to her, Nawab Sahib." All this, I should tell you, was said in Urdu. I hope the Governor's daughter doesn't understand Urdu. Anyway, I introduced the Nawab Sahib to her, and he talked to her for a solid hour. The poor girl sat there and never once got up to dance. She was so taken up with him. . . .'

'Really, Nawab Sahib!' Sarvari laughed.

'Yes, he's a dark horse, our Nawab Sahib. Ask anyone you like. Every day he puts a silver pill in his tea. He says it's ambergris, but my private opinion is that it's a rejuvenator specially prepared by the *hakims*. . . .'

'Nawab Sahib!' said Sarvari, reddening slightly. She seized the hand of Nuruddin Zangi, who was standing close by, still discussing the same legal controversy with Shahtir Jang.

Mutmain Jang glanced quickly at her hand and then turned away. This girl was no credit to his old friend Zijah Jang. There were all sorts of scandals about her. He must have brought her

115

up very badly. (Mutmain Jang liked listening to scandal, which, however, he always professed to disbelieve. 'No! I don't believe it! I can't think that that's true.' Thus, while he sinned with his ears, he simultaneously acquired merit with his tongue.)

Kulsum now brought across a fourteen-year-old girl and introduced her to the Nawab. 'This is Huma, Mr Zubair Samdani's daughter.' The Nawab Sahib studied his friend's daughter out of the corner of his eye. She wore no make-up and was wearing the Panjabi *shalvar qamis*, a purely Islamic style of dress, rarely seen in Farkhundanagar, except in a few Panjabi families. Auspicious signs. But her hair was bobbed, and her manners westernized, and she spoke more English than Urdu – inauspicious signs. But it was not her fault, poor girl. Her parents had sent her to convent school, and that, too, in Bombay. And anyway she was his friend's daughter, and there was still time to save her. He began talking to her about Islamic history, about the pious caliphs and the saintly women of Islam, and he was bringing the conversation round to the unpleasant subject of westernization, when a remark of Rajah Bajpai distracted his attention. The Rajah was talking to an English colonel, and was complaining about his brother. 'He has taken possession of the whole estate,' he was saying.

The Nawab laughed. 'Rajah, try again! Try again!' he called out.

The Rajah turned to him and said in English, 'Nawab Sahib, if you are going to start that again I shall leave.'

The Nawab laughed and again said, 'Try again, Rajah! Try again!'

The English colonel was mystified. 'Is there a story behind this, Nawab Sahib?'

'There is indeed,' said the Nawab laughing. Poor Huma was staring at them uncomprehendingly. 'Well Rajah, shall I tell him?'

'No, Colonel, there is no story behind it,' the Rajah cleared his throat and went across to the veranda to spit. (This was a habit of his and he had suppressed it all this time only out of consideration for the ladies.)

'He's a nice chap,' said the Colonel. 'I like him.'

'Yes, he's a nice chap,' said the Nawab changing his smile into one of suave politeness.

As a matter of fact Rajah Bajpai was dying to hear the Nawab Sahib repeat the story. The moment he returned he again said,

'No, Colonel, there's no story behind it. It's a peg for one of Nawab Mutmain Jang's stories. But what would people say – what would the Khan Hazrat think? – if they got wind of it?'

'It's a true story. There can't be any harm in telling it. Well, Rajah, shall I tell the Colonel?'

'All right, tell him then. It's not as though I'd done anything wrong,' the Rajah laughed.

The Colonel offered the Nawab a cigarette, 'Do you smoke?'

'Only in bad company, and the Rajah's here, so I don't mind if I do.' And then he continued, 'What happened was that our Rajah sent his elder brother some bananas from his garden . . .'

'Colonel, you mustn't believe a word of this.'

'His brother ate the bananas, dropped the skins on the stairs, and then slipped on them and fell and hurt himself. So I always tell the Rajah, "Try again, Rajah, try again! One day your brother will slip again and break his neck. . . ." '

The Colonel laughed, and Huma smiled. Nazir and Kulsum announced that the buffet supper was ready.

Nawab Mutmain Jang now turned to Zubair Samdani and began talking about a new hydro-electric station near Farkhundanagar. Sartaj was chattering to Shahtir Jang who was standing next to her, a serviette in his hand, and a plate on the serviette, and a little fish on the plate, with which he was toying with his fork. 'Allah, Shahtir, why don't you marry again? Just give the word and see what a fine girl I'll find for you. It was a good day when you sent that mem-sahib packing. . . .'

This last remark was rather tactless. It was not he that had left her, but she that had left him. He had met her in Italy and given her to understand that in Farkhundanagar he was somewhat more influential than the ministers. She had given him to understand that she was a millionairess. After the marriage they were both disappointed. Her rich imagination had been attracted by a brown man; now when she came to India, she discovered that all of two hundred million men were brown. So she craved for white men again. Shahtir Jang was ambitious, and had hoped that his mem-sahib's smiles would help him on with the ministers and the powers that be. . . . It did not work. They were at cross purposes. They argued, and were jealous, and fell out more and more frequently; until in the beginning of 1940 the Italian Consul-General wrote to her from Calcutta that if she intended to go home she had better go quickly. So she left for Italy before the fall of

117

Paris and Italy's entry into the war. Shahtir Jang had a nervous breakdown.

'Let's drop that subject,' he said quietly.

Sartaj realized her mistake and at once changed the subject. 'Allah, Shahtir, how well you play bridge. I still can't understand Culbertson's rules. Allah, Shahtir, how well every one in Ala Kausar Nawaz Jang's family plays bridge. After all it is the Prime Minister's family.'

'Yes, they all play very well,' he said; 'so did Ala Kausar Nawaz Jang himself, but nowadays he's too busy.' He moved towards the table. 'Can I get you anything?' he asked. 'Chicken? Pulao? Something else? . . .'

Nur Jahan was sitting on a chair by the wall, with a plate in her lap, eating slowly. Her brother-in-law, the Black Railway Engine, had brought her some food and was saying, 'Nur Jahan, you should come to parties more often. Doesn't that tyrant let you?'

'You're a fine one to call my husband a tyrant,' she said with mock aggressiveness. 'Wait till he comes back. I'll tell him.'

'If he gave you any encouragement, God knows what you'd do. As it is you always take his part. All right young lady, go and sit in purdah. Shall I send you a good thick canvas curtain for your car?'

'Use the canvas curtains for your own ramshackle Rolls. They'll go well together.'

Sartaj reddened with anger as she heard her Rolls being made fun of, but she continued talking to Shahtir Jang. 'Allah, Shahtir, what a good film *Gone with the Wind* is! I've been to see it twice.'

At the far end of the room Athar was talking to Huma. The panther and the doe, the falcon and the dove. Dozens of times he had promised to reform himself, but every time he saw a new girl he forgot his resolution. How unfair nature was. Day and night more and more pretty girls were growing up all the time, and each more beautiful than the last. Even so he could not help looking at Nur Jahan and catching her eye. What magnetic eyes she had, this old playmate of his. She was nothing to look at, though, and he wondered why he felt so strongly attracted to her.

After supper there was an exhibition of the classical Indian dance by a Bengali girl, Mohini, the daughter of a station-master in one of the outlying districts of Farkhundanagar. She had often been with the members of her family to Rajah Bajpai's parties, and it was at his persuasion that she had come this evening. She was a wonderful dancer. The eyes of everybody, including even

Mutmain Jang, were on this little girl as she danced as a devotee of Kali, the goddess of destruction. How supple her body was. Nur Jahan, even though she felt the weight of her eight months' baby within her, forgot her impending motherhood, and felt herself responding to the rhythm of the dance, and a desire to move her own body with the same suppleness and the same freedom.

The ladies got down to their card playing. Kulsum said to Nazir, 'Begum Ahdi Husnkar Jang's looking for a fourth to make up her table. Shall I ask Begum Samdani?'

'She hardly ever plays. Where's Sartaj?'

'She's in the other room playing bridge with the men. She's cheap.' Kulsum said.

'Hush, darling,' said Nazir. 'All right, go and ask Begum Samdani then.'

Begum Samdani was preparing betel – one for her husband, one for Ahdi Husnkar Jang and one for Mutmain Jang. She licked the lime from one end of the little spoon, and having spread the perfumed tobacco paste with the other, was on the point of licking that, too. She refused Kulsum's invitation and Ahdi Husnkar Jang agreed to make a fourth. After all it was his wife's table. His cigarette in its holder stuck up at right angles to the table. Huma was with them. He asked her, 'Well, Huma, are you enjoying the party?'

'Very much!' said Huma, as she took up her cards. What a hopeless hand, she thought to herself.

Begum Ahdi Husnkar Jang said, 'Ninety per cent of the time Huma has been talking to Mutmain Jang.'

'Yes,' said Huma looking despairingly at her cards.

'No bid.'

'No.'

'No bid.'

Ahdi Husnkar Jang threw down his cards on the table. They were dealt again. He asked, 'What was Mutmain Jang talking to you about, Huma? . . .'

'Mostly religious things, Uncle. I don't remember now. There was some pious caliph.'

Begum Ahdi Husnkar Jang belonged to the Shia sect which does not care for the 'pious caliphs'. Ahdi Husnkar Jang said hastily, 'Yes, yes. Mutmain Jang is a very nice man, very interesting.'

Nur Jahan was feeling sleepy. She made her excuses to Kulsum and asked her brother-in-law, the Black Railway Engine, to take her home.

'Stay a bit longer,' he said. 'We'll all be going soon. Your beloved's away. What's the hurry?'

'No, Haidar. Sartaj'll go on playing till two in the morning, and I shall be half dead. You can take me home and come back.'

'Shall I order my car?' Kulsum asked.

'Yes, would you, darling?'

Athar, who had been talking to Rajah Bajpai, came up and said, 'I'm going to Mahtab Manzil. I promised Uncle I'd be back by half-past eleven. Can't I drop you at your house?'

'No, thank you,' said Nur Jahan. 'Kulsum, will you order your car, please.'

Athar looked at Kulsum beseechingly and Nur Jahan noticed it. She remembered how on her own wedding-day her brother Asghar had beseeched her mother to let him drive Zinat home. He had been kissing Zinat without caring who saw it. He ought to have been ashamed of himself. Her husband had not been dead eight months. In a second the drama of Zinat's life passed before Nur Jahan's eyes. How fast she had been, both before and after her marriage. On the very day when her damn fool of a husband had found her out – Anyway he is dead now, poor fellow – he was killed in the crash at the level crossing. It was a miracle that the chauffeur escaped with his life. At the scene of the accident Zinat had wept and thrown herself about; and now they say that she is marrying some Englishman, who already follows her around carrying her betel-box for her. With sudden decision she said, 'Kulsum, could you order your car right away? If not, Haidar will drive me home.'

But Kulsum's car had already come. As she got in, Nur Jahan thought to herself, 'I'm married now, and going to have a baby; but that rogue Athar has no shame. A fine thing if I had gone with him, alone, and at this time of night! Though he's always behaved himself with us, poor boy.' And in her heart of hearts she forgave him.

10

Sultan Husain returned from his tour on the evening of the following day to find that Nur Jahan was still resting. He felt rather put out. His idea of a dutiful wife was one who greeted her husband smiling the moment he set foot in the house, sensed his mood, and entertained him accordingly, slaving like any maid-servant to meet his every need. And come to think of it, he said to himself, what difference is there between the two except that a wife wears better clothes and talks better, and sits down to table with you. She's only a glorified housekeeper, and very often a nuisance into the bargain, because she pesters you when you want to work. He thought of all the times he had had important plans to get ready for the next day, and Nur Jahan had appeared in the doorway before it was even ten o'clock and said, 'Let's go to bed, darling! I'm sleepy.' He would say, 'You go to bed if you're sleepy.' But no, that wouldn't do. 'I'm afraid to go to bed alone.' Afraid to go alone! The lady is educated. She has been to Panchgani. She moves in society. But the moment darkness falls she feels afraid. And what is she afraid of? Not of snakes, or scorpions or thieves. She's afraid that Satan will get her! As soon as evening comes, it seems, Satan drops all his really important tasks, such as seducing the offspring of Adam and Eve, and turns all his attention to the single task of frightening my lady. . . .

He called out from the bathroom, 'Nur Jahan, Nuri, Nuri.'

'Yes?' answered Nur Jahan in a listless voice.

He mimicked her tone and said, 'What's the matter? Don't you feel well?'

Nur Jahan went into the other bathroom, which was still unpaved, and was sick. When her nausea and headache had ceased a little, she came into the dining-room and began to pour tea.

Sultan was munching potato crisps and talking about his tour, grumbling about the dusty tracks and the jolting bullock-carts, when Nur Jahan interrupted him to say, 'Oh, I forgot to tell you, Nazir and Kulsum gave a party last night, and I . . .'

'You went?' he cut in, and his face suddenly became stern.

'Yes. Why? Shouldn't I have gone?' she asked coldly.

'Of course, why not? Of course you should, especially when your husband was away on tour.'

'I didn't want to go. I *told* them you were away and that I couldn't come. But Kulsum absolutely insisted. She came to fetch me herself.'

'Wonderful! My wife is becoming a great social figure. Darling, what difference does it make whether I'm there or not? That's what husbands are for, to go to work and earn money to bring to their wives, so that they can go about flirting with other men.' He went on munching his potato crisps.

Nur Jahan was angry. 'Now look here. That's going too far. If that's how you wanted it, you should never have introduced me into society.' She felt her temper rising, too. 'What a man! First he lugs me around himself to people's parties; then he gets angry because I go to them. But I know why you're angry. It's because your precious Araish Jang doesn't go to Nazir's parties, isn't it? That's the reason, isn't it? Otherwise you'd have been the first to want me to go, and the more I charmed the men the better you'd have liked it.'

'Shut up, you bitch.' He brought his clenched fist down on the table with such force that the tea splashed on to the doily and the polished table.

'You swine! Watch your tongue when you talk to me. Do you think I'm your slave? He's a scoundrel of the first water himself, and then he turns round and torments me!'

Tears were already flowing down her cheeks, and her face was distorted and red with anguish. The pallor of her pregnancy seemed to have suddenly vanished, and she looked strangely beautiful.

Sultan felt a sadistic pleasure. He ground his teeth and said again, 'Shut up, you bitch! or I'll give you such a thrashing that. . . .'

Angrily, in tears, she shouted back, 'You'll thrash me, will you? You swine! You contemptible scoundrel! Just try and touch me!'

Sultan felt the intoxication of tyranny rising in him. He lashed out and slapped her hard on the face.

Something in Nur Jahan flared up for a second and then as suddenly died out. Her anger ebbed away and a sense of her deep humiliation, a bitter awareness of her utter helplessness such as she had never felt before, took its place. She looked at her husband like a wounded animal. She could not speak. A strange depression

122

came upon her, as if she were sinking to the uttermost depths of the oceans, and with it a stark realization that it was possible for someone to strike her and humiliate her like this.

She stopped thinking. For a few moments she was in a vacuum where nothing mattered, and nothing existed – neither she herself, nor Sultan, nor her mother, nor the unborn child in her womb. All seemed like a dream which had vanished, leaving only a faint recollection. A pain was clutching at her heart. The slap on her cheek seemed to have penetrated to her mind and paralysed it. Her soul seemed to have melted into sobs. She felt as though she had just died.

Sultan went to his own room, feeling a little sorry, a little self-satisfied. What was that Persian proverb? 'If you're going to kill the cat, kill it the first night.' What a wealth of experience there lay behind it! Yes, he'd given her too much rope.

It was a curious chance that Nur Jahan's first visitor, only a few hours after this incident, was Zinat Rikab Jang, the Zinat whom her brother Asghar had once been so keen on, and whom she had thought about when Athar had been so eager to take her home from the party.

'Darling! Your snapdragons are glorious! Where did you get the seeds? From Poona? I'm thinking of getting some, too. I ought to plant some annuals. Since Rikab died the garden's a shambles.'

'I hear you're marrying again, Zinat,' said Nur Jahan. Her eyes were still red and her eyelids swollen, and her cheek, where Sultan had slapped it, was hot and burning.

'Hee, hee, hee,' laughed Zinat, and her layers of fat shook with her laughter. 'Nuri, darling, from what I've seen, one man's as good as another. Rikab used to think I didn't love him. He was wrong. I did love him in my own way. He was jealous because I used to flirt with other men. But what has that got to do with love? Anyway, I can tell you, Nuri darling, that some people in Farkhundanagar like talking dirt. True, I've flirted with plenty of men and made love to them, too. I'm not ashamed of it. But in a way I always thought that my home and my husband and family were very sweet. It was a peaceful life. Home's a kind of anchor. Now that poor Rikab's dead, I'm marrying again. Yes, it's true; I am marrying again.' And she (and her layers of fat) laughed heartily.

Nur Jahan glanced at her enviously. Zinat was not beautiful in any way. She had no charm. She was born into the most 'advanced' family of Farkhundanagar, had been to school at Lausanne for a few months and spent two or three years in England. No very extraordinary background; but in the art of enslaving men she had no equal. And she gave herself so freely to her lovers that she was always surrounded by men. She drank like a fish. Modesty and reserve are for girls who are out to catch a husband. She had no need of all that. She came from a rich family and when poor old Rikab Jang crashed into the train she inherited all his property, too. The dilatory, slow-moving, meandering kind of love-making was not for her. If she liked a man, she liked him. If she did not, she did not. Let purdah girls play the men up; all she wanted was to amuse herself.

This was why, when she drove at fifty miles an hour along the Shahid Sagar embankment in her streamlined Packard, her foot on the accelerator, the wind rustling through her clothes, and her heavily made-up lips tingling with the memory of recent kisses, Nazir coming the other way in his little second-hand Ford would turn to his wife and say, 'The Dirty Buffalo.'

He was applying the proverb, 'One dirty buffalo makes all the rest dirty'. Neither he nor anyone else would have dared to call her this to her face. All the weapons that people use against women were ineffective against her. Her retorts were brazen enough to put the most ribald of men to shame. In any case she did not worry. Scandal was the universal theme in this society, just emerging from purdah, and the men wallowed in it as much as the women, if not more. No woman was safe from their tongues, and Zinat refused to be bothered by anything people said about her.

In the Tabindanagar Club she was always surrounded by a crowd of young officers, mainly Indian, though with a sprinkling of British, too. In time it became noticeable that a young British captain named Lewis was particularly attentive to her. People wondered why. What did he see in her? He was fair-haired, well-built and handsome, and for some time had been going around with Ada Carruthers, the parson's daughter. Ada was charming, and nice to talk to. The trouble (from Lewis's point of view) was that she was too serious. You could not just play around with her. The first man to take her in his arms must be her intended husband. She would not have been a bad bargain either, for she had a remarkable virginal beauty. But Alfred Lewis wanted amusement, too, and that was why he first took up with Zinat. Then gradually some piquant, exotic attraction in her light brown colouring, or some indefinable sex appeal in her, began to draw him to her, and he found himself spending more and more time with her.

Lewis was the second son of a solid, prosperous British business man, but something in his nature had made him singularly free of national prejudices. He first came into contact with Indians – some returning students – during the voyage to India. At first he just watched them from a distance like all the other English officers. Then he plucked up courage to speak to one of them, who was sitting in a deck-chair reading Laski's *Liberty in the Modern State*. Shipboard friendships do not last, but this hob-nobbing with native students excited the disapproval of his fellow-officers. They discussed him at the bridge table. 'He's a funny chap, talking to those native students. Can't understand what he finds to talk about.' When one of them put it to him he said that he 'found them interesting'. 'Interesting!' his fellow-officer had replied. 'Interesting my foot!' But Lewis was quite a handsome young man, and most of the middle-aged mem-sahibs prophesied, 'Give him time. When he gets there he'll soon became a pucka sahib.' And perhaps he would, but for the fact that he had hardly taken his first steps in that direction when Zinat came along.

Zinat bestowed her favours on him with her usual generosity. By that time she had grown tired of Nur Jahan's brother Asghar. He was becoming more and more a slave to the 'daughter of the vine'. It was no longer mere 'Whisky and beer, have no fear'. He now mixed his drinks in such weird combinations and devised such strange cocktails that even a born tippler like Abul Hashim sometimes doubted his sanity. Zinat had liked him. Girls generally did. With them he found his tongue. He was not handsome, but he was 'forward' and 'pushing' with them. And when the whisky inside him spoke, his tongue and his hands were difficult to resist. Zinat did not mind the 'daughter of the vine' as a rival. But she could not accept Asghar so long as Sunbul was his concubine. The situation was aesthetically unacceptable. In a way Asghar was responsible for her meeting Alfred Lewis, for it was he who had taken her to the Tabindanagar Club on the fateful evening when she had first met this unnecessarily handsome British captain.

Zinat's party often used to go to the second showing of the 'English' (that is, American) films. Usually it was she and Asghar and Nazli; and sometimes when the party was more respectable it would include Sartaj and her Black Railway Engine. Now Alfred Lewis became a permanent addition. Asghar still followed her around, though Zinat was edging away from him, and there were even one or two pitched battles. But he had not 'fixed up' any other 'decent' girl yet. Sunbul was after all a household concubine; she did not count. As a matter of fact he was running after several 'decent girls' at the same time, and was pretty sure to 'catch' one of them. But for the moment he was 'marking time' with Zinat. A diverting feature of these cinema parties was that Alfred Lewis was often seen carrying Zinat's betel-box. No casual lover would have done that. And that was why on this memorable evening Nur Jahan asked her, 'Is it true that you're marrying again?'

Nur Jahan's head was splitting, and she still felt in all her being her shame and humiliation. But with contrived and unnatural politeness she hid her feelings and went on chatting to her visitor.

Zinat chirruped on. 'Nuri darling, I'm reading a very interesting book, a collection of B.B.C. talks called *What I Believe*. What some of the great writers believe. "I believe in humanity." And "I believe in – oh, God knows what else." Nuri darling! Shall I tell you what I believe in?'

Miserable though she was, Nur Jahan could not resist the opportunity. 'You believe in Mae West,' she said.

Zinat laughed. 'No! Nuri darling! You don't think I could be so vulgar, do you? You'd be surprised how intellectual I've become. That's my Alfred's influence. . . .'

Despite her headache and the deep feeling of humiliation, Nur Jahan felt herself brightening up. 'Tell me, Zinat darling,' she said, 'does he still carry your betel-box around for you?'

'Oh, shut up Nuri! Stop it! Alfred says that sex (what's "sex" in Urdu?) sex isn't anybody's private property. That's what I believe; that sex isn't anybody's private property. Every man is as good as every other man. You understand, my dear? What is all this love, etcetera? A lot of rot. I like Alfred. I like him a lot. More than Asghar. Asghar has such vulgar tastes. Just look at him – that girl Sunbul.'

'That was all Mamma's fault. If she hadn't brought those creatures into the house, Asghar would have married. And he'd have married you.'

'No, thank you, Nuri darling! I'm very fond of Asghar as you know, but I wouldn't marry him. He'd make a rotten husband. No darling. Marriage is really a sort of convenience.' And Zinat snapped her fingers with their bright-red nails. 'What do you call "convenience" in Urdu? Anyway, it's a kind of happiness, a domestic happiness, which an unmarried woman doesn't have.'

At the word 'happiness', Nur Jahan could no longer control herself. The brief spark that had kindled within her suddenly died out, and she could not suppress her sobs.

Quite mystified, Zinat did her best to comfort her. What a difference there was between them, the one living to enjoy life, to whom a new man was no more important than a new saree; the other, who was sobbing so helplessly, so pure, even by old-fashioned standards, that the very angels might worship at the hem of her garment.

Suddenly Zinat realized what was wrong. 'Darling, have you and Sultan . . . ?'

Nur Jahan did not answer. Zinat rummaged in the sideboard, took out a packet of glucose and gave her a drink. Gradually her sobbing subsided. After a while Zinat asked her, 'How do you feel, Nuri darling?'

Nur Jahan felt rather ashamed, and did not at first reply. At last she asked, 'Zinat darling, will you take me to my mother's?'

'Yes, of course I will, dear.'

Nur Jahan changed into a light net saree, combed her hair, and looked at her face and her bloodshot eyes in the mirror.

Outside Sultan was walking up and down in the yard questioning the foreman about the details of the day's work. He was expecting some sort of a storm, but he greeted Zinat as she and Nur Jahan passed. She was feeling very sorry for Nur Jahan, but was not quite aware of the nature of the quarrel. She replied rather curtly to his greeting. Then she told her chauffeur to get in the back and took the wheel herself, seating Nur Jahan beside her.

Sultan Husain watched the beige, streamlined Packard as regally it turned the corner and disappeared from view.

The following day Khurshid Zamani launched a full-scale invasion. She did not need to marshal an army of relations; she took an army of servant-girls instead. Completely ignoring Sultan, she went straight to his mother, who was at that moment saying her prayers. Without a word of greeting she struck her first blow. 'You hypocritical old hag, bobbing up and down on your prayer-carpet. Why did you take my girl for your daughter-in-law? So that your swine of a son could beat her? You bitch, you old sow, you mother of a swine!'

Sultan's mother did not even know that Sultan and his wife had quarrelled, and that Sultan had slapped her face. But in any case, she could not lie down under Khurshid Zamani's torrent of abuse. Her toothless mouth accustomed to holy recitations, turned, albeit with the minimum loss of dignity, to revilings. 'Are you out of your mind, old woman? Have you gone mad?'

Her daughter Zubaida entered the battle on her behalf, 'You come here without as much as a word of greeting and start swearing at us? Mother of a swine yourself!'

Khurshid Zamani did not have to say any more. That was why she had brought the servant-girls. Sunbul hit back at Zubaida. 'Your watch your tongue, lady. We don't let any old whore talk to our mistress like that; look out or you'll get a good thrashing from us.'

Neither Sultan's mother nor his sister were prepared for this. They had their maids and their servants, but it was not safe to provoke the invading servant-girls. If one of these wretched girls did strike her or her widowed daughter before their own servants could come to the rescue it would be a disgrace they could never live down. So they both turned their wrath upon Sultan. Mother and daughter both began to cry. And Sultan's mother in her anger and tears called out to him and began to curse him. 'You wretch, I wish you had never been born! Because of you I have lived to see the day when other people's servant-girls threaten to beat my poor widowed daughter. I wish you were dead!'

While this uproar was going on inside the house, some of Sultan's friends had come to see him. In Kishanpalli's open spaces you only had to raise your voice for the echo to resound all over the hills. His friends departed with an ironic smile or in even more ironic silence; and Sultan went inside to his mother feeling very crestfallen. What with his mother's sobs and curses and Khurshid Zamani's roarings, he was completely unnerved.

Khurshid Zamani had plenty to say to him, too, but she changed her tone and vocabulary. 'My boy, does one marry a girl of good family to beat her as though she was a concubine or a servant-girl? And you call yourself a gentleman! Shame upon you!'

Amid the din of the quarrel the situation gradually became clearer to Sultan's mother. Only now did she understand that Sultan had struck Nur Jahan and that this was the counterattack. The quarrel began to subside. Sultan's mother began to scold him. 'It's because of you that your old mother and your widowed sister have seen this day. Shame upon you! Can't you understand that if you insult other people's daughters your own mother and sister will have to suffer for it?'

Sultan tried to pacify his mother-in-law. 'Husbands and wives do quarrel. Their parents shouldn't worry much about it.' And he told her that he was ready to come with her and make it up with Nur Jahan.

Khurshid Zamani also softened. Of course the daughter of Qabil Jang could not apologize, because the daughter of Qabil Jang could never be in the wrong; but she did try to be nice to Sultan's mother. 'Sister, put your hand on your heart and tell me. Your daughter Zubaida here – God keep her, what a sweet face she has! – if her husband (may his soul rest in peace) had struck her, how would you have felt? This is no way for gentlefolk to behave.'

But Sultan's mother was still inconsolable. Poor woman, she had suffered a great deal – the loss of her own husband and her daughter's widowhood. Besides she did not know how to quarrel.

But at any rate Sultan was quite willing to go back with his mother-in-law and be reconciled to Nur Jahan.

When Khurshid Zamani returned home with her son-in-law and her three servant-girls, she could hear the sound of a gramophone coming from the room where Mashur, Sartaj and Nur Jahan had spent their childhood. Nur Jahan was playing a record, 'My love and I could not agree. . .'. She had played it again and again all morning, weeping all the time.

Sultan tried to make up to her, but she went on crying and saying, 'I hate the sight of you.' Whenever he came near her, she shook him off. 'These eight months of marriage have been like eight years.' She felt the unborn child move in her womb, and hated herself, and her husband and the unborn child. Sultan tried to take her in his arms, but she again shook him off. 'If you think I'm a whore, why do you want to take me back home? I've told you already it would serve you right if your wife really was a whore. I don't care about your honour, but I do care about my parents' good name. I won't have people saying that Sanjar Beg's daughter . . . otherwise I'd have shown you.'

Her anger began to prevail over her grief and tears; and Khurshid Zamani, who was listening at the keyhole, judged that this was the moment to intervene. She came in and took Nur Jahan in her arms as she burst out crying again, her whole body shaking with sobs. Khurshid Zamani herself had difficulty in restraining her tears. 'My child, he is your husband and you have to live with him. God will help you. My boy, it's a holiday for you today, isn't it? Stay and have lunch with us and then take your wife home with you.'

Nur Jahan's sobs died away. She was lying with her face to the wall, her eyes shut and her face covered. Every now and then her whole body would shake with a sob.

11

This kind of compromise could not last. Temperamentally Sultan and Nur Jahan were poles apart, and the latent tensions in their marriage could at any time put them at loggerheads. At one time it would have been possible for Nur Jahan to love him and so to overcome this temperamental difference between them, but that plant had withered and died at the very outset because of Kamala Paresh. The heart, like the mind, abhors a vacuum. Nur Jahan began to think sometimes of Athar, her childhood friend and companion. At first she thought of him with amusement. But gradually 'that scoundrel' struck deeper roots in her heart. The more Sultan tormented her, the more she felt Athar's attraction. The Persians say that 'ghosts move into empty houses'; Athar's vague form moved into Nur Jahan's empty heart, at a time when it seemed that there was no place for him in her life. Nur Jahan had inherited a divided nature; part of her was the legacy of Mashur ul Mulk, restraint, dignity, aristocratic regard for her good name and the honour of her family; the other part was the legacy of Qabil Jang, a certain hauteur, and a certain subdued longing for freedom and enjoyment. But the granddaughter of Mashur ul Mulk was stronger and more resolute than the grand-daughter of Qabil Jang, and she resisted this 'sinful' attraction, tried to drive it out of her heart, and was at pains to behave with exemplary correctness. But there was one thing she could do nothing about: Athar on his side was falling desperately in love with her.

At this time he had begun to frequent Zinat Rikab Jang's parties. He did his best to persuade her somehow or other to get Nur Jahan included, too, in these parties and visits to the cinema. Zinat was evasive. 'Her husband's a real tyrant,' she would say. 'He wouldn't do anything to you, but he'd kill her.' Or else, 'She's nearly nine months pregnant; she can't get about much.'

At last Nur Jahan gave birth to a pretty little girl, like a little doll. At long last nature had given her all the pain and all the joy of motherhood. For some time everything except her child seemed unreal to her – Sultan, Athar, her home, everything. The baby was named Sultan Jahan, after the names of both parents, and everyone thought it a happy choice.

For several months Nur Jahan's whole life revolved around her baby. There was a sort of temporary truce with Sultan, and for a while it seemed that she had at last settled down to married life.

The child was now two years old. And Nur Jahan again began to be seen at parties, but never without Sultan. She was always rather reserved, and although her heart sometimes beat a little faster when she saw him, as far as possible she avoided talking with Athar. Zinat was married at last to Lewis. Her old father and one or two of the older members of the family did not come to the wedding, but most of her 'advanced' family did. With all the wealth of Rikab Jang she became Mrs Lewis, and went to Naini Tal for her honeymoon, where the government officials of U.P. thought her Farkhundanagar dialect amusing, and found her parties the greatest fun.

When Zinat returned to Farkhundanagar, she insisted that Sultan (albeit with a long face) and Nur Jahan must come to her parties. And still Athar's eyes were constantly upon Nur Jahan; while everyone else's eyes (and only their eyes) were on Sartaj.

The spark of jealousy again kindled in Sultan's heart. When Athar's and Nur Jahan's eyes met, it was as though a current still passed between them, until Nur Jahan would lower her eyes and break contact. The more Sultan restrained himself, the more he boiled inwardly, until one day he erupted. They had all gone with Zinat Lewis to the cinema, and it so happened that Athar and Nur Jahan found themselves sitting side by side, although generally Nur Jahan was exceedingly careful to avoid this. Nur Jahan got up to move, but Zinat, who was sitting on her left, got hold of her hand and made her sit down again. She was whispering something to her, and Sultan repeatedly turned to look at them. Athar had the reputation of flirting with every girl he met. He should never have started going around – and letting Nur Jahan go around – in such company. Zinat was quite capable of acting as go-between for them. 'One dirty buffalo makes all the rest dirty.'

He sat there writhing with anger, and on the way back they began quarrelling in the car. He started driving at breakneck speed hoping that they would crash and both be killed. But somehow the lamp-posts, walls, trees whizzed safely by, and even on

Kishanpalli the car held the road and did not plunge down the hillside. He kept his foot down on the accelerator, but not the slightest trace of fear showed on Nur Jahan's face. Her hair seemed even more beautiful as it streamed in the wind; and Sultan got more and more angry as they got nearer home.

The little girl was sleeping quietly. Nur Jahan went into the bedroom to kiss her, and began to change ready for bed.

Sultan said, abruptly, 'At the cinema you were practically sitting in Athar's lap.'

Nur Jahan turned on him angrily. 'Look here, just watch your tongue when you talk to me. What do you think I am?'

'A whore.'

'Why don't you leave me then?'

'I'm quite prepared to; it's you who's so shameless that you won't go.'

'All right, send for the car. I'll go this very moment.'

'What difference will that make? Tomorrow your mother'll be here with her army of servant-girls. A whore's mother's worse than the whore.'

'Don't you dare call my mother a whore! She hasn't done you any harm. Why don't you call your own mother a whore?'

Sultan flushed red with anger and thundered, 'What did you say?'

Nur Jahan could control herself no longer. 'And what did *you* say? Didn't you insult *my* mother?'

'Yes, and she *is* a whore's mother.'

Unflinchingly Nur Jahan hit back, 'And so is your mother – and your grandmother, and your great grandmother.'

Before she had spoken the words Sultan slapped her face with such force that her ear went numb. She felt as though she had gone deaf. But this time she, too, was ready to fight. She dug her teeth into Sultan's wrists and began to scratch his face with her long, polished nails.

The contest became one of sheer physical strength. She scratched and hit, and Sultan hit her repeatedly, with his fists, with his open hand, on the face, on the back, on the bosom. Then she bit his ear, as hard as she could, and he cried out in pain and flung her off so violently that her head struck the steel safe as she fell, and she lost consciousness.

Sultan felt a sudden panic. He hardly knew what had happened, and he felt a cold chill run up his spine. Was she dead? With a

133

belated feeling of remorse came the terrifying thought that he would be tried for murder, and on a sudden impulse he thought of killing himself, too.

In the open door stood his mother. It must all be a dream. This was not his mother standing at the door. He was not Sultan Husain. And that was not his wife Nur Jahan lying on the floor, perhaps dead.

'What have you done?' Have you killed her?' His mother came into the room. She had heard the quarrel; but at the scene which now confronted her she nearly fainted.

She and Zubaida felt Nur Jahan's pulse, which still beat shamelessly. With difficulty they lifted her up and lay her on the bed. Sultan awoke from his trance and tried to help them. But his mother shouted at him, 'Get out of here, you murderer!'

And he went out of the room, every now and then reappearing at the door to see if Nur Jahan had recovered consciousness. His mother and sister were rubbing her hands, splashing water on her face, and short of calling a doctor – that would have caused a dreadful scandal – doing all they could to revive her.

At this extreme of her humiliation, Nur Jahan was happily unconscious. The one good thing about pain and grief is that there comes a point beyond which they cannot increase. She had fallen unconscious before that point had been reached. Her mind was a blank, unaware of her helplessness and of the insult to her human dignity. She could not reflect that she was no more than a piece of property, and that this was the reward of her purity. Athar, too, whom she could not get out of her mind, but whose body she had kept at an impeccable distance, was also far from her consciousness. Nor could she think, what she had often thought before, that sometimes the one who loves you does not make his appearance at all, and sometimes he comes, but so late that his coming is of no avail – the thought that when it is the time to love, the loving one is not there, and when he is there, then the time for love is past.

Slowly she regained consciousness. She saw her mother-in-law and Zubaida, and felt the cool air of the electric fan and again closed her tired, uncomprehending eyes.

Next morning Nur Jahan awoke with a splitting headache and a large lump on her head. She told her mother-in-law again and again, 'I want to go home to Mamma.' She did not cry until she was in the car, and then the tears flowed as though they would never stop. She had not even asked to see the child before she left. It was Sultan Husain's child.

This time Khurshid Zamani launched no counterattack. At Sultan's an invasion was expected all day, but the evening came and all was still ominously quiet. Sultan paced up and down all night. He had eaten nothing. He felt ashamed and miserable, and at the same time tried to justify himself before his conscience. But he was beginning to feel that this time the gulf was almost certainly too wide to be bridged.

When Nur Jahan reached her mother's home, everyone was shocked to see the state she was in. This time she convinced not only her mother but her circumspect sister Mashur that there was nothing for it but a divorce. Things had gone too far. Khurshid Zamani was weeping even more bitterly than her unhappy daughter, and the thought of counterattack never entered her mind. 'The bastard! May God revenge me on his people for what he has done to my daughter.'

Sartaj was more upset than any of them, and they had the greatest difficulty in restraining her. 'I'll go myself and give the big bully a thrashing that he'll remember all his days.' Mashur managed to dissuade her. 'Don't descend to his level. If he could hit Nuri he can hit you, and what a disgrace that would be.'

The next day Asghar returned home from Bombay. (These days he was running after a rather moth-eaten actress named Chaya Devi, and when he was in Farkhundanagar had taken to beating Sunbul, mostly for the crime of not being Chaya.) When he entered the house he found everyone in a state of gloom. All three sisters were there. It was still only tea-time, too early to start drinking; and so even he realized that something serious had happened. Khurshid Zamani told him the whole story and said, 'Some day that madman will kill my little girl . . . I have had enough. . . . Asghar you must arrange for her divorce as soon as possible, and there is the child to be fetched, too. . . .'

Asghar tried to reason with his mother. 'Mother, think it over before you decide. It's not so unusual for a husband and wife to quarrel; only this time it was rather violent. Besides, what will become of Nur Jahan?'

Before his mother could reply, Nur Jahan burst into tears and said, 'Asghar, you provide for your servants and servant-girls and dogs. Give me the same as you give them. I promise you I won't ask for more.'

His anger at once flared up. 'Mamma, I'll go and shoot the bastard!' The others managed to calm him down, and they all began to discuss what was to be done. In the end it was decided that Araish Jang or Mahtab Jang should be asked to help arrange the divorce.

Once they had all agreed that this was the only solution, Nur Jahan began to feel a longing for her little girl. The child must be pining for her. And even if she was Sultan's child, it was she who had carried her in her womb. Her mother's anguish rose in her heart, 'O God! I must get her here somehow. She'll be pining for me.'

The next day while Sultan was at the office, Sartaj descended on his house, taking Nur Jahan with her. She had made meticulous preparations for the raid, and her Black Railway Engine had sent a truck-load of servants on ahead.

The child was in her grandmother's arms when the ayah came and announced, 'The Mistress is here.' And before Sultan's mother or Zubaida could prepare themselves, Nur Jahan and Sartaj were there in front of them. Nur Jahan snatched the child to her, as one snatches his dearest possession from the clutches of an enemy. Sultan's mother said, 'My dear, I am ashamed for what my son has done to you, but you cannot take the child away like this. You must discuss it with Sultan first. I shall not stop you. But he is at the office now. And I cannot let you take the child like this.'

'You can't damn well stop her,' said Sartaj. 'Legally the child belongs to her mother until she is seven – or was it nine, Nuri? I've forgotten. What did Uncle Mahtab say?'

Zubaida said, 'That's all very well. But wait till after Sultan comes back. It's between him and Nur Jahan.'

Nur Jahan hugged the child tight and said, 'If either of you come near me, I'll kill you. Do you understand?' Sartaj shouted to the servants to come and fetch all the furniture which Nur Jahan had brought as part of her dowry. Zubaida telephoned Sultan at the office. But before he could get there, Nur Jahan had handed over the child to Sartaj, and told the servants to bring outside all her jewellery, the bed, the dressing-table, the writing-table, wardrobe, clothes, sofas, everything. They began loading them on the truck. When she saw the safe on which she had struck her head, she started crying. She could still see the blood-stains on the bedroom carpet where her nose had bled. When Sultan

136

arrived both sisters were standing in the hot sun by Sartaj's Rolls supervising the loading and dripping with perspiration. Sultan saw them and stopped his car. Nur Jahan got into Sartaj's Rolls and turned her face the other way. 'Ugly devil!' Sartaj said to her. 'He's got a nerve. Look, he's coming to speak to us.' She adjusted her saree stylishly and put such a charming smile on her face that Sultan did not know whether to order the servants to stop loading the furniture or to enlist Sartaj's aid in mollifying Nur Jahan. So he tried to do both at once, and said with a smile, 'Good day, Sartaj! Where are you running off to with my home?'

Sartaj smiled as sweetly as ever. 'There's your home, Sultan, still standing. A beautiful house. A real consultant engineer's house. We're not taking a stick of your furniture. This is all my poor sister's dowry. And now will you kindly stand aside, or shall I call the police?' Her sweet smile grew even more entrancing, and she said in a polite and endearing tone, 'Ruffian, hooligan, scoundrel, get out of my way!', and got into her car beside Nur Jahan.

It was decided to ask Araish Jang to arrange the divorce. The main reason was that he had always taken Sultan under his wing, and carried great weight with him. Nur Jahan's bride-money[1] had been fifty-thousand rupees; but they were ready to forgo this, just to be rid of him. Sanjar Beg's estate had not yet been divided up, but it was certain that when it was, Nur Jahan would not be in want, even if her brothers did not help her.

The days passed by, and at last the divorce was finalized.

Abul Hashim and Mashur un Nisa – his 'Tom' – had been happily married for some years now, and there were three children playing in the black-tiled rooms of 'al-Khizra'. Mashur took good care of them and brought them up well. In recent years their father had taken to drinking very heavily, quite often going without his dinner to sit and drink solidly from five o'clock until bedtime. It had seriously affected his liver, so much so that at one time his friends had managed to persuade him to see a doctor. As a result he had given up drink for a while, but only to start again with even greater recklessness. By now drink had played havoc with his constitution and his appearance alike. His face had grown long and drawn; there were circles under his eyes; his eyes were bloodshot and sometimes so yellow that you would think he had

---

[1] The money which, in a Muslim marriage, the bridegroom contracts to pay the wife in the event of the dissolution of the marriage.

jaundice; the creases on his face and around his lips were oily with perspiration. Nowadays he opened his unique 'American' bar at five o'clock. Sometimes Nayazi and Asghar were there to keep him company. Otherwise he would be alone with the 'daughter of the vine'. Mashur, though she had three ayahs, always bathed the children herself and dressed them in their pretty little frocks and suits. Then she would bring her knitting and come and sit with her husband. At one time she had done all she could to break him of his drinking habits, but she had given up in despair long ago. Abul Hashim had been very good to her throughout their married life. In a way she was more fortunate than her sisters. She had not married such wealth as Sartaj; but she had an inner peace of mind and a contentment which contrasted sharply with Sartaj's exuberant snobbery, and made her proof against social jealousies and heart-burnings.

Now Abul Hashim had begun to drink so heavily that the doctors had warned him that at this rate he could not hope to live much longer. But this was not the first time; for some years past the doctors had been making these dismal prophecies. 'To hell with you!' he would say, and fill up his glass. Now it had become his invariable routine to drink without a break from five in the evening until ten at night. He had stopped taking dinner, and if Mashur pleaded with him he would wave her away with an impatient gesture. He was getting into a vicious circle. Unless he drank, he could not get about or concentrate on his work; and because he drank, all his energies were steadily being impaired.

The end came suddenly, after an illness of only eighteen hours. Several doctors were called to him, and Mashur beseeched them, one by one, to save her husband's life. But the 'daughter of the vine' had poisoned him, and robbed him of all his strength. And now she swept his life away.

The mourners came. The innumerable bougainvilias brought from Sylhet and Bangalore and Japan and Texas and Mexico, swayed mournfully in the rain. It was raining so torrentially that they had difficulty in digging his grave. On the rococo veranda the poor of the locality recited the Qur'ān to bring blessings on his soul, and were charitably fed. The bar with its stock of Scotch whisky was closed, and Asghar, though he sincerely grieved for his widowed sister and her orphaned children, also felt a suppressed and most improper wish that the bar had been open, and that he could have had a drink.

Abul Hashim's death was untimely. He was not so very old and it would have been several years yet before he could draw his pension. Moreover, his death had come within a few months of Nur Jahan's divorce.

Sultan came to pay his respects. After all he had been Mashur's brother-in-law. He had condoled with Mashur and was going out to help with the funeral arrangements, when he came face to face on the black winding staircase with Nur Jahan, who was carrying her youngest niece in her arms. For a minute their eyes met. Hers were lustreless, devoid of hatred, devoid of all feeling. She lowered her glance and quickly went on up the stairs. Her heart was beating, without hate, without love. It all seemed like a dream. Everything was unreal: she, Sultan, her little girl Sultan Jahan, Mashur, Abul Hashim. No home seemed to have any real foundation, no ship any moorings. All was irrelevant, like a dream, as if one's own story was somebody else's, and somebody else's one's own, and both were unreal, unsubstantial. A strange, unnatural weariness came over her and she said to herself, 'O God! If only I were dead.'

It was a heavy blow to Khurshid Zamani. Nur Jahan had, so to speak, been widowed by her divorce. And now Mashur was really a widow. Even now her pride was undiminished. There was no power, not even destiny, that could bow the head of Qabil Jang's daughter. Mashur and her children were no burden to anybody. Abul Hashim had earned plenty and had left her enough to provide for the children's education, and for her own comfort for the rest of her life. But seeing the homes of two of her daughters in ruins, she decided to come to terms with fate. She gave up her close-fitting, bright blouses and took to wearing long, loose chemises and to spending much of her time in prayer and in reciting the Qur'ān.

12

Another two years passed. Athar laid constant siege to Nur Jahan's heart. She never went anywhere alone with him, but she saw him frequently at Zinat Lewis's parties. Sultan had often seen them together at Zinat's outings to the cinema.

About this time Mahtab Jang began to take an interest in the matter. He, too, took his parties to the cinema, but the routine was quite different from Zinat's. Hers followed a strict time-table: first, cocktails at the Tabindanagar Club; then dinner at her house, where peas *pulao* and Lewis's jokes were always on the menu; and finally the last showing at the cinema. Sartaj used to tell her admiringly, 'Allah, Zinat, what heavenly parties you give. Always the same routine, and yet one never gets bored.' Whereas Mahtab Jang, with all his nephews and nieces, always went to the matinée showing. Though his monthly income was something over four thousand rupees, he and his party always went in the one rupee seats, and a whole row was reserved for him. As he arrived, the cinema manager would bow to him. He would take off his felt hat and hand it, together with his stick, to the chauffeur to put in the car. The chauffeur would then fetch the cigarette tin from the car and offer it to him, holding it on the crossed palms of his hands. He never smoked expensive cigarettes. Cavander's was his chosen brand, and no one had ever known him smoke anything else. The one rupee seats and the Cavender's cigarettes were the signs not of parsimony or avarice, but rather of an aristocratic modesty. It must be added that there were no other discernible signs. Before the war all his suits came from Saville Row, and his ties were specially made for him in London and Vienna. To build his imposing house he had borrowed thousands.

In these days Mahtab Jang was in the autumn of his masculine charm. His crop of nephews and nieces seemed to have suddenly grown up before his eyes; and he now taught them the art of love as an old fisherman teaches a novice. He did not really have to teach them; his life was a lesson in itself. In the aura of his greying hair, his fair and handsome face, with its long nose, its little red mouth and its sharp shining teeth, seemed to have acquired an enhanced lustre. Besides the maharanis, whom autumn had mellowed but not yet withered, even young girls fell in love with his handsome face, with the glow of his little eyes, with his incomparable courtliness, the way he laughed, and the polish of his conversation. He regarded them with a fatherly kindness, joked a little at their expense, advised them on subjects that he himself knew nothing about, and holding his tin of Cavander's with aristocratic dignity, would turn his attention to some riper society beauty whose heart would beat a little faster as her red, over-painted lips pronounced his name. The adolescent girls would look on, halting uncertainly at the crossroads of emotion, as they tried to decide what relationship with this handsome middle-aged man would be most appropriate. Should they see him as a lover? Or a father or uncle? Sartaj, who had the reputation of being, so far as anyone could see, quite impeccable in her morals, would exclaim, 'Allah! Uncle Mahtab, I've never seen a more charming man than you. Allah! how sweet you are! No woman can resist you.' In spite of his popularity with women, Mahtab had been no Casanova. He had had very few affairs, no more than you could count on the fingers of both hands. But every one of those affairs was an evergreen scandal in Indian high society – a scandal with romantic appeal, for society sympathized both with him and with the heroine of every case. No harm had come to any of his mistresses, for he managed all his love affairs with amazing adroitness. They became pregnant and bore his children; but there were no divorces. The population was increased without homes being wrecked in consequence; for the homes where he sought love were too exalted for affairs like these to damage them.

There was a remarkable stability in his parties and in the whole social group of which he was the head, a stability which could not be disturbed by love or sex or cards or dancing; and Khurshid Zamani made no objection when he began to take Nur Jahan under his wing. After all, Sartaj had married into his family, and if Nur Jahan accompanied her in her social round what was the harm? Besides, Khurshid Zamani with a woman's instinct felt that this could lead to re-marriage for her divorced daughter – perhaps to a marriage to Athar. It was always difficult for a girl who had divorced one husband to find another; she could only hope that someone would fall in love with her and marry her; only in this way might she get the chance to make something of her life.

In the beginning Mahtab Jang watched Nur Jahan closely. It

was no deep psychological study; he lacked the capacity for that. His feeling for her was really based on simple human sympathy, and this and his perceptive glances showed him what was happening. He watched the clouds of gloom gradually disperse from the girl's face. The old record 'My love and I could not agree' was worn out by now, and its music had vanished into thin air. He watched her at Zinat Lewis's parties, as she gradually emerged from her depression and became gay – gay, but never more than that. Her cheeks gradually lost their pallor, and the dark circles under her eyes began to disappear. Mahtab noticed how when her eyes met Athar's a current seemed to pass between the two 'children'. But she still danced only with Uncle Mahtab or with Lewis – except once, when she did dance with Athar, but disengaged herself the moment the music stopped. She did not want to surrender her body to Athar even in dancing, for in his arms she felt herself melting like wax, and she did not trust herself. She knew that in the last resort she could not resist him, and she did not dance with him again. She would talk to him for hours, her eyes watching him spellbound, but she feared his touch as if it were a sweet but deadly poison. Despite all his persuasions she never went out alone with him. What she had told Sultan was true; she really was concerned for the good name of her family; and it was a fact that had she not held herself at a distance, she would never have won this dashing nephew of Mahtab Jang. He knew no Persian, or he could have seen his own plight described in Kalim's verse:

> I am the sea-shore, she the ocean wave –
> Ever approaching, ever fleeing me.

He was 'in love' but he went on flirting with other girls, sometimes just to make Nur Jahan jealous. But Nur Jahan had ceased to expect anything from anyone and there was no trace of reproach in her glance.

One day at breakfast Mahtab Jang suddenly said to his nephew, 'Athar, why don't you marry her? . . . Sartaj dear, pass me the jam. No, not the strawberry, I don't like it; the pineapple, please . . . thank you!'

Marry her! Now Athar realized what he had been wanting. In his own idiom he told himself, 'I've had my fling, here and in Europe, too. Now it's time to settle down.' 'Yes, Uncle,' he smiled, adding in English. 'Yes, I have had my fling.'

'You were very rude to Nur Jahan yesterday,' said Haidar Muhiuddin, the Railway Engine. 'It was shocking taste to flirt like that with the "merry widow". It's time you pensioned her off.'

'Please, Haidar darling!' protested Sartaj, 'I won't hear a word against my Aunt. Do you understand? And I know Athar. Poor Athar! You were flirting with Auntie Kahkashan just to make Nur Jahan jealous. Allah! What a cold-blooded girl she is! Haidar, just you try and flirt with someone and see what I do to you . . .'

'Well, come on, Haidar. She's challenged you. Do you accept or not?' said Athar.

Mahtab Jang smiled, his knife and fork poised in elegant parallel.

'Uncle Mahtab dropped the hint to Athar today', said Sartaj to Nur Jahan. 'Allah! What a cultured man Uncle Mahtab is. I think Athar will propose to you any day now.'

Nur Jahan's eyes lit up and she felt herself blushing. Before the proposal Nur Jahan rehearsed it all to herself. Should she be 'cruel', or should she be 'coy'? She would say, 'This is so sudden, Athar. Give me time to think it over.' No, that would be too hackneyed. She closed her eyes and thought, 'Why shouldn't I say, "Of course, I will Athar, a thousand times yes".' Or should she punish him for flirting with Auntie Kahkashan? 'Athar you're much too fast for me. I could never marry you . . . never. . . .'

She was still absorbed in these day-dreams, when at Zinat's party Athar looked at her so lovingly that she felt embarrassed. Her heart beat violently. 'Now he's going to propose', she thought. He came up to her and remarked, 'What lovely weather we're having, Nuri.'

Zinat was in her element, chirping like a song bird. 'Dirty Buffalo', thought Nur Jahan. 'What a stupid name for such a nice woman. She was quite right to marry her Englishman. It's nobody else's business. Love is the most important thing.'

'Cheer up, Nuri darling.' The cocktail glass gleamed in Zinat's hand. 'Cheer up!' She mimicked Nur Jahan's long face. 'What's the good of worrying? You're only young once.'

'Oh, shut up,' said Nur Jahan.

Lewis was a handsome sight in his officer's uniform. All of them looked handsome in their uniforms and their bush-shirts with the stars and crowns on their shoulders and their clipped black moustaches. The butler came in and stared intently at Lewis as if the end of the world had come. But this only meant that dinner was ready. 'What's the matter, Rajanna?' asked Lewis in broken Urdu. 'Why are you staring at me like that? Has something bitten you? Don't stare at me like an idiot.'

'Cheer up, Rajanna!' said Zinat raising her glass and laughing.

Rajanna grinned stupidly showing all his teeth. 'Cheer up!' said Zinat again, and several others joined in in the chorus, 'Cheer up, Rajanna!' Lewis gave him a playful punch and said to his guests, 'Let's go in.'

As they went into the dining-room Athar seized Nur Jahan's fingers. She had always flinched from his touch and she tried to pull her hand away, but he tightened his grip and she felt quite helpless. He said to her in English, 'Nur Jahan, Nuri, I love you very much.' Something rose in her throat and she could not speak.

A strange sensation came over her, which she had so far experienced with only one man, a man whom she now hated. She trembled at the thought of going through all that again. But then why not?

At table Zinat had as usual seated them together.

'How is the little girl?' he asked her.

'She's all right. Why?'

'I hate your little girl.'

'Who are you to hate her? And why? What has she done to you?'

'She's his child – Sultan's,' he said shortly, and Nur Jahan at once realized that there would always be a barrier between them.

'But I'm very fond of children,' he continued, 'and I shall love *our* children, I promise you.'

Her veneer of modern sophistication suddenly vanished. She put down her knife and fork and hid her face in her hands.

13

The wound in Sultan's heart was now almost healed. The last two or three years had been a terrible strain. Few men, he said to himself, could have borne as much as he had and still survived. Or rather, as Surendar would have put it, few middle-class men could. Funny, that his first wife had left him, that *she* had divorced *him*. He had loved her in his own way though, in spite of all the jealousy and quarrelling and beatings. Perhaps there was a streak of sadism in him after all. Perhaps he liked torturing her because she fought back. Khadija now was quite different. She was naturally submissive – submissive, and obedient, and very young. Luck had brought him two beautiful young women for his wives when he himself was over forty. He had not had to make any particular effort; they had just dropped into his lap, so to speak. Why? Because of his social position? No, that was nonsense. Well-trimmed little moustaches? There was more in him than in youngsters of twenty. . . . 'I wonder where Kamala Paresh is now?' he thought. 'In Farkhundanagar a man has only his wife, he's starved of other women. What a wretched place to live in. No mixed clubs. No decent hotels where you can dance. Nothing except the cinemas and those tiresome private parties. God damn these private parties that wrecked my home. Anyway, now I've got Khadija. She'd be happy looking after the house, even if there were a thousand Kamala Pareshes. . . . Poor girl, she wouldn't even know.'

At that moment the 'poor girl' was making carrot halwa in the kitchen. After the first two or three months of marriage, she had confined herself to two tasks – knitting for the coming baby, and making all sorts of sweets for her husband. What an extraordinary feat Sultan Husain had accomplished. From the twentieth century – God damn twentieth-century India! – he had stepped back comfortably into the middle ages. Into medieval marital bliss. Not one wife, four if you like; or even a harem if you want it. Well, no, not quite that. The age of the harems is past. . . .

He did not really believe in marrying again, but Zubaida had forced him to it. 'Sultan dear, I can't bear to see you like this.

Why do you pine so much for that witch? She always was a bad lot. I said so the very first day I saw her, when we went to have a look at her for you. She giggled at the idea of being married, as though if ever she got a man, she would gobble him up. Stop thinking about the wretch. I'll find you someone much nicer.'

And his old mother, who in spite of all his persuasions, would never get false teeth – at this moment she must be at her orisons on the prayer-carpet – she, too, had been insistent, and Sultan had to give in. Another leap in the dark. But this time he had made sure that it would be a leap onto soft ground.

He pushed away the files in his office and rolled up the blue-prints. He opened the window and looked across the valley to Kishanpalli, where the lake was playing hide-and-seek with the lemon-groves in Dr Qurban Husain's orchard. An unseasonable cloud hung over the hill. It was still early evening, but the first floor of Mahtab Jang's house was already brilliantly lit up. In the corner room of that first floor would be Nur Jahan with that other man. Sultan felt a revulsion rising within him, like the nausea you feel on a stormy sea when the ship gives a sudden lurch.

He wanted to hate Nur Jahan, to hate her with all his heart. But he could not. In every contest the victory had always been hers. At the time, eight months after their marriage, when he had first struck her, and she had only said 'These eight months have been like eight years to me'; and on the day when she had declared her resolve to divorce him; and again when she had come to fetch the child while he was at the office, and when his mother and Zubaida had tried to stop her, and she had rounded on them like a tigress. The divorce, too, was her victory. True, in an old-fashioned place like Farkhundanagar her good name suffered by it; but he was not only disgraced but cruelly mocked as well. A strange thing, he thought, *you* suffer defeat, *your* life is ruined – and it is *you* they laugh at.

He did not close the window, defying the blazing lights in Nur Jahan's room across the valley. What an architectural monstrosity that house of Mahtab Jang's was, like a hideous crab sprawling over a quarter of an acre of land. What an exhibition of crankish individualism. And all of it mortgaged to the hilt to the money-lenders. He smiled contentedly and began to turn the pages of a recent American magazine. On the cover was a Hollywood actor in army uniform, standing at a table. Again, he could not help thinking of Athar. Why do women fall for men in uniform? If only

Athar had fooled around with Nur Jahan and then dropped her. On the table in the picture was a miniature clock-tower, and across it ran the legend 'Welcome home, Jim'. Welcome home Athar, you, the light of the eyes of Sir Taj ul Muluk's house. Next was an advertisement for Ethyl. An orange and chocolate car refilling at the petrol pump. What wonderful days those were when he was studying at the Columbia Institute of Engineering, and neither Nur Jahan nor Khadija existed for him, and he knew nothing about Indian women. There were two women in the Ethyl advertisement. He again thought of the light burning in Nur Jahan's bedroom, where she was probably changing her clothes in front of the other man. Sultan closed his eyes. That helpless look in Nur Jahan's eyes, like those of a stricken deer. Her slim body, and the two apples of her breasts, now denied to him for ever. He compared her body with Khadija's plump young body, fresh with the bloom of early youth . . . and he again turned to the magazine.

The next few pages bloomed with beauty. Miss San Diego, with her hair drawn back, and a string of pearls around her neck. Pearl-white teeth, pointed nose. Miss Chicago. Typical American chorus-girl. Pin-up. Nineteen. A year at Cornell. Hobbies, playing the piano and collecting restaurant menus. Miss Tennessee, a blonde with mermaid eyes. Just Sultan's type. Miss Wisconsin in a *fin de siècle* hat. Dimpled cheeks. Not his type. Miss New York City, now chosen Miss America, sitting on her throne with a crown on her head, her shoulders wrapped in a big fur, but her neck and arms bare. Close-fitting swimsuit. Pointed breasts, bare legs, shiny shoes, sceptre in hand and a broad smile on her face. Sultan thought of that verse by Dagh about the cruel beauty with sceptre and sword in hand, about to strike her hapless lover dead. And he again thought of the rebellious Nur Jahan. He sighed deeply. Khadija must be in the pantry, setting out the plates of halwa.

He turned another page and found himself in the land of the Incas. In Peru lie the ruins of a great culture. A fast-flowing river forces its way through densely-wooded hills. The Incas lived in the mountains. There lies their village spread over two pages. The village is a mass of red flowers. The rich lived on the high ground, the poor on the low. As it should be. They knew how to bond stone to stone without lime. They carved the stone like the masons of Ellora. They rolled heavy rocks up to the summits of the

147

mountains like the builders of the Pyramids. They also built a great empire. But then the Spaniards came. The Incas' was a culture of leisure. They polished stones with sand. There was the Great Inca, royal, sacred, divine. All the land was his, the state's. When the Spaniards came, saw and conquered, the Incas kept up their resistance for twenty years. Their descendants still worshipped the Great Inca God, and sun and moon and stars and thunder.

For a while Sultan forgot Nur Jahan and Khadija. He was walking a tightrope stretched between the mountains of Peru and the testing ground of the atom bomb. On that tightrope he walked blindfolded, parasol in hand, balancing with uncertain steps. He dared not stop to reflect, on this tightrope stretched between two kinds of civilization, what his own place was and where he really belonged.

14

The Frontier Mail was very late. The war was over. Delhi station was swarming with American and British soldiers going back home, and with W.A.C.(I.) girls in uniform, who had entertained them during the long years. On the trains, every compartment – first, second and third – was crammed to the roof. Rashid and Fatima had had great difficulty in getting an air-conditioned coupé from Rawalpindi to Delhi. A little doll of a girl, three or four months old, lay on the mattress. The saliva was dribbling from her mouth. Perhaps she was just old enough to distinguish things, and perhaps even knew that the smiling face bent over her was her mother's. Anyway she knew that it was some friendly food provider. Rashid, who was afraid to touch the baby, sat on a corner of the berth watching her, joking with his wife and kissing her whenever the ayah went into the toilet.

Their connection was already overdue, and there was no point in going to a hotel. So Rashid escorted Fatima, the ayah and the baby to the first class ladies' waiting-room, and went off to the men's waiting-room to shave.

When he returned Fatima had got the baby off to sleep, and she now left the ayah in charge while she and Rashid went to lunch. As they were leaving the waiting-room they saw a couple come out of the retiring-room opposite, hand in hand. Fatima stopped short. She had recognized Nur Jahan at once, though it was seven years since they had last met in Mussoorie. But the young man with her was a stranger. He could not possibly be Sultan. This man was younger, and not so handsome. Nur Jahan spotted her too and exclaimed, 'Fatima!'

'Nur Jahan!'

'What a coincidence,' said Nur Jahan; 'I *am* delighted. Meet my husband.'

'Your hus. . . .'

'Yes, my husband, Athar. It's a long story. But tell me, how are you?'

Once her first shock of surprise had passed, Fatima remembered her manners and said, 'You and Rashid have met in Mussoorie, haven't you?'

'No, but I've heard a lot about him from you. Rashid you're very lucky to have such a wife, especially these days. You'd told her not to go out too much while you were away, and she hardly ever went to Hackman's or to the Standard; and if she did, she never danced.'

'Yes, I remember that year', said Fatima. 'First Rashid wrote that he was coming on May 22nd. Then it was the 25th; then the 27th; then the first of June. Before June 1st I never even went to a dance hall. After that I used to go with Mums and Jalis, and you sometimes used to come with us, Nuri darling. But I never danced. And do you know, Nuri darling, when Rashid reached Mussoorie? The first of June went by. The first of July went by. And in August when we were getting ready to come home he turned up.'

Athar laughed as he shook hands with Rashid. 'The ladies have forgotten to introduce us. Anyway you seem a very irresponsible sort of husband.'

Fatima and Nur Jahan laughed and Fatima said, 'Yes, very irresponsible.' Her two fang-like teeth gleamed between her painted lips. 'He kept on writing he was too busy in the Courts to come. And do you know what the real reason was? There was some play he was producing. And he stayed two whole months sweltering in the heat to rehearse it.'

'Where have you come from?' Fatima turned to Nur Jahan.

'Ludhiana. His regiment's stationed there. We're going on a month's leave to Farkhundanagar. And you?'

'We've been on holiday to Kashmir.'

'It must have been very nice there.'

'The place is swarming with Americans and tourists,' Rashid said.

They went together to the refreshment room.

After lunch Athar went down to reserve their seats. At Nur Jahan's insistence, Fatima had moved the baby from the ladies' waiting-room into the retiring-room where it was cooler and the beds were rather more comfortable.

There Nur Jahan briefly told her the whole story.

Fatima listended, deeply interested. At the end she just asked her, 'And now you're happy, Nuri darling?'

'Very happy. More happy than I can tell you.'

'I'm so glad you're happy. And if Mums had been alive she would have been very glad, too.'

'Has Begum Mashhadi passed away then?' Nur Jahan got up from her chair and came and sat on the bed, clutching the pillow nervously.

'Yes, five years ago. Consumption is a terrible thing. And then Jalis married that boy Samuel in the end.'

'But that must have been after Auntie's death? She promised me,' said Nur Jahan.

'No, as soon as he returned to India. She went off to Delhi. You remember what Mums and I always told you? How unreliable Jalis was? And do you know how she used to argue in the end? Jinnah's daughter married a non-Muslim. Nehru's daughter married a non-Hindu. What's so special about the Mashhadis? Anyway, her obstinacy brought Mums to her grave a little before her time.'

'I'm very sorry to hear that. And I'm really sorry that I couldn't write to all of you. But after we got back from Mussoorie, Sultan got so suspicious that even if I had written to you, he would have thought that I was using you as a means of contacting some lover.'

'Good heavens! Did things get as bad as that?'

'Yes, they did.'

'And now?'

'Now things are quite different. Life is heaven.' And Nur Jahan put the pillow under her head and lay down next to the baby, and began stroking its face with her fingers.

'Is Athar very fond of you?'

'Very; he won't spend a day away from me. Just see, while he's been at Ludhiana, I've been with him. True it's a family station. But life is pretty uncomfortable there.'

'Do you remember how Mums and I always had a poor opinion of Sultan?'

'It used to wear me out keeping him in a good humour. And to the last I never knew why he was cross, or why I was humouring him.'

'Anyway, that's all over now.'

'Yes, when I think of those days, it all seems like a bad dream.' And for a moment both of them were silent.

Then Nur Jahan suddenly said, 'But you haven't told me anything about yourself. How are things with you?'

'The same as ever. He is in the Courts all day. In the evenings people come to visit us, and sometimes we go out visiting. About once a month there is a cocktail party. Now we have the baby. After eight years. We've named her Iffat. Do you like the name? But we call her Amy.'

'I like her name. It's a very nice name. But, Fatima darling, don't call her Amy! I don't like these English nicknames at all.'

Fatima laughed and cooed as she kissed the baby, 'You're our darling Iffat, aren't you? You're our darling Amy, aren't you? Auntie says she doesn't like the nickname Amy. She will call you Iffat, darling. And your Papa and Mamma will call you Amy, darling.'

'And you and Rashid are happy?' Nur Jahan asked.

'Yes, it's quite a successful marriage. Rashid's very fond of me and we hardly ever quarrel. We've only quarrelled twice; once it was about the upholstery of our suite. He likes plush and I told him he was a barbarian. And anyway he had no right to interfere in these things. He gave in in the end, and I got rid of all the plush. And the other quarrel was about the curtains.'

Athar came back to tell them that the train had come in, and Nur Jahan said good-bye. A chance meeting after seven years. Like the Khalji caravans which come from Kabul and Kashmir and the Frontier and Baluchistan and Persia, and wander from country to country. The beautiful Khalji caravans, with their camels, and women dressed all in black, their black clothes enhancing their pink and white beauty. Their camels laden with food and merchandise, and all their worldly belongings. All their lives the Khaljis wander. And sometimes by chance one caravan passes another. There are intermarriages. The girl departs with her stranger-husband in the strange caravan. And then each caravan goes its own way. Once or twice in a lifetime the two caravans meet again, and the girl will see her father and mother and brothers again. And thus their life passes.

But neither Nur Jahan nor Fatima compared their meeting with the Khalji caravans. Fatima it is true had seen the caravans in Kashmir. But Nur Jahan had never even seen them.

At night in their coupé when Rashid had shut all the windows and was putting out the lights, Fatima said to him as she made room for the baby on the lower berth, 'Nur Jahan hardly ever used to eat betel. It looks as though she eats plenty now.'

'You ought to eat it occasionally. It makes your breath smell nice.'

'Yes, but it stains your teeth.'

Smoothing out his bedding on the top berth, Rashid answered, 'But it makes your breath smell nice'.

Fatima laughed, 'You should spend your time kissing Amy's ayah. She's always eating it.'

In their train, eating their dinner in their compartment, Nur Jahan smiled. Athar, mischievous boy, asked her, 'Why are you laughing?'

'Oh, nothing.'

'But why?'

'Good Heavens, is it a sin to laugh?'

'Well, laugh then,' and he began to tickle her. She felt very happy. This unexpected meeting with Fatima had suddenly brought back memories of the past. The Mall at Mussoorie. The forest fire at Dehra Dun. Lies. Love. Poor Begum Mashhadi. The laughable mixture of tragedy and comedy in her life. Now, like Sultan Husain, all these things had receded from her. All except her child, who was Sultan's child, too, and whom she loved. Why was Athar so insanely jealous of her?

When she lay down to sleep, she called out from the lower berth, 'Athar?'

'Yes, darling, what is it?'

'Are you asleep?'

'No,' he said in a sleepy voice. (How quickly these soldiers drop off to sleep. Her brothers Asghar and Khaqan were just the same.)

'What is it? Go to sleep now, darling.'

'I don't feel sleepy. Athar, promise me one thing.'

'What?'

'My little girl. After all she's mine. What has she done wrong? Why are you so jealous of her?'

'Go to sleep darling.'

'When we get to Farkhundanagar you must love her.'

'All right,' said Athar sleepily. And Nur Jahan's heart sank. In this world no happiness was unalloyed. If only the girl had been hers and Athar's. She thought of her innocent helpless look, as though the little girl knew that there was no place for her, and of the innocent way in which she said, 'I've got two Papas and two Mammas'.

'Athar!' she again said in a voice full of love and pain.

But Athar was asleep. Nur Jahan turned over and looked at him with a fond smile. He was snoring now, and she again felt a thrill of happiness, thinking of how the moment she reached

Farkhundanagar she would send for her child from Sartaj's house and hug her to her bosom. And then saddened by the thought that in this world no happiness is unalloyed, while every sorrow is complete in itself, her eyes filled with tears.

15

A few days previously the official order had come listing Sultan Husain's appointment as Deputy Chief Engineer. He had not done too badly in his twenty years of service. True, he had always had the favour of Araish Jang, but that was not the only reason for his advancement. He had had a hand in the building of dams and reservoirs and roads, and he was happy that at last his worth had been recognized. For the last two days the employees on his staff had been garlanding him. Some of his friends had given parties in his honour and others were hinting that he should celebrate the occasion by entertaining them. And his home life, too, was now just as he wanted it to be.

Between Khadija and Nur Jahan there was a world of difference. Khadija was better educated, but more conservatively brought up than Nur Jahan, and his house was no longer the scene of a continuous round of mixed parties, no longer subject to the invasion of 'dirty buffaloes'. His right to the sole ownership of his wife was now undisputed. She was his property, as completely and absolutely as his house and land. As for Khadija, the idea had never crossed her mind that she was anything else. She knew that the problem of finding her a husband had been worrying her parents for many years, for a grown-up daughter was a heavy responsibility. Her father's financial position had never been too sound, and during the war it had grown shakier. Her mother was practically an invalid. The economics of the situation had held her long in bondage, and now in the whole world she could see nothing beyond her husband. Now for the first time in her life she felt she had nothing to worry about. In her own estimation she loved Sultan deeply. The economic motive of the marriage had receded and a strong sexual attachment had taken its place. Sultan's hair was turning grey, but she liked it like that. She was only half his age, but she would sit in her armchair as he sat working at his blueprints and gaze at him with eyes full of adoration: 'Allah, darling! How handsome you looked a minute ago. Stay like that, like you were before. Sometimes I love you so much that I could eat you.'

She especially liked the nape of his neck. There was nothing remarkable about it. No one else had ever found it attractive. But she would kiss it again and again and say, 'My love, I love the back of your neck. I would give my life for it.' And he would laugh and answer, 'Well cut it off and pickle it then.' She would give him a gentle slap and say, 'You're teasing me again. Don't say such dreadful things.'

Their two children were the fruits of her love for him. He, too, had changed with time, and was no longer young enough to go running after a new Kamala Paresh every day. Happiness had at last come to him, and his home was a paradise to him. For the first time in his life he was feeling what it was like not only to love, but to be loved. He would be working, and Khadija would come up to him before putting the children to bed, put her arms round his neck, press her cheek against his head and say, 'Just one kiss.' With an air of resignation he would lift his face; her lips would meet his and he would feel a sort of warmth and tenderness. Then with a resigned but tender air he would say, 'Put the children to bed, darling; I have work to do.' She would pretend to be cross and say, 'If you don't like me coming into your office, I won't come any more . . . not ever.' And he would take her into his arms and kiss her again.

But this was not the same spontaneous passion as he had felt for Nur Jahan – Nur Jahan, whose spirit had eluded him even when he held her body in his embrace. Sometimes Khadija felt desperately jealous of her. Her woman's instinct told her that despite the fact that Sultan was so happy with her, despite all the thought he took for her comfort, it was not really love that he felt for her. Sometimes she would burst into tears and say, 'All that you feel is a sort of regard for me; you've never really loved me.' And this was not all. She was wounded by a deeper and a more painful feeling that even though Nur Jahan had spat in his face and left him, it was still she who held the central place in his heart.

In point of fact, to say that Sultan was even now in love with Nur Jahan would have been an exaggeration. He was not in love with her, because he had never possessed that intellectual and moral capacity for sacrifice which love demands. He had suffered defeat at Nur Jahan's hands, and he felt the same kind of frustration as a fowler experiences when a quail escapes from his net, or as a rake feels when he has squandered all his fortune in dissipation.

156

That morning Khadija had fried him *khagina* for breakfast. They had an excellent cook, but Khadija never felt satisfied unless she cooked him something herself. She gazed at him adoringly, as he sat there in their elegantly furnished dining-room, with his back to the polished sideboard, on which stood a cut glass dish piled with fruit. He looked back at her and smiled. She had not yet done her hair and it fell over her shoulders in attractive disorder. She never bothered about her dress. Steam rose from the tea-cup as she poured him some tea. The sound of a child crying could be heard from the nursery, and the voice of the ayah rocking him and trying to quieten him. 'Ooi . . . ooi . . . urru . . . urru . . . o . . . aa . . . no baba . . . don't cry.' Khadija and Sultan looked at each other and smiled.

Then Sultan Husain left for his office and Khadija busied herself with the children and the housework.

At the office Sultan worked for two hours or so and then remembered that a file he had sent for had not been brought. It concerned a case which had to be submitted the next day to Nawab Araish Jang. He rang the bell again and it was answered by a peon, who in his bright red sherwani, embroidered belt and voluminous turban looked like King Porus mounted on his elephant. Like Alexander the Great, the Deputy Chief Engineer thundered, 'The Superintendent has not brought the files I asked for; ask him to come here.'

The Superintendent came, but without the file. The Deputy Chief Engineer thundered again, and was informed that the record-keeper had been given the day off and the file in question could not be traced. Sultan felt his temper rising. This inefficiency in his office irked him more than anything else. He got up and went out of his room to look for the file himself. Forty clerks in the record section rose from their seats to salute him. The Superintendent opened the cupboard and began to search for the file, which he at length succeeded in finding. Sultan took it in both hands and began to read it. Suddenly it slipped from his hands, and before anyone could come forward to pick it up for him, he himself fell to the ground. When the clerks rushed to help him up, he was already dead.

They cleared the table in his own room and laid him out on it. A doctor was called, but Sultan Husain's heart had long since ceased to beat. The news was telephoned to his home. Khadija was completely stunned. She simply could not comprehend what had happened, and no tears came to her eyes. Preparations for his burial were put in hand.

Nur Jahan heard the news from Athar when he came home. She felt strangely affected. A man who had been her husband, whose body had been at one with hers, was dead. The whole thing seemed unreal. But her nerves felt a kind of relief. The woman in her remembered all the experiences of the past and she forgave him with all her heart. She felt very sorry for his young widow. She felt that she herself had only escaped by a miracle; otherwise not Khadija, but she would have been widowed. Man's life is uncertain, she thought; God keep Athar safe. She did not go to offer her condolences. Sultan's old mother and Zubaida would be cursing both her and Khadija for having eaten away the life of their darling boy. Nur Jahan sat there as though dazed and did not eat any lunch, and at night, in bed with Athar, she could not sleep. She again and again embraced Sultan's little girl and kissed her. Athar hated his step-child, but today he said nothing about it. In the middle of the night she left Athar's bed and, weeping softly, went to sleep with the child.

People talked about Sultan Husain's sudden death for quite a while, and everyone who heard about it felt sorry. Such a promising, talented engineer! Khadija made up her mind that she would mourn him all her life. She had saved enough from his earnings to take care of the children until they had been through college and got married. She was firmly resolved not to marry again. She again started attending college. She wanted to complete her education, so that if anything worse should happen she would not have to be dependent on anybody. She had been her husband's willing slave, dependent in all things upon his will; but for all that she knew how to fight the battle of life. As for the future, who could say? Perhaps she would forget after all, and one day, on the insistence of her parents and her friends, would agree to marry again.

A few months after Sultan's death Araish Jang came to Delhi to negotiate a joint enterprise for hydro-electric power, and found the city so hot that he went up to spend a few days at Mussoorie. On the evening of the third of June he was sitting on the veranda of the Savoy Hotel, playing bridge. A few fools – in fact, more than a few – were sitting inside the lounge listening to the radio. The voice of India's last Viceroy came across the air, out of the lounge to the bridge tables on the veranda. Araish Jang said to his partner Diwan Bahadur Kol Bhushan, 'The higher an Englishman's class, the more courteously he behaves. There is no living being more contemptible than the tommy, and I have never met a greater gentleman than Lord Mountbatten. After all, he belongs to the British royal family.'

'Have you ever attended the King-Emperor's levée?' asked the Diwan Bahadur.

'No, have you? Sorry partner, no spades.'

'Yes, I was in England at the time of the Coronation. I agree with you. The higher an Englishman's class, the more of a gentleman he is. I once met Lord Mountbatten myself in Kashmir at a Residency lunch. In those days he was the head of S.E.A.C., and was there on leave. Whose deal is it?'

'Cut for partners,' said Surendar smiling. As they cut he said, 'Diwan Bahadur, I don't agree with you. In every country it is the middle classes who decide what constitutes a gentleman. It's my opinion that the world's greatest gentlemen are you and I. . . . True, you're a Diwan Bahadur now, but still. . . .'

Diwan Bahadur laughed.'Our Surendar is a great cynic.' he said to Nawab Araish Jang. 'He's a bit crazy, too. He's got a complex about the middle class.'

Nawab Araish Jang smiled aristocratically.

'What's happened?' Diwan Bahadur asked one of the fools who had been listening to the radio in the lounge.

'Partition. A truncated Pakistan.'

'Bengal and Punjab have been partitioned, too,' someone said.

'Well, that's all right,' commented the Diwan Bahadur unemotionally. He took up his cards again and said, 'No bid.' And the game went on.

'Who gets Lahore?' someone asked someone else.

'For the moment they do, but there's going to be a commission to settle the boundaries.'

The game continued. No matter where Lahore went, no matter how many partitions took place, the Diwan Bahadur and Araish Jang knew that the administration would still be in their hands. There was no point in getting excited like their opposites and calling 'Three no trumps'. They played dummy turn by turn and helped their partners out.

Three Sikhs came out, frowning and aggressive.

'Why did you come out so soon, Ajit?'

'Well, I heard Pandit Nehru's speech. Who wants to listen to

Mr Jinnah? When Sardar Baldev Singh speaks I'll go in and listen again.'

'Well done,' said Surendar, 'a fine finish.'

When the cards were being dealt again, Surendar asked the Diwan Bahadur, 'Well, Diwan Bahadur Ji, what do you think of it all?'

'I was playing bridge,' smiled the Diwan Bahadur; 'I didn't hear all they were saying.'

'India and Pakistan will be separate dominions from August 15th this year.' Ajit was full of detailed information. 'But in the Frontier and Sylhet there will be a plebiscite.'

'What of it?' said Surendar. 'There's not going to be one here in Mussoorie. One heart.'

'Two spades.'

'Three no trumps.'

'Four hearts.'

'No.'

'No.'

'No.'

The radio droned on in the lounge. On the veranda the game went on.

At length Ajit came out again and briefly announced, 'Practically everyone has agreed, Ji. Sardar Baldev Singh says this is not an imposed settlement but a real solution. Pandit Jawaharlal says the Congress has accepted it. But Ji, Mr Jinnah has, of course, repeated his famous formula that it will be the subject to approval of the Muslim League Council.'

'In short, they've all agreed to disagree.'

'At any rate the riots will end.'

'Partner, what on earth have you done? You ought to have kept back the king till last.'

They threw down their cards on the table. As they were being dealt again Surendar bared his yellow teeth in a smile and said, 'Bravo! What a wonderful solution! India and Pakistan both Dominions! There'll be rioting from Kashmir to Calcutta, but the King of India will not be at war with the King of Pakistan. A wonderful solution! No coronation of Nehru in Delhi or of Mr Jinnah in Lahore. Clever men! What'll be the capital of Pakistan? Lahore? Karachi? Calcutta?'

'Calcutta stays in India,' shouted Ajit indignantly.

'Well! Anyway. . . . One no trump.'

'You haven't expressed any opinion,' said Surendar to Araish Jang.

'Four diamonds,' he replied briefly, and smiled.

Even on the fashionable veranda of the Savoy the atmosphere was charged with political emotion. The Nawab's tactful silence amused Surendar. 'Where do you come from, Nawab Sahib?' he asked.

'No bid.'

'Four hearts.'

'No.'

'No.'

At last the Nawab replied graciously, 'I come from Farkhundanagar.'

'I have a friend who lives in Farkhundanagar,' said Surendar. 'I got to know him when he was a student in Germany. . . .'

'His name?'

'Sultan Husain.'

'He's dead, poor fellow.'

'Dead? When?' Surendar was shocked. Even now, so late in the autumn, he could see Kamala Paresh walking between her two admirers. 'Ye-es,' he could hear her saying in her musical voice.

When the game was finished, Surendar paid his debts and left. Kamala was sitting on a stool at the bar. On one side stood Hasan, looking very smart in his R.I.A.F. uniform and on the other was Balmukand, as dark and monkey-jowled as Surendar himself. But Balmukand had a flourishing lock factory in Ludhiana, and Kamala quite naturally was more inclined towards him.

'Have a drink, little one,' she invited Surendar.

'Thanks! Whisky and soda.'

He drank one glass after another. Kamala had long ago finished her cherry brandy, and was holding her empty glass in her hand. 'You boys have started drinking like fish. I wouldn't feel safe with you even from here to the dining-room.'

Surendar's yellow jowls shone in the light. Suddenly he said, 'Did you know that Sultan Husain is dead?'

'No! Not really! I am shocked. Poor darling! When? How?' She put her hand on her bosom and smiled.

'Whisky will outlive us all,' said Balmukand sententiously. 'Boy, three chhota pegs.'

Surendar finished his fifteenth glass of whisky and a tin of

Black and White cigarettes, and in memory of his dead friend quoted T. S. Eliot:

I said to my soul, be still, and wait without hope.

I, you, Sultan Husain. In my beginning is my end. Birth, copulation and death. To me all three are meaningless. Because I'm a middle-class agnostic. I don't believe in flowing water or baptism or the sacred thread or the beads of the rosary. I read the forbidden Manifesto, but I cannot break with my class. But it wasn't me. It was Sultan Husain who just passed across the open field, leaving the deep lane shuttered with branches, dark in the afternoon. Damn the middle classes, and the Scotch whisky, and my excellent memory:

> In that open field
> If you do not come too close, if you do not come too close,
> On a summer midnight, you can hear the music
> Of the weak pipe and the little drum
> And see them dancing around the bonfire
> The association of man and woman
> In daunsinge, signifying matrimonie . . .

I used to tell him: Don't be a damn fool, Sultan Husain. Stay a bachelor like me. Drink your whisky. Take a month's holiday in Mussoorie every year. Flirt with Kamala Paresh or any so-and-so. But the bloody fool got it into his head that he must get married. First it was Nur Jahan . . . Shahdara by the glowing Ravi, the flowing water. Then he broke his first fetters and put on others. A dignified and commodious sacrament. Sex. Copulation. Sex! Sex!! Go, make love, Sultan Husain. My boy, you never knew how to live or how to love. Inside you were rotten to the core like all of us. A rotten egg. . . .

If only he could swallow that whisky neat. But the rim of the glass seemed to be warning him, 'Surendar, my beloved, don't drink so much'. If Sultan Husain wanted to die, well then, to hell with him. What was he to you? Plenty more of your bloody friends have died anyway. Surendar, my friend – his yellow teeth smiled at him in the mirror – Surendar, my friend, it's not you who's dead. It's him. You're alive. Let's go out. Out into the dark.

> They all go into the dark
> The vacant interstellar spaces, the vacant into the vacant . . .

162

Etcetera, etcetera. Yes, they all go into the dark. So what? Surendar, my friend, this is all nonsense.

I, Surendar, shall forget you, Sultan Husain. I shall forget the merchant bankers and the interstellar spaces. I promise I shall forget all which is not flesh, fur and faeces, I shall now talk of other things. Such as twenty years wasted, the years between the wars. But now the inter-war years have gone the way of interstellar spaces and they say the English are anxious to quit India. And Gandhi and Jinnah are imploring them in chorus:

> 'Don't go away,
> You looked into my eyes and set my heart on fire,
> Don't go away.'

These days even the orchestra at the Savoy plays this tune. Sultan Husain, my friend, you chose the right time to die. The day is not far off when snake-charmers will perform cobra dances at the Savoy and we shall be deprived for ever of the bare fleshy thighs of the Anglo-Indian cabaret. Now you can watch the dance of the houris in your Muslim paradise. It's out of bounds for me, because I'm a pagan. I shall keep on watching at the Savoy the dance of the lamps, and the language of the hands; and perhaps one day a dancing bear may come in and hug a dancing couple in the ball-room. That'll be a sight worth seeing. Yes! Yes!! Ram Raj in India and Allah's rule in Pakistan. Lucky man! to founder on the Dry Rocks. Only a problem for the builder of bridges to solve. Now build your bridges across the streams of milk and honey to your palace in Paradise.

> And piece together the past and the future,
> Between midnight and dawn, when the past is all deception,
> The future futureless . . .

Surendar, my friend, Scotch whisky has been your undoing, otherwise you wouldn't play bridge and worry your head about time. Instead of the Savoy, you could have stayed every year in Pandit Tankwah's Kashmir Hotel and watched his nine-year-old daughter grow from year to year into a beautiful maiden of nineteen. The gift of time, which time alone can take away. The bitter apple and the bite in the apple. Instead you have drunk seventeen pegs of whisky, and finished a whole box of cigarettes in memory of your friend. Why observe disease in signatures, why evoke biography from the wrinkles of the palm? It's dinner-time.

Eating is the greatest pleasure of your favourite middle class. Fruition, fulfilment, security or affection. Or even a very good dinner. Not hungry like the poor, nor yet like the rich, entertaining uncongenial strangers. I'm sorry for the poor Viceroy, and even more for the poor Vicereine. I expect she has to dine at least three times a week with Sir Narsinghakrishna Gopalamangalam Chetty and other uninspiring ministers. So good-bye, Sultan Husain, you who preferred meat to vegetables, a woman's breasts to a woman's hair. Come on Surendar, my friend, finish up your whisky; otherwise you'll think of some obscene verse; and that would be an insult to your friend's memory.

The action of the greater part of the novel takes place in the city of Farkhundanagar, capital of a princely state of that name in central India. The period is that of the Second World War. Farkhundanagar has a twin city, Tabindanagar, and the great lake of Shahid Sagar lies adjacent to both. Overlooking the city is the hill of Kishanpalli, where many of the nobility and the wealthy families are having their houses built.

The ruler of the state is entitled the Khan Hazrat. His Prime Minister is the Rajah of Rajahs Sir Shujaat Shamsher Singh Bahadur. He is later succeeded by Ala Kausar Nawaz Jang, who in the earlier part of the story is Finance Minister. Other political figures which appear prominently in the story are Zijah Jang, the Home Secretary and a great rival of Ala Kausar Nawaz Jang, and Ahdi Husnkar Jang, Secretary-in-Waiting to the Rajah of Rajahs, and originator of the project to build on Kishanpalli Hill.

The main characters of the novel belong to the families of Sir Taj ul Muluk, Qabil Jang, and Mashur ul Mulk – three nobles who had been political rivals in Farkhundanagar half a century earlier. By this time the traditional family rivalries have been largely overcome by inter-marriage.

The words 'Jang' and 'Mulk' that recur in the names of the characters, are not personal names, but titles of the state aristocracy. Of those which occur frequently in the novel 'Jang' represents the lowest rank. The next above it is 'Mulk', and higher still is 'Daula', though this rank is only referred to once. 'Nawab', which, unlike these, precedes the name or title, is roughly comparable to the English 'Lord'.

Muslim personal names also present some difficulty to those un-familiar with them. This is mainly because there is no conception of surname amongst them, so that members of a single family normally have names which have no element in common. Often the personal name consists of a single word, e.g. Athar; sometimes of two, e.g. Sultan Husain. A married woman is sometimes called by her own name, e.g. in this story the wife of Sanjar Beg is always called Khurshid Zamani. Sometimes, however, a woman is called by her husband's name with 'Begum' ('Lady' – or simply 'Mrs') prefixed, as in (for example) Begum Ahdi Husnkar Jang.

The main Farkhundanagar characters

(a) *Related to Nur Jahan* (the central woman character of the novel), cf. Chapters 2 and 3.

Qabil Jang	Nur Jahan's maternal grandfather.
Khurshid Zamani	Nur Jahan's mother; daughter of Qabil Jang by his first marriage.

Grace Crewe (Sikandar Begum)	Qabil Jang's wife by his second marriage, made five years after the death of his first wife.
Nayazi Mahmud Shaukat	Qabil Jang's sons by his second marriage.
Nazli Nazima Kahkashan	Qabil Jang's daughters by his second marriage.
Mashur ul Mulk	Nur Jahan's paternal grandfather. At first a political rival of Qabil Jang, later allied to him by the marriage of his son, Sanjar Beg, to Qabil Jang's daughter, Khurshid Zamani, so that the two families might join forces against their common rival, Sir Taj ul Muluk.
Sanjar Beg	Mashur ul Mulk's eldest son.
Khaqan Asghar	Sons of Sanjar Beg and Khurshid Zamani.
Mashur un Nisa Sartaj Nur Jahan	Daughters of Sanjar Beg and Khurshid Zamani.

(*Nur Jahan is the central character of the novel*)

(b) *Mostly connected by marriage with Nur Jahan's sisters* (cf. Chapters 4–6).

Athar	A grandson of Sir Taj ul Muluk. Childhood playmate and second husband of Nur Jahan.
Sunbul	A chokri, one of three servant girls bought by Khurshid Zamani. Becomes Asghar's concubine.
Sarwari	Daughter of Zijah Jang, Home Secretary in the Farkhundanagar government; married to Khaqan.
Abul Hashim	A consultant engineer. Marries Mashur un Nisa, Nur Jahan's eldest sister.
Nadir Beg	Sanjar Beg's younger brother, married to Nazli, eldest daughter of Qabil Jang and Sikandar Begum.
Dil Afroz	Daughter of Nadir Beg. Courted by Asghar, but married to a nawab of Coromandel.
Haidar Muhiuddin	A grandson of Sir Taj ul Muluk. Husband of Sartaj, Nur Jahan's sister.
Sultan Hussain	A consultant engineer; Nur Jahan's first husband.
Zubaida	Sultan Husain's widowed sister.

The main Mussoorie characters (cf. Chapters 6 and 14).

Kamala Paresh	Daughter of an elderly Sikh, Professor Tochi, and an old flame of Sultan Husain.
Surendar	An employee of All-India Radio, and a close friend of Sultan Husain.
Begum Mashhadi, and her two daughters, Fatima and Jalis. Kazim Mashhadi, her husband.	
Rashid	Fatima's husband.

Other characters (cf. Chapters 8 and 15).

Mahtab Jang	Son of Sir Taj ul Muluk, and head of the family after his death.
Araish Jang	Earlier in the story (Chapter 4), before he gained his title, appears as Araish Husain, an official in the Public Works Department. He is now Minister of Works, and a special patron of Sultan Husain.
Zinat ('The Dirty Buffalo')	Widow of a Farkhundanagar noble, Rikab Jang. Later marries Alfred Lewis, a British Army officer.
Khadija	Sultan Husain's second wife.
Khan Hazrat	Ruler of Farkhundanagar State.
Ala Kausar Nawaz Jang Zijah Jang Ahdi Husnkar Jang	Political figures. See second paragraph on page 165.